THE GRIFFIN BRAIN

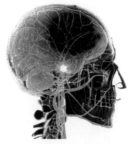

THE GRIFFIN BRAIN

&

OTHER STORIES

JAMES RUSSELL

grand
IOTA

Published by
grand**IOTA**

2 Shoreline, St Margaret's Rd, St Leonards TN37 6FB
&
37 Downsway, North Woodingdean, Brighton BN2 6BD

www.grandiota.co.uk

First edition 2023

Cover image courtesy of Creative Commons
Typesetting & book design by Reality Street

A catalogue record for this book is available from the British Library

ISBN: 978-1-874400-90-5

For Charlotte

Contents

The Griffin Brain

1. Leaving the gym to find out who you are

Outside the grass was green all over under the trees, except those bits like ticks or smooth brackets looking ready for digging up or burned with an iron and the rest.

Yes, after the rowing cable to pull that didn't move you and the changing room where I matched the rubber number round the angle key with the metal one on the door square, I pulled out wearing-clothes. As it was for the best, I had dressed up and left.

The sky was a wall above the green, white and hot, and seemed like a place after a holiday flight where you don't speak the language and no one at all is known. There was a sitting bench on which I put my body to open the inner jacket to the wallet, and my head felt like a big flower against all this hard.

Money for my lunch or dinner (good) and money cards, a gym member one, driving licence with an address giving me somewhere to go for the best, and it had a little photo of a peering man so I can check against the mirror of me when I get home somewhere. This feeling belongs to me, so I relaxed, as if my weight had been left on a bus driving away, but I learned the address by heart for the asking.

"Do you know where Flat 4 Benchley Court is, please?" I ask some little football boys and they laugh me off. Other ones I ask hand me on the shoulder with a worried touch. At the end, a nice lady drew me a map and said best to bus it, surely. I walked, thanking her, followed the streets that were in fact nothing to me.

Another bench before the roadway: bus bench. In the heat of the afternoon I got out the wallet again. The same name on all the cards, name of the man who owned the clothes and gym bag and daps, and a bigger photo on the FRISBY-ORLEANS ACADEMY card. Name equalled Mr Michael Griffin, so him on the photo, so me, so bright-eyed of a bossy man. What a tight tie, striped for the day. I supposed to get to know this man and all his things and people. Maybe so.

A bus pulled up and I thought I'd ask the driver to take me to Benchley Court, then I knew, I knew suddenly that it doesn't work like that. Here was map-fodder enough, and that saw me on for the walking. Here was incline enough with bigger trees and the quiet of stories while I found the road's offshoot in the end. To what must be an important street for me, running on the seam of the earth, was what I thought, as I angled my body into it. All of a sudden there was a happy feeling that people sleep beside the streets and trust them.

Benchley Court not letting me in through its gate. I pushed some of the numbers in different orders but all was null. I pushed what was for me a talking button to say, but a man's voice said "Hello" so I said:

"Please let me in to Flat 4 of Michael Griffin."

It went silent and he said after a silence, "Is that Mr Griffin speaking?"

And I said back, "In a way, yes, it is."

"I'll come out," he said, and I got in in the end.

People keep asking me "Are you alright?" and I keep saying "Never better."

The keys were in the trousers and the door opened with a single push. What freshness after the niffy gym and the stale of the street heavy in my lungs. Then, to be in the middle of all these clear and sharp and shiny things electrical, things so placed that wherever you stand you stand right near everything you need. Yes, it was a bedsit or studio. Not big: a bed, a kitchen corner and chairs like big dice. Some exercise weights lay under his desk, and on it a giant computer before little pads with neat notes sheltered by three computer screens like black mirrors. It was like screens that electric people could get undressed behind. (I laughed it)

No wine or beer in the fridge and no treats at all. In me, there was the need for cake and wine (and baked beans) and to take some of this place apart. But first to go right to the bathroom for its mirror to hold my face beside the ACADEMY card. Yes, the same. Completely different as well: me as an open window and him as a fine-steel grill, polished to a sparkle about the teeth of him ... And those burning eyes. I washed our face and hands ready for a short trial of the place. Nothing there I could turn on that I wanted on. The mobile phone kept ringing but I did not want to answer to someone the name of Milly. Why try to turn on the computer, because what is in that for me? The coffee machine impossible; the TV too. He lived like this: somewhere you could not imagine music. The glass-topped table made me shiver. Oh, we could be doubles, maybe, but never one.

Nobody could throw a lifeline between me and what was laid out here in cold. How so? Maybe a little dog could jump from the drawbridge before it was pulled up for good; but that is all. The dog would fall into the moat, and this start is a new one, a different one, from a new point, blank as his white walls. Good luck to him, I say; but let's make the most of it by shopping outside.

Turning left, back at the main road, saying over and over to myself 5492: the code to get back in to the Court. Looking forward to wine, beans, cake, more wine, while trying to get the telly to work. It was cool in the Food-and-Wine, encouraging me into buying other things: clothes pegs, imitation squirt cream, pink indigestion drink, keyrings. How rare it is for something you looked forward to to be as happy as the image of it. True, the telly did not work in my way of doing, and I could not turn up the volume in my way. But I could think in the TV quiet of the sand in which I reclined. Can you float in sand, hot on the surface, cool under? Yes, blue sand, or sea if you like, with an approaching shark that could not harm you as it was bound for somebody else.

2. Back to school

I let the light come down on me bit by bit across the bed. So heavy with it, I managed to sleep through the mobile ringing (that Milly still?), till I was fresh from the night, looking across at the kitchen and my breakfast (the rest of the ginger cake). The feeling of the first day of a holiday. So I, I mean me as Michael Griffin (though that makes no sense, as I explained), must have had holidays. Just imagine him on holiday! No. Impossible. But here I am lying across it, across a new morning.

Books. He has some, partially sighted on sly shelving here and there. Books on school teaching: It's OK to be a teacher-tyrant. Teaching as a form of extreme cooking. Books like *The Leadership Mandate*, *The Audacity of Dominance*, *The Audacity of Example-Setting*, and others in that frame. Books on French – textbooks, no novels. Nor novels in English either. Computer books, lots of.

My instant coffee was not very nice, like liquid sawdust before the cake. The phone went again. I answered it from foreseeing loneliness.

I say, "Hello."

And the Milly said, "What do you mean, hello? Where the hell have you been? We were supposed to meet with the builders yesterday."

"I was in the gym," I said, "and walking here and at a Food-and-Wine."

"You sound funny, sort of dopey," she said. "Look: be ready. I'll be right round."

So I dressed up in one of his suits and shirt and a tie so I felt and looked like a tight gawk. I didn't sit down for fear of spoiling the suit. I tried to turn the radio on: impossible. The doorbell rang lots of time as I was digging out cake crumbs from the tie-knot.

Open door. There! Very nice. Blonde hair in a back bunch and twin lines of fall across the brow, and the same boiling eyes as Griffin. Was it his sister? I thought at first she was leaping in to hit me, but she forced her tongue into my head and grabbed me between the legs (no sister!) and said, "We've got time for a quickie."

"Yes-yes, we have," I said. (even happier now)

But then she said, "Christ, have you been burgled? Who's been dossing here?" She looked at the cubbyhole kitchen, picked up the bean pan, removed the slice of medium white I'd used to mop up the bean juice, and looked at the wine bottles all around and at the cake destruction. "Why are all those keyrings on the chopping board?" she said, to which I said:

"Special offers!"

She started to tidy up and clean and I followed her around, saying, "What about the quickie, then? Stop!" (she did) Eyes more boiling at me now.

"You been taking something? You must be on it now," she said. "I'll sort you out later."

"How do you mean, sort me out?" I said, in a hopeful way.

"You may need a doctor."

"No," I said.

"And why are you in that bloody suit?"

"Shall I take it off?" I said, in a hopeful way.

"No," she said.

Her car was a little world with all you need bar a bar and a toilet. Any car could bash into you and you'd be fine, like a dummy. I asked for the radio on.

"For God's sake!" she said, and I played with the dials, loud, to stop her talking in that sour-milk voice of hers. I looked down at her legs moving to work the pedals and wished I had cleaned and tidied up.

We drove out of the treeline zone into a brick zone, a cement and boarded-up zone that made me worry for her car (but not much). Then, of a sudden, there was a corner of rubbly brick, colour of dried blood and soot, and round the corner the brave face of a grey, smooth, clean building. A shopping centre? Made of the same stuff as Griffin's studio. It looked plastic, and was of grey and red patches with an electric feel to it.

Through a gate and in the same colours:

FRISBY-ORLEANS ACADEMY – WHERE EXCELLENCE IS THE DEFAULT

"They'd better not try to fob us off again," she said. "We need," she said, "to find the guy, name of Vince, I think, the one you told you'd put his balls in a vice if the labs weren't ready by this week."

"I'll say it again, if you like," I said.

"Yeah, why not say it to me now," she said in her sour way, "and I'll pass it on."

It was not going well. Which was fine, cool by me. But cool as it was, work was involved, walking work for one thing. As Milly strode to the right, I strove to stay beside her. She was silent now and I missed her sour remarks.

There were two men stained from work and stained more general in the huge Science Block. Amid the sinks and benches and Bunsen burners, there were buckets on the floor, presumably to catch last-night's rainwater.

"Can you tell me where I can find Vince?" (Milly)

"He's not in today, love."

"Don't call me love! I'm Ms Ball, one of the deputy heads, and this is Mr Griffin, our head teacher."

I waved and said "Hi!" adding, "So you managed to collect some rainwater. Very good for washing the hair, I'm told." It was supposed to be a joke.

She went on about being "exercised" about the fact that they had done so little given that term would begin in just over three weeks' time ... and more of that kind of thing, so I uh-huhed and quite-ed, adding that it would be "great" if the roof didn't leak during lessons.

They looked at me and smiled in that slight way, glancing at each other. I could have played the Teacher Tyrant and boiled them as an example of Extreme Cooking, but really my heart would not have been in it. It would have been like blowing hard at an armed assailant to make him go away. Instead *we* went away, with her swearing at me in all the standard ways.

Wherever she ended up and whichever builder she launched her fury at, I stood or sidled beside her, adding my "quites," my "that's-it-in-a-nutshells" and a few "there's-no-getting-around-its." Meanwhile, it wasn't the obviously slow progress that struck me: it was the building itself. More like a battleship: a nightmare of fragmented battleship designed to wage war not on ignorance but on the homely municipal outside-bogs epoch. (I knew this like I knew how to ride a bike.) It had the riveted hide of a ship though the sheets were of a kind of plastic, as I said before, not boiler- but Lego-plated, and the builders were engaged not in stone-wood-metal management but in bolting, clicking together and crack filling.

She was losing patience with me, to the extent of almost running away. We entered the main admin block or bunker. The Staff Room was a work in progress, in which a guy Milly recognised as a bossman was taking tea. His name was Tipper, and I sang, not quite to myself, "They Call Him Tipper, Tipper, faster than ..." (why?) and meanwhile saw a door with my photo and Michael Griffin's name on it.

I entered the office and something shifted inside me or rather collapsed, to be replaced by a terrible friendship: a meeting-up between me and Griffin. (If you can call a solar eclipse an alliance: the sunny form of me and the dark moon of him.)

Here was evidence of just how much builders *enjoy* the *de*structions that precede their *con*structions. Here was a feast of ripping out guts and letting them spill over Turkish rugs; a jokey disdain for the delicate of life; product misplacement, misplacement and muck.

The focal thing was a can of emulsion resting on a copy of *The Sun* on our (yes, why not – *our*) desk. But this, *this* was a compass point to the heart: the brush had dripped magnolia onto our copy of *The Audacity of Reasonable Force*. Now, I'd rather eat gravel than read the books he reads, but in that instant it was my or our most treasured possession.

I raced out to Tipper and dragged him into the room by his elbow, saying more or less this: "Tell me what you think of this Tipper ... huh? It's a shithouse. It'll take months to restore our" (he probably thought this was the regal plural) "office. Not only is your gang of Eastern-European retards failing for all it's worth, but they treat the *engine room* of this fine school with the utmost contempt.

"Listen … I shall be attending a conference of my fellow super-heads" (yes, now *where* did *that* come from?) "in a few weeks' time, where I shall, if things don't improve immediately, drop some poison into certain powerful ears about the bovine fucking uselessness of your firm. If you don't pull your finger out of your fat arse NOW you'd better begin looking for a new job because this firm's name will be shit!

"And do NOT use our staffroom for brewing up the precious cuppas you drink to pass the time. Bring your own troughs and billycans.

"Now fuck off back to work!"

I strode away with Milly hot on my heels and with my first thought in the good backwash from this being that at least one quickie or a slowie was now on the cards.

3. You're not the one, love – sorry

Funny how you can snap from that back to this, I thought, in her car in a cocoon of gentle rays, passive and happy, happy in my way. No anger left to think of and her rummaging among her CDs for one by – was it? incongruously? – Tina Turnip. "Simply the Best" blasted out as I watched her thighs rub against each other as she worked the pedals of the car. Nothing urgent now for either quickie or slowie.

The best I could do was to pretend strong-and-silent, staring straight ahead, not daring to speak in what I knew would be exactly the wrong voice … Then doing that felt wrong. Passive could not be the ticket, so I began to punch the air in time with the music, not chancing a glance at her for approval or not.

No. Mistake. First I punched the posh wood above the glove compartment (who would put gloves in there?) and then the sun guard over the windscreen. Doing this reminded me to flip it over to look in the mirror. (Did I have boiling eyes? No.) Another mistake.

"Jesus-God!" I heard her say under her breath as she turned off Mrs Turnip.

Her front garden, which could have been nice, had been cemented over for cars, but she smiled at me and talked about a "much-needed" drink as she unlocked her front door. Better. I stepped indoors onto something like a lawn, all cream, just as she shouted "SHOES!" I took them off while she took off (disappointingly) her high heels. I had expected her to sit beside me on the also-cream leather sofa but she sat opposite, her with her gin-and-tonic and me with mine.

She asked me what the hell had happened and said how serious it was, how bad things were for me. Then she said she knew, or thought she knew, what was up: I'd been to see Nicole and the kids.

"Who are *they*?" I said. "Are they a new band?"

She finished her drink in one gulp, like me, and gave one of those builder half-smiles, and said she'd better call the emergency services.

"Eh?" I said.

"They're your wife and children, old chap" was what she said.

Yes, that was the other name (Nicole) that came up on the phone-screen, but with a different ringtone.

I told her I'd not seen them since going to the gym.

"That means nothing, as you go every day" was her response.

As if to make her point by other means, she then jumped

over to the sofa and started kissing me, till everything took its course on the sofa.

I don't know why, but I thought that would sort of shake something loose in me; but after we'd finished and she was running her fingers through Michael Griffin's chest hair, all I was thinking was: Would there be the chance for another one before I took off for the flat via a Food-and-Wine, and would she be able to get my telly going and drop me off at a bookshop where I could stock up on novels?

It was awkward but OK till she began to speak Foreign. French, I guessed.

"What are you on about, Milly? I don't understand a word."

Wet eyes looked at me and her mouth said, "But you used to be Head of French, for fuck's sake. You really must see a doctor, Mike."

I think I must have looked scared then, because I felt it. I detest hospitals and the word doctor. "So long as," she added, "you've not forgotten you love me."

"You're very good indeed," I said. "But you're not the one, love. Sorry."

These words spoke themselves, and in the speaking of them I learned their truth for myself. It knocked me sideways saying that. It knocked her sideways, too, of course, and her being knocked sideways knocked me further that way.

She sniffed hard, and got all sarky, saying, "Thank you very much, headmaster, sir." Took a swig from the gin bottle and paused, then said coolly, "So what DID happen to the divorce-her-marry-me project, my presently fucked-up super-head gym bunny?"

I said: could we put it on the back-burner for now and could we possibly have a bit of music on?

"Get dressed." (Milly) "Your taxi will be here in 15 minutes. Where's my bloody phone?"

We'd broken its screen on the sofa, as it turned out, but it still worked; and yes, the taxi did arrive quickly, and she said, "Off you pop!"

Luckily I had the address in his wallet and recognised the approach to the flats and my Food-and-Wine. "Stop!"

There was some confusion in the shop: I didn't have much cash left, so the chap explained to me I could get £30-worth of stuff without knowing my card code called a pin; and £30-worth on *each* card. Great! So I was well away with staples: cake, wine, milk, bread, fruit-and-nut bars, plus some squirting cream on special offer and nail clippers on special offer, also beans. I really wanted some novels, too, so the chap said he'd keep the stuff while I walked to a bookshop name of Waterstones. He drew a map. I went back later for the cake, wine and so forth.

Home. I settled down to a read and a drink. Barbara Pym goes very well with angel cake and Riesling it turns out. Funny feeling, like when you think you're still in your depth in the sea but you're not, but you can swim really strongly so it's OK. *But for how long?* you think. Nobody worries about how long he can keep walking or she can keep walking ... but swimming!

I really should (I thought), as it grew dark, find the phone code so I could speak to Nicole (to find out what she's like), especially as Milly was on the way to falling away. What was obvious was that Michael Griffin, unlike me, was very organised and neat, very spic and very span, armylike; so it was a good bet he'd written down his passwords and codes and stuff.

I set to work on his desk drawers, found a little book covered in patent leather like a turtle shell. It contained the neatest handwriting I had ever seen. In the front of it it said

Michael Griffin (BA Hons, York). Beside the word iPhone there were a couple of passwords and four digits. Tried them. One worked.

I didn't know much. Almost nothing. I mean, in the way that sentences are formed in books, but some kind of sensible-ness steered me. So I found the phone's address book and the name Nicole, with a little photo of her at the top. Looked good. Brunette. Right then I spilled some Malbec (I'd switched vins) onto the screen, and wiping it away made the image bigger, so I sort of stretched it out so I could get a proper look at her. Then, as his wife's face got bigger, I heard myself saying aloud, "You're not the one, love. Sorry." Was so glad I was not saying it straight at her. She looked a nice lady, so I didn't want to hurt her feelings.

Decided I'd phone in the morning. First, I looked through the turtle book for TV codes. Nothing. So I experimented more with the remote controls till my hero of sense got me as far as a menu and loads of programmes. Watched some-thing called "Friday Night Dinner." Really good. The phone confirmed that it was Friday. Best day of the week. Every-one's favourite, really.

4. Trouble in mind

Her voice wasn't at all the Milly bully-girl. When she told me that Griffin – she called me Mikey (I liked that) – had forgotten to take "the kids" swimming yesterday, she seemed to blame herself, coming up with excuses for me. Sweet is the word.

When I said I'd come over right away (I had what was probably his old scored-out address in the turtle book, and a taxi card), she got all excited and said she'd cook my favourite. I wondered what his favourite was. Raw beef and filtered water? – ha-ha. She said how excited the kids would be.

It was not a suburban house like Milly's. Was a big old terrace where the cab could not pull up to the kerb (jam-parking). Two faces (boys) were at the window and, seeing them, I thought what a bad idea it was to come here. A peck on each cheek from the petite darling with honest blue eyes who smelt flowery in her weird kind of embarrassment – stilted, like a bad actor, wooden but very very aware of me, too aware for her own good. Lovely, really.

Yes, it was two boys (more later of them), and just in time I stopped myself putting on a commanding voice and saying to them "So what do they call you, then?" I listened hard when Nicole talked to them. Mark and Billy, I gathered; but which was which?

After a glass of whisky and ice (his drink, it seems), I took a chance, but called Billy Mark. Then I asked where the toilet was. When she said, again, that she'd cooked my favourite, I said, "What's that?" (Fish pie, worst luck.) Then she said we'd better put the fish pie on hold and have a talk in the front room.

Never mind about me: *she* was strange ... How can you pour a drink apologetically? She could. With me, of course, she was bound to get a lot of things wrong – about the new me, the non-Griffin. She served Chardonnay with the pie I don't like ... She said, "Of course, so silly." She said "How is the new car going?" I said I'd taken a cab and she said, "Of course, so silly." Or she would tell an anecdote about her making a mistake, like putting the bins out on the wrong day, adding, "So silly." Each time it was as if she'd tripped over herself, apologising to herself, and it was – odd word to use – heartbreaking how her lips turned down and her breath lengthened and tailed off: *So sillehh. A*nd especially how she was trying and failing to make light of something nagging at the heart of her.

Anyway, I'm getting ahead of myself. Our talk:

"You're so different," she said. "In a way you're better; but there's something broken ... so silly ... I mean *disordered* about you."

"Memory problems after a gym session," I said. She forgot to be her strange way and looked straight at me with mothery eyes. Was silent for a long time.

"Is Milly helping you?"

"No, she's not helping. In fact, I think she's on the way out."

"Dying?" (was there hope in her voice?)

"No, I meant *we* are not working. It's not working out."

"Oh, so sill–" Silence then. Eyes down to the carpet. "So you might be coming back to us?"

"Sorry, no."

"Of course not. So silly."

I felt like saying, "Sorry, I mean yes, I will come back," but my heart wasn't in it. My *heart?* All over the shop. How wonderful, I thought, it would be to take her in my arms and make both of us happy. *Happy?* In a way I already felt happy. The world was fresh and exciting, alive. Mentally I was undressed or dressed mentally and ready to go. But sand down the surface and there it was: the immoral murmur and horrid slop. She wasn't the one, you see.

Don't ask me (was what went through the mind) who *the one* is. Maybe I could go back to the school acting all "super," maybe line up all the female teachers like an identification parade, maybe wander the immediate locale of the flat and Food-and-Wine for women who looked *the one*, scan the phone's address book for women tagged by first name only.

Her eyes looked to the side of me, and the longer they

looked the more tears were filling them. Don't blink, I told her without speaking. She blinked and I watched the fat tears hit the colourful rug beneath, just as the bigger boy (Billy?) poked his head round the door. "Mum's crying!" he shouted back to his brother, as if she had just served an ace. Up she stood, acting the mother now. Brisk, almost poker.

We went to eat the pie. Pino Gris came to the rescue after the Chardonnay debacle. Billy was bossy to his little brother and knowing, always on the brink of saying something more than the usual child-stuff about fair shares and what's for pudding (apple pie and ice-cream, in fact – nice) but not saying it because we were all caught in invisible taut wires. Mark was only five or six, delicate of feature. Delicate all over, really. He looked upset but also impatient. "What's Daddy doing here?" he asked.

"He's come to see you two because he couldn't make swimming," she said.

"Right, then he can play me at chess!"

"OK, we'll play after dinner," I said.

He beat me fair and square. I remembered all the moves but when I looked at the board I just felt a fuzzy boredom. God, was he happy to win; probably for the first time against his dad. Billy just carried on racing a car on the TV round a circuit, a crashing circuit with chicanes and balloons, using a remote control. Sometimes the screen would be splattered with ink spots and pause. "NO!" he would yell, ignoring us completely. So he really wasn't interested in me at all; or he was interested, was upset, and pretending not to care. My "hero" common sense decided the latter. Mark took me up to show me the jet he'd made, and I said I'd better be going.

Nicole put them to bed, told them she was popping out, went next door for a babysitting daughter ("Oh. Hi Mike!")

and said she'd give me a lift home. Dry eyed and different, she was; but I didn't suggest a Food-and-Wine stop-off.

Shocked is what she was when she saw the inside of the flat: wine bottles strewn across the floor, cake plates, cake wrappers as bookmarks, drawers spilling out, spillage from hot drinks on upholstery. A pongy pawl over all.

She told me to sit down and sat across from me. "Who is our current Prime Minister?"

"No idea," I said.

"Count back from 100 in threes." (that was easy)

"Where are we now?"

"London, England, I'm pretty sure."

"Whereabouts?"

"Um, Fulham? Tottenham? Chelsea? West Ham? Crystal Palace?"

"I'll phone Fawcett Medical and get you an appointment. I'll take you there."

As it turns out, that did happen, as we shall see. But more to the point, her nervous little-girl apologeticness had gone. I missed her. But I missed the whole of her more when she left the flat, first brushing my lips with a kiss much too quick; no hug.

I was lonely for the first time as whoever I was, living a dislike of Mr Griffin, "Super-head." No mind for wine that evening.

5. A piece of cake

All I knew for certain that morning was that somebody had woken up. Do children ever feel in two minds, hovering about options, drowning in big thoughts? I'd hovered between TV channels and drinks and eats but not, since whenever, had I hovered about which lumbering background of mind to embrace, which mountain range to live in the shadow of.

Nicole surely didn't hover when she let go of the little girl, the self-excuser; but there I was a kind of matured boy waiting to be taken to the doctor.

Fried eggs on toast would have been nice.

Filter coffee with hot milk would have been great.

I phoned her and one of the kids answered (must not be her mobile then). "It's Daddy!" he shouted out from me. She came, harassed, to the phone and, terse to me, said I was seeing the doc at 4.00 p.m. and she'd pick me up at 3.45.

So to do what with my day till then?

Using my "hero" common sense, and after overhearing things said in my Food-and-Wine, and reading signs, and, well, just generally phone-fiddling too, I worked out that his wallet card called Oyster would work on the Tube, so I decided to go for a ride. Finding the Tube was easy, reading the map a piece of cake, so I headed for Piccadilly Circus.

After a few stops an oldish lady, smiley but tense, got on, sharp of feature, skinny, briskly moving, plus two children, boy and girl. She sat between them. Incredibly miserable, contemplating the end, was how they looked, the poor nippers. Moving, as refugees move. Sat across from me, their eyes wide, as if afraid to blink (see above on Nicole).

Catching the eyes of me was the woman's pink straw trilby, pulled brim-down over her eyes like a rock chick or detective or rich lady irritable in a posh deli. Then a younger woman swaggered on, in boxer-into-the-ring mode, tight clothes, short skirt over big thick legs. She sat next to me, opposite them (got the picture?), engrossed or engorged in eating grapes from a transparent box as the older lady (her mum?) kept trying to talk to her – I think about an exhibition she and the kids had just been to. Well, wouldn't you be miserable if the one next to me was *your* mother?

Every inch and twitch of her was bully. Pushed my elbow off the armrest. Made me feel like a whipped whippet. She was a hard pig, tanned and bleach-blonde. She dropped the empty grape box into her bag and got out a box of watermelon chunks to feed her face. The kids hungrily watched her eat them, and then ... Well, then she got out a magazine and read an interview, I think to discourage her mother's conversation gambits. The interview was the keyhole or rabbithole. It was the meat of it all for me – or that's what it became.

Let me explain ... Filling half a page was a full-face photo of a black-eyed woman: black bob, pale skin, bright red lips. Something about the ensemble or face-terrain, something in the way she ate me up with her eyes, told me it was she who was "the one" – the barrier against Nicole (and that other one, too). The text (yes, there was text) said her name was Valerie or Veronique or Valerianne Something-or-other. She lived in Paris, was French, while the phrase "loved Chabrol" or "lived Chabrol" was there.

Then we stopped at a station. The person next to the girl got up to leave, and somebody got on (a black guy) and was about to take the seat, but piggy leapt up, grabbed the seat herself, telling him, with a poisonous tone, "I'm going to sit with my mother, IF YOU DON'T MIND," and pointed to her empty seat. Meanwhile, somebody else had taken her seat, so I stood up to give the black guy mine. After all, I was getting off and heading home for a good think.

I got off and tried the nearest pub, picked up a paper lying around and read it to calm me; also on the off chance that Val-or-Ver was in it. No such luck. But Mistress Piggy was in it – both male and female versions. The male was Boris Johnson. The female one was called Jennifer Arcuri –

bulky, of equivalent build, so hard-fleshed and big and unconscious. I don't know what a soul is but they showed the body and body-in-motion performance of lack of one. And to be frank, Milly was somewhat in that image too. The paper caught the two Piggies in New York eating lunch one year on from news of what they'd done.

Tried the beer. So heavy on the mouth, filtering some-thing into the throat; treacle, blended with something that made me feel dirty. Ordered some Sauvignon Blanc. Diabol-ical. But I had to drink to calm me down. Brandy, the great leveller. Much better. Had two and wandered back by way of the tube again.

It wasn't euphoria (re Val-or-Ver X) I felt, more like open-ing a door onto a cupboard full of muddled stuff, hidden inside of which is the simple guarantee of permanent happi-ness. When I saw Val-or-Ver's picture, I felt neither love nor lust. More like being given a diploma – sorry, shall I go on? – knowing that now I'd have to practise my First Class in Luck. Whew! Is that OK? Bought some different instant coffee in my Food-and-Wine. Made a joke: "I'll take a jar of your insolent coffee, if I may." "Of course you will, sir." (He seemed a bit peeved I was not flashing my £30 card limit.) Back to my novels. I had some Elizabeth Taylors, some Penelope Fitzgeralds, the aforementioned Barbara Pyms, plus some William books (for a laugh). You may ask: Was it reading or rereading? No idea at all. Have not a clue. (A joy in itself.)

After a read plus coffee and cake, Nicole turned up. A kiss on both cheeks, not too brisk this time. "You've tidied up in an ... original way," she said. I'd lined up all the wine bottles round the skirting board, hid the dishes in the sink with two cushions, and lined my novels spine-out along the back of the couch like it was a bookshelf.

Later I had a kind of rush all over me, the kind I maybe ought to have had seeing Val-or-Ver X. I had it in the car. Nicole suddenly gave out a "So silly" to me when I'd corrected her (no, I'm not keen on lager and don't know who Bear Grylls is). It was a warm rush. Old Fitzgerald (Scott, not Penelope) compares running into the sea on a very hot day to drinking cold white wine after a hot curry. This was the other way round: a warm mindful after the chilly stuff. Warmth also in the surgery, with me saying lots of never-betters to "How is your this, that and the other doing?" But some questions got the better of me. The doc said he'd phone Nicole (not me!) about my hospital appointment for scanning my head.

"I do have a phone," I said.

"Can you use it?"

"Never better," I said.

I invited Nicole in for a bite. "By *bite,* do you mean a piece of cake?" To my Yes, she touched me on the cheek and said "Ciao" and dropped a few tears. It really is all more complicated than I thought. I bet my brain will be too, when they get its photos in.

6. Nobody in the world

Now here was a model of what it was like to be me. Walking through a graveyard in fog so thick there was a continuous Nowness of sensation, past strangers' names on stones. Live people appearing out of the fog suddenly, rushing to and from Barons Court tube station. Lots of fresh new doctors and tip-tapping business women were looming and sinking back. You (I) speak to them: "Which way to the hospital, please?" And they are so nice and well-meaning and clear and articulate in this soupy fog. But you – again, I mean me – are living in the fog, ignorant as much as I was of who owned these chiselled names. Was I downhearted, and did I even know what it was to be downhearted? No. The fog suited me, and I was looking forward to being scanned (my brain).

I was wrong: it was nothing like interest or fun. It revived someone's memories of an electric ham- or bacon-slicer in a grocer's shop: *neeeeong! yeeekong!* but amplified as under a jumbo's flight path. Then it may stop and change to the rumble of a train in a tunnel, where the train inexplicably goes over a cattle grid. No little jokes with the scanning people – boffins all, young and electronic, not appreciating my joke about forgetting I had metal teeth or a ball-bearing stuck in my left ear. Didn't crack a smile.

Then to wait, treading water, finding a good supermarket with better arrays of wines and eats (chocolate cheesecake – like something I'd dreamt of – creamy curry you actually don't need to heat up (better eaten cold). To own up: after some wine I'd sometimes feel like phoning Billy and Mark, to tell them a joke I'd come across. They'd have been in bed for three hours and Nicole was not patient (the reverse). But she took me back to the hospital as a bag of nerves (her) to hear about my brain. Well, it looked all present and correct to me. Yes, it looked perfectly good, all wrinkly and squashed and grey, dark in places, light in others. Walnut-like? The doc mentioned "issues" to me while looking at Nicole. "Issues" did not sound serious to me. The doc asked to speak to Nicole alone. She took me home (hers).

Look, I'm bored with this. It's bad to relay, to dredge the desert numb. Me, sitting, feeling as if my hands should be folded in my lap and my knees pressed together as if a coin was trapped between them, and listening to the creamy words, God-help-us. So I broke the sympathy pool, shattered the sponge-cake world ... "I'm off to Paris," I said.

Before Nicole had a chance to collect her thoughts, I told her about somebody's memory of reading a book about a boy who woke up one day to find nobody around at all. No mum, no dad, and the cat yowlingly unfed. Silent roads. No school. (Yippee!) Walked into town (no buses). Empty, not a soul or sausage. He walks and walks and walks, enjoying the King-feeling, the free-access euphoria, and gets to the airport. Nobody landing at all.

A bright boy, he takes this to show it's worldwide. He sees a single-seater monoplane, like a blue toy, with its key in the ignition and the fuel-gauge on full. What's he got to lose! Off he goes. Whoosh ... he's in the air, heading away from the sun. To the continent. Flying just below the clouds so he can see what's on the ground. The Eiffel Tower is below. (Yippee!) He lands on the Champs Elysées ... imagine that! Alone in Paris. Imagine! Where did he go? To a cake shop, of course, or to what they call over there a patteeseree. Just look at all those cakes. Different kinds of cakes, different from the English ones. Prettier, finer, lines of yellow and green, chocolate in dots and thin layers, butterfly tops, shades of yellow and brown, fruits rearranged from their normal state on top, snowfields of sugar; and, what's more, the wonderful aroma of coffee.

He simply picked the closest thing he could find to a boring old currant bun. (Not tough-chewy like the English ones, and complicated inside.) Lack of imagination? No. He wanted something to remind him of home. It tasted of nothing, but he chewed and chewed in the hope that some taste would crack loose, until the chewing became the saying of words:

"Mum! Dad!"

Mum wakes him up. "Bad dream, darling?"

"Not *all* bad, Mum."

"Why," said Nicole, "does this make you want go to Paris?"

"Now there you have me." You see, I'd kept quiet about Val-or-Ver X. But that book had sown the seed in someone (me) of Paris-love (so it was not a terrible lie, now, was it?).

Before she had a chance to reply, before she had a chance to stop staring, I asked her if she could get her husband's radio working. I'd heard (it turns out) of Radio Six Music. "Will you," she said, "be alright over there?"

"Why not? I'm a grown man!"

"Yes, of course, so silly. Actually the consultant did war –" Her tongue bitten.

"Did war what? War work? – ha-ha!" I was as nervous as she was.

I'm not (was not) stupid, and I knew that the chances of meeting Val-or-Ver X over there were not high, but – I took a while over what's coming up – what's worse? Trying and failing or failing to try? Eh? I was about to share this gem with her. Didn't. You can only upset the apple cart once and then you have to bend down and pick up all the apples – bruised, they may turn rotten, and I didn't want to hang around anyway.

Wanted to see Mark and Billy for a game or two and some chat and jokes; wanted to get Nicole to cook my favourites (I won't go on). But there you have it: what the wind stirs up won't settle, if you get my drift. You don't need to know about our discussions of when to go (soonest) and when if ever to come back (it's complicated).

Should I describe her printing off my tickets, the trip to St Pancras?

But I will discuss how it was to go to the station alone

(she had to take Billy to A&E after a minor fall).

The chaos around Marks and Spencer: imagine! Poking your ticket into the slot (which way up?) as the queue queued behind you. His passport and my face, then the hall of people, and at the stage-end Café Nerd (was it?). No faith at all for me in the snaky train going under the sea, so I focused on the buffet car and which direction to walk to it, then focused on my Elizabeth Taylor. Nicole had packed me a little bag, plus my phone charger. "Keep in touch," she said.

Loved the Taylor for a strange kind of reason ... A woman marries the wrong man and the right man returns but really is not much better / to write home about / use, so being happy seems an impossible dream for all of them really. But there's a but, which is that all the fallings-short and down-right pain happen in a firm and carpentered terrain. I think of Harriet's hallway, bannister, dado rail, dining-room door and the rest of it, as being of beautifully chiselled oak. *There* was a structure as solid as the rules of action – greeting, farewell, meals. The polished coachwork of Charles's motor: imagine! A frame to be lived in and suffered in.

Now, I'd had a bit of happiness recently, but not like that solid carpentered kind. Tacky-rickety is, was, and cheap. Sorry to be a bore ... I cheered up after a couple of little bottles of nice red and a cheese-and-ham French toastie. Came into the Gare du Nord. I tell you: it would have been improved with nobody there.

7. Under a pillbox hat

I struggled and squeezed out to the big entrance, bubble-wrapped in my private self, bubble-housed for all it was worth. There, from within my bubble-house, it was impossible to take in this place as Paris. But I relished the lovely dark-blue of the street names, hardly visible on the tall grey buildings, which seemed all the same height. At street level, the usual mish-mash. Was happy inside my bubble-wrap house in the tacky way I mentioned, and I felt confident that if it eroded to nothing the bubble-wrap itself would buoy me up. I hoped so, anyway.

I wandered along in the thought that if we came in from the north I would be heading south, knowing the river was south, the river I fancied more than the mish-mash – downhill slightly. Now this was more the feeling I needed. Imagine being on the back of one of these scooters and scooting up and down these little Rues. Imagine! So many little particulars for drinks and eats. The people? Not so French, it turns out. Quick and young, plus some fellow strugglers.

This was nice: a columned church above a square-cum-thoroughfare. A Roman temple, it seemed to me, proud of itself. The square called Place Franz Liszt – traffic-jam square, ha-ha! I sat on the top of the columned steps, looked across the circus to a café below the slight slope of the expected kind: cane chairs, yellow brass bits, waiters in white shirts and black waistcoats. The business!

Thanking Nicole to myself for the phrase book, I asked for the green drink I could see being drunk ("leh mem shows") that looked so French ... and steak frites. Tea, yuk, sweet mint. Ordered a carafe of rooge. All around me French-speak, not the multi-glot of the concourse. The failing to understand was really not too bad. To explain and put it this way:

TooAnnetoo AHfor.

Here at last was a solid memory, though unanchored:

TooAnnetoo AHfor.

the first line of a school-kids' chorus (children's song).

TooAnnetoo AHfor.

To some past child (let's say, for argument's sake, me) it was an incantation and collapsing wave of comfortable sadness, a lullaby that masked some adult secret, before Danny Kaye comes in singing "Inchworm, inchworm / Measuring the marigolds."

Maybe I was as slow as a kid as I am now as new Griffin. As a kid I didn't work out that they were singing *two and two are four*, though it was obvious as the next words were *four and four eight*. But that wasn't me being a slow kid only. It was the pure sound of it I wanted, like a sad lullaby from the singing children, an inviting eiderdown. I did not want it to mean anything, just sound an echo inside me.

Lost? You should be. I mean, the sea of French was filtering down through my bubble, washing me in waves of English or non-meaning. I might hear "Kes curtsy," "Johnny Marr" (rang a bell, this; from the mouth of a disheartened-looking boy), "Un-fray Amy," and as people nattered on I might hear about Benny Hill's plaid sheets, about knocking over a jam jelly, about wrapping a fridge in steam. More to the "Inchworm" point, was the mouth music, for a fancy, settling onto my mood of hope, so light, so concocted, so daft that it could be blown away by the wing-wind of a passing butterfly.

Things were nice there but they weren't easy like they are when you mooch around your Food-and-Wine in the afternoon. In short, it stopped, and I thought about why I was here: Val-or-Ver X. For goodness sake, let's head to the river. Find a hotel was the first idea after the adissyown.

Turned left and left and along where I looked up to admire the lovely dark-blue street name: *Rue de Chabrol*. Well, shiver me timbers and hi dee hi! With a wind behind me of a million of those butterflies, I was off, safely of the view that my mind had only been testing me. I was on-track. Here I come, Miss V Something. OK, I don't like pretend tension, only the real kind. Yes, I did find her a little way along Chabrol, in a corner café that looked as if it had been made from offcuts of some of the proper bistros.

The first thing I noticed was the large (for such a small, black-bobbed head) high-pink pillbox hat of someone sitting between a guy and a woman. Was it her? I sleepwalked into the café. The guy looked like he had to shave twice a day. The other woman was in the domain of Mistress Piggy. It COULD be her, and this WAS after all Rue de Chabrol. To still my heart-flutter I ordered a bootay of van blonk.

I took up position and watched and watched and drank and ordered more van blonk till a glow emerged from within me and what felt like certainty wrapped in velvet. Her movements were super-feminine: flutters of eyelashes, slight touches on the couple's arms, heavenward glances mid-sentence, poutings, hand-claspings in mock entreaty; but such a stillness default that only the best drama-schools can teach.

A split in the bubble, and the gel of me seeped out towards her, and I spoke almost in a single word: "Do-you-speak-English-and-does-your-Christian-name-begin-with-a-V?" Shock. Silence (of course) and then a smile (lovely) from

her. Her friends looked at me with the boiling eyes encoun-
tered (do recall) in other scenes, and wide grins from them
that did quite shrivel me for the moment.

Her voice was very breathy and very low in pitch and volume and not easily understood. "Eh?" I said.

"I sayed I speek eet quite good and yes my name is Virginie. Seet down, please."

She introduced me to her friends, laughing friends.
"They doan speek as good as me."

At this point it came to my attention that I needed lay
twahlets, wine and fizzy water indeed); but how could I
trust them not to leave? Part of me knew the atmosphere
was eccentric, walking-quickly-over-broken-glass eccentric. I excused myself and looked for lay twahlets with fingers crossed. Returned to find her alone, smoking (looked
great, cigarette held away from her, from *us*).

We didn't exactly talk: I interviewed her. Was she making a film at the moment? "Feelming in Spain next meunth
... verrrr secret." Where did she live? "A beeg, gruend 'ows
in San Cloo, but I 'ave a leetle playce jeust along street."
(eyes cast coyly down)

After a bit more of this, I told her my name and life story
– I mean from the last few days. I thought what I had to say
would fascinate her: my Food-and-Wine, fast sex on the
cream leather sofa, the kids teaching me the "Baby Shark
Dance" song, all that stuff.

I thought her eyes would be eating me up just like they
had in the Tube photo. They hardly met mine (trapped
flies). The only time she spoke was to ask the waiter for a
cognac – "Beeg glass 'ennessey" – and she ordered two. The
gel or sap that ran from me or was me made everything
sticky, blurring the contours. I shelved the autobio project
and the interviewing feeling to cut through the stickiness to
the euphoria that ought to be there, right then and now.

"I love you," I said, statuelike (the drink), loudly, lonely.

"I loved you before I ever saw you on Mistress Piggy's lap behind the watermelon chunks near South Ken. Do you understand me, Virginie?"

"Eeet mayke PERRRfik since to me." Her eyes met mine at last, though blurrily. "I knowed zehr was a man for me, just a filling: Eenglish, handsome. No picture of eem. But wayte! Do you know za Goya painting of Duke of Wellington but wiz yoor beeg blonde queef of' 'air? My eemaj of the man to come. You for sure now."

The machine had paid out in full. Lap now full of gold coins (maybe chocolate ones). What to do? I was all over myself with happiness.

"Zing me a zong to celebrate us, Greefeen!"

OK. I sang the "Baby Shark Dance" but it did not hit the spot. Ah! "Inchworm." All went well until I reached ...

"Could it be, you stop and see / How beautiful they are"

I choked at that point. Not crying (unlike my wife), I just seized up. She took my hand. "Brayve buoy. You are my brayve buoy, my preety deer. We pay and leave? – I theenk so."

I paid the huge bill, including for her and her friends' evening. So why the choking? Beauty? No. This was Paris and she WAS the one, attractive and very sexy. But *beauty* in all this? – do me a favour! All this? Hysteria of chocolate gold, low-key of crazy gang, no flower could flourish in this rickety darkness (fallen now). She stood up to show her flowing Spanish-like wide black skirt (getting into character?), carefully adjusted her hat, and we were off back down Chabrol towards Franz Liszt.

8. Do I hear your cistern?

Losing touch. Something out of reach. I mean, this was Paris, but there was an *Indian restaurant* side by side with a *hardware store*, like we were in Ealing or somewhere. And, to be honest, I was feeling out of touch with her too, for reasons less easy to touch. She took my arm while walking. Into her flat, my excitement still afloat in the drunkenness. Inside, she clicked on two small table lamps, but we were still in semi-darkness; just enough light to see the mess of it – a mountain range of fluffy trash, small sofa, huge TV. She stood before me, head to one side. "Brave boy!"

"Not at all brave," I slurred at her. She pulled me into a hug (no kiss; I didn't press the point).

Have you ever been in a butcher's shop that also is a florist? Me neither; but that was how she smelt. I was passive, and she spoke again:

"Not the perrfek time for eus tonight, I think so, sweet. Can neut say why at large. Tomorrow, Virginie will have a abondeunce of leuvlee theengs feur you t'enjoy."

Eh?

"You slip on sofa and be fresh for euz tomorrow."

Quick peck on the cheek and she vanished into the bedroom.

This outcome was one I was happy with. Had to assimilate it, though. Let it settle. Though, I have to say, the room was not settling, with its fairground circuit. Managed to slop onto the sofa – small, as I said. I, however, am long and skinny, almost willowy. (So how could I be a gym bunny, Milly, eh?) I floored the sofa cushions and all the rather pongy soft furnishings that complemented them and gained repose on the floor. Dreamless sleep, as all my sleeps so far; then bang awake mid-morning with my head in a vice and joy in my heart. I lay there, watching the motes of dust floating up from room rubbish, at peace in the beamed sun of Paris, knowing that this day would set me on the road to the "true me" uniting with the "true one." Planned to tiptoe in to wake her with a kiss.

Strange noises coming from the corridor, where the loo was; a torrent gush. Could she have a problem with her cistern? Imagined the floor of the bog awash.

The door was open and this I saw. Rather, this was my overall impression. A balding man dressed in Virginie's clothes, his back to me, pissing into the toilet. I could have said "like a stallion filling a tin bath from a great height" (no, I've never seen that happen). Urination petered out followed by a thunderclap fart, then, with that airlock cleared, a further short flow, then vigorous shaking and him smoothing down her dress. He turned ...

"Sah vah?" he said.

It was Virginie. I mean a man who called himself that. No hat on head to hide the big bald spot; exactly like a clot of yogurt on coal dust. Here, in the daylight, was the makeup as applied by a child, the "breasts" now at an angle, and the firm male voice.

"You're a man!" (What else could I say?)

"No! Ham a wohman. Name of Jaqueline or Jacky."

"Well if you're a woman, what are you doing with a penis?" (Slight leap of faith here.)

It's hard to think of a laugh being patronising when the laugher has approximate Panda eyes, approximate red gash of mouth-paint, drag queen eyelashes at risk of falling off, and skin like the surface of Nicole's fish pie.

"Lemee explin: Eet ees a woman's penis. I feel a woman, so ham one."

"A *woman's* penis!" (What else could I say?) *"It doesn't work like that.* You *know* it doesn't work like that. You know it *never could* work like that. You are a thoroughly nasty, lying piece of furniture and a ridiculous oaf."

"Doan call me reedeecleeuz loaf! YOU are reedeecleeuz!"

"A little, maybe, but YOU ARE A MAN!"

Then he tried to tell me, as he pottered around looking for his pillbox hat, that in years to come babies' brains will be scanned ("pictured") and they will be "given genderrr" as male or female from that. The brain expresses what sex you really are. "Zah body we muz ruhize aboeuve."

I laughed (what else could I do?), but only for a short spell as it hurt my head.

"Get out!" he added.

Having put on my shoes and jacket, I turned finally to him and started to say, "In fact, you look–"

Mistake!

He grabbed me by the hair with one hand, opened the door with the other, and threw me out, chucking my bag after me.

Call me irresponsible but it turns out I felt relief. Here was a brand new chunk of reality. Always good or goodish to find another bit.

It was more like time for lunch than breakfast, so I ordered a ham omelette and coffee in a café, and yes, you guessed, when it came to pay – no wallet. Also no phone. Delved deep in my bag. No turtle book. So he'd been creeping around my sleeping body.

Luckily I had a €20 note in my shirt pocket.

Maybe I'd left essential items there, in my pissedness ... I could maybe go back.

All my novels were gone bar one; all the ones I'd bought by women were gone. Maybe he wanted to read them to learn womanly ways.

I could try to get around him, call him Jacqueline and tell him how lovely he looked ... If he could just give me one card, the one I knew the code for by heart. Prevail (funny word) on his better nature. Or, once inside, threaten him with the police.

No, not that!

Went back and rang the entry bell. "Ello!" from the rusty grill.

"Uh, hello, Jacqueline, my lovely girl, it's your brave boy."

"Feuk oeuf!"

9. *Untender are the streets*

Numb. No feeling. Next question? Why didn't I find a policeman and try to explain it all? No confidence that it would help (touch of shame, of course of course). Second reason – numb. Third – a rash feeling of freedom, curious to find out how I would cope.

Back to Liszt and the Roman-temple church steps. The only novel left was one Nicole had given me "because some of it happens in Paris." Not one of the books I like much; in fact, just then, I resented *Tender is the Night*. Even the title ground me down.

I tried rereading a bit ... the Shah of Persia's bloody car (Shah Vah? Ha-ha!) with its fur carpet and silver frame. Mad as poor Jack. And then this sentence:

"It was fun spending money in the sunlight of a foreign city, with healthy bodies under them that sent streams of colour up to their faces, with arms and legs ..."

I can't go on. Mad, as I say, as poor Jack.

The reading made my head worse. Maybe Nicole had packed headache pills. Looked inside the little zipped pockets of the bag. No. But she had written these words on a scrap of paper: "For emergencies!" And folded inside it was a hundred euros. Thank you! Thank you! Thank you!

That my first thought was to head for my local across the roundabout and order a variety of cheeses and a bottle of their best Bordeaux (plus cakes) for a celebration may come as no surprise. Given that my mind was still in the fog of the Baron's-Court-to-hospital transit, it really was no surprise at all.

More directly at it: Imagine being short-sighted in this way. Twenty yards before you and the world is crisp and spry, otherwise a curtain of blur; so you travel forward, unravelling a clear present, hoping for the best. You look behind you – same idea. Where you have been is guesswork beyond twenty yards, and you infer for the best. Within this ring of bright pavements you can continue and construe the serious pantomime of your life; but you are without two further gadgets.

1. As for the past, you cannot cast your rod back into the memory pool. Events and facts beyond the blur-curtain wire you to bright knowledge (Danny Kaye, novels you like and may have read, monoplane to Paris, certain cakes), but they only *happen* to you – like weather and lust.

2. As for the future, you lack the slightest inkling of what to *do* in right-now's ring of bright accidents that will have any effect on possible futures in the forward blur and misty world. So the very idea of conserving money, of asking for central or scattered aid, was not there – if you follow – and d'you know what? (a horrid phrase for my purpose found on

TV channels I don't enjoy) *it was fine*. Exciting. Inevitable.

Cheeses were ordered by how much I liked their names beyond camembert and brie; lovely bread, OK salad, a powerful metallic red. Sweating (the wine and head-throb) over the phrase book, I asked them to bring "deuh gattowe fantasteek." A predictable custardy thing and a little knob of cakelette arrived like – and here's a case of wiring to the past again – those carved ridged acorns of bannister-top (yes, OK, Elizabeth Taylor's lady's staircase) but much, much smaller. Chewy on the "varnished" outside and a delicious rubberiness inside. I asked for three more and offered the custard to the waiter, who showed no interest.

Breathing deep and slow in the traffic fumes, I sat for a while over coffee, then set off back down Chabrol. There I saw an old beggar woman sitting on the pavement, legs tucked under her, hand out, entreating face tilted up and a "bonjewer" to each passerby in hardly a voice. I said "Sah vah?" and into her hand placed a twenty euro note. Her "Mehrsee" was a quiet shriek of shock at my munificence, and I toddled on.

A couple of scruffs (I was in hardy tweed jacket and cords, despite the summer) in track suits saw this. No, they didn't take her money. But after a very serious, very short confab with her, they walked in my direction.

Did not look back, feeling I could smell the river, or was it the Gare d'Est? Yes, another station with all the mucky circuits, cries and mingle of a station, with its (let's be honest) promise of escape. After I'd crossed a wide Boulevard that almost blew the pokiness of Chabrol away, I quickly looked back in station-transit to see the track-suiters speed-confab with a further scruff-pocket.

Ah! The river, the river! Here was the Seine itself, narrow at this point, more like a canal ... Actually it WAS a canal as it turned out: an Amsterdam theme-park in a bit of Paris that could be anywhere in Europe.

On my crowded side, young legs dangled over the stone bank, free and easy, seeming to know all about one another, drinking from cans. On the other side, a pleasant strip of green, neat and tended bushes that looked like the gym-surround where I came in.

I crossed the bridge and sat on a bench with my irritating book. Began to look for scab sentences to pick at, not having much success at the thinking option. The newly-formed scruff-knot, formed of the two originals and three more dark-skinned shufflers, soon crossed to my side, circuited beside the water, glancing or glaring over their shoulders me-wards in a way that looked fearful – but how could that have been? They wandered on and I relaxed till one of them appeared behind my bench.

"Eel fare bow," he said.

I knew it was not a password but replied: "The eagle flies up the chimney tonight at 9.00."

"Eegleesh?"

"Correct. What are you?"

"I hungry, boss. Not eat for two week dying on hungry."

I looked behind and saw the other scruffs in a snigger-huddle, watching the one who'd drawn the short or long straw. Five euros were pushed shiftily over to him but were rejected in dramatic sorrow. I gave him ten and he returned to the snigger-knot. They all came over. "We all hungry too, boss." More money would have eased them away – whilst glueing them to me, unless I could convince them I was spent out. So I had to pretend this. I wanted to keep some euros for dinner, breakfast, maybe a few beers.

They obviously did not believe I was spent. Oh, their disbelief! Arabs, I assumed. A kind of dance round the maypole of me. Semi-and-deadly serious, or a game. A heavy challenge for them; their knowing oh-so-well that I was on the way down, weak as water, cursed by helpfulness and beyond self-care. I was a piece of cheese nibbled away by mice ...
   "You tried dat pocket, boss? I help you, boss."

The only money I salvaged – I add that many young ones around me looked on laughingly, whereas oldsters averted their faces, disgusted; my embarrassment throbbing with Englishness – was in the back pocket of my cords. "You stand up, boss." "No! Piss off!" And off they did, like school's out.

Why didn't I try that earlier? Because now I had only 12 euros 65 and this bloody book about rich people's worries in idleness and brilliance displayed through the wrong end of a telescope. Wanted to throw it into the canal. Instead, I walked and walked till I was ready for a couple of beers, having decided to develop a taste for the lagery stuff over there and keep the wolf, the where-do-I-spend-the-night-thoughts wolf, from the door.

After the beers, I streeted my feet and heard English spoken by a blooming young family. "Oh, hello there," I beerily said and they more or less ran away. Filled the rest of the day with numb hours, chewing a ham baguette.

10. Dark camaraderie

Do you like silence? I know I do. Do you like warmth and a pillow? How about a mattress that is not made of paving-stones, a duvet that's not non-existent? I know I do.

Did I sleep at all under the solid canopy of the Roman-temple church? No idea. Sleeping with many other uncaged birds who were hardened sleepers, I lay awake mainly. I was staring at the blurry circus of the Place Franz Liszt. You shift position, buttock to buttock, hip to hip, thinking how good it would be to cuddle up with one of the more substantial female dossers, or to that shaggy dog. Maybe a couple of those small children would make a decent eiderdown. Breakfast in bed: the hamless tip of yesterday's ham baguette.

Stiff of limb, pains in my calves and coccyx, knees seized up, my walk now felt like a shuffle and, reflected in a shop window, looked like a stumble. To sum up: the white night heralded a black morning. Yes-yes, I know: "Melodrama," you'll say. But if you had been me for ten minutes the melo would be redacted, retracted, disenacted, and point made I believe.

I walked off in a new direction: south then west, not east along Chabrol, away from all the steam of so far. New streets, more from the central casting of Paree – smells of bread, coffee, mouth too dry to water so my eyes and brain watered instead. You pass so close to couples sipping and nibbling, their having the flaming cheek sometimes to ignore their food and kiss. You almost brush a cup handle, almost detect croissant-heat on the back of your hand. A bit of numbness then would have gone down a treat.

You know those novels, usually by males, where the writer has recently visited a city (Lisbon, Marseilles, Berlin, but never Leicester – ha-ha) where his characters traverse named streets, named parks and squares, visit named churches and galleries (paintings described, quivered before or despised), with transport idiosyncrasies revealed? Well, even if I could recall the rues and boulevards I walked, and fine bistros sniffed past, I wouldn't tell. Call me irresponsible. Likewise my hunger contours. They were simply the hole in the ring-doughnut I would have loved to eat.

"Don't we all, ha-ha!" I'd replied to the doc who'd asked me if I ever had suicidal thoughts. Give me a chance, I should have said, I'm only six days (is it?) old. For the thoughts that then filled the world along my unveiling walk were keeping-alive thoughts; and so, as I said before, not all bad. There was then a weird sunniness until the sun curdled suddenly, late afternoon.

It was geese I heard around me, honking honk eugh, honk eee, honk-honk eunk. No wonder, it came to me, they torture geese for food. Maybe they also torture the geese for mimicking their accent – ha-ha. Oh how I would have loved to stick the cardboard inner tube of some kitchen roll (£1.25 for two in my Food-and-Wine) down certain voice-boxes sounding from table to table, corner to corner, and force some four-square English down their throats instead of honk-honk-bloody-honk. Yes, I was turning sour-bad from all the lack.

Thus I energised me into a swagger, then ... "Hello, cowboy!"
　　What?
　　She walked beside me, falling into step, a tiny blonde in a duffed-up leather jacket, rather cute. "Eenglish, no?"

"Yes, and you?"

"Bulgaria. You have a place sleep night?"

"Sorry, I have no money." (I thought she was a prostitute with poor discrimination.)

"For sure. None of us do. I show you free hostel just down along here."

Fair enough, I thought.

We went down an alleyway, which I assumed was the back entrance to a building, and heard a man speak in rough foreign behind me, replied to by her. I turned to see the shaved head of a dosser I recognised from last night, plus another dodgy Herbert.

Baldy banged me up against the wall in a wake-up call. "Passieporty! Passieporty! NOW!"

Now that's a thought ... was passieporty still there in a zipped pocket of my bag? I hugged it to me, reminding myself of one of those young dads with their baby slung before them. By looking down at the bag end, as if it were the cutie-chops of a delightful babba, I thus gave the duo a fine clue. On cue, the dodgy Herbert whips out a knife and presses the point of it to the tip of my nose. I wasn't scared exactly so much as stilled, freeze-framed. Yes, if this had been an action movie there would have appeared at the entrance to the alley, back-lit, the black triangular form (long coat winged out) of an avenging hero.

Which was more or less what happened, as it happens. A man who was a breathing 3-D silhouette, not brown but actually black, rushed up, poked baldy in the eye, chopped his hand down onto Herbert's wrist – knife clanked down and stepped upon – punched Herbert in the belly, then kicked baldy up the arse. They ran off, followed by blondie, after whom the black triangle called a name something like "Putin!" He picked up the knife slowly, as if to calm himself, turned to me and said in almost unaccented English, "Let's get a drink."

My wishful image of a cocktail in a dive bar with an eccentric aristocrat and amateur avenger was not fulfilled. The drink was from a tin cup at a public fountain. "Let's sit," he said, and we sat on a bench. "My name is" (could not catch it) "but please call me Tash." He said:

"You must be careful. You are a sore thumb, and you look well off but collapsing."

I told him something of my story of coming there, to which he said nothing but "Let's have a couple of days of fun, then we'll get you back home."

"Fun?" I said. "What do I live on in the meantime?"

"You'll live on tar factory pills," he said and made the kind of laugh actors use to signal insanity. He very sanely wiped his eyes. He explained something of the politics of the street community, all forgotten bar this: in the 10th arrondissement there was conflict between Africans like him and Easterners (European and Middle Easterners). Being seen with him meant I was in danger from the latter, so ... Keep your eyes and bowels open – more mad laughing.

First, he told me to smarten up. I got a clean shirt from my bag, wetted a comb in the fountain, brushed myself down, polished shoes on trouser-backs. He said his coat was "pocket central." (more laughs) This was the plan: I would go up to a stallholder (the market just around the corner), try to make him understand some impossible request in loud English and sign language, while Tash pocketed baguettes, fruit, etc. We'd then repair to the canal to enjoy our feast.

"Just view this" (he couldn't contain himself) "as an adventure holiday, Michael."

It worked a treat, and soon we were marching back past the Chabrol hardware store above which poor Jack could have been, and may well have been, adjusting his hat.

11. Lookee here! ... number eleven!

"What a terrible time you all must have had with the negroes. The wisdom they have is all moulded up in their personas into masks they face the world with: Irish and romantic, illogical. They do let Baby speak for herself as one often lets women raise their voices over issues not in their hands. They become suddenly their fathers – cool and experimental."

F. Scott Fitzgerald

It was a cold night in the park (I'll explain) and I'd decided to stuff pages of *Tender is the Night* between my shirt and skin instead of a vest. Then, in the strong moonlight, I pulled out scraps from sweaty armpits left and right and read, thus concocting the above pre-dream sequence.

This was swallowed at once by an image from Tash's story. (Be patient: I'll explain, I'll explain.)

Sea surface full of banknotes, no longer marking the spot where a baby drowned.

This was undercut by sudden sub-verbal shouts, and Tash saying to stay where I was, whatever. Outlines of men fighting, and women's shrieks. Eventual departures with jeers; an almost silence, then grumbling speech.

The sea surface image returned, rising above my absolute exhaustion as I lay there. A prelude to my dream. (Never tell your boring dreams, I've heard tell. What … not ever?)

I dreamt I was on the crest of a low hill leading down to the Eiffel Tower. On the long, mild slope were fountains that could have been rows of stupendous cats' eyes, each giving off brilliant light. It was the dream of a glittering allotment that somehow outshone Versailles. The sky above, as rendered by a Renaissance master, was soundtracked by violin music that unforgettably showed me what people go for in classical music (to which I am or was deaf). This was not an image of peace and beauty, it was peace and beauty itself.

Unwelcome awakening. I'll bring you up to speed.

Tash had taken me to a park near the canal (funny kind of place, containing a vegetable garden as well as all the usual park deposits but on a grand scale). Funny and lovely, in fact. Quite a lot of fellow uncaged-ones there. He said it was a good place to sleep – locked at night so "you're less likely to wake up to find a comedy troupe emptying its bladder onto you." (Manic laughter from him; thoughts of Poor Jack from me.)

We had eaten as he talked. He was from a French-speaking West African country where he found things very bad. He taught English in school and lots of other things (clever guy but unreadable; silent then crazed, mostly as still as wood).

He and his wife had sold their home and converted the money to US dollars, planning to take a boat to France from Tunisia. Did so. The boat was flooded (overcrowded) and capsized a mile from the Spanish coast. The wife couldn't swim and drowned clutching their 12-month-old son. They'd decided not to keep the cash on themselves for fear of being robbed while asleep, so they'd stuffed $100 bills into their son's romper suit. Tash swam ashore alone, with some notes between his teeth like a money-dog.

What possible intelligent, sensitive reply could be made to this? I find it hard to meet talk with silence (I gibber, I witter, I make falling-through-the-ice wisecracks). I patted him on the shoulder after a mighty effort. He showed me the place behind a shed in the vegetable garden where he kept what would pass for a thick blanket.

"Put this on the ground," he said. "Otherwise the soil will enter your soul." (grim laugh this time)

He slept on a bench, me under it. Early hour later, he took me off for a pre-breakfast march. (The usual theft routine ensued.) Both of us tall and skinny, black and white, we were like piano keys – elongated wavering ones.

Passing some fellow uncageds (friendly), I heard them shout: "Vwallagh noomero onz."

I told him my dream. "Luxembourg Gardens," he said. No, surely not. In *Tender is the Night* they moon, they introspect, they suffer a pushy youth in a restaurant at the top of it. No, please. But he had some Metro tickets and who was I ... etc.

Loved the Metro – clean, Parisian. I felt dirty and was very. Yes!

I saw what he meant. We sat on the grass, looking down towards the centre of the city, with confected raw materials in place.

"This," he said, "will help you connect something with something." (wry laugh this time; versatile) He fumbled in "pocket central" and brought out a cigar tube and pulled from it a long roll-up. "Now," he said, "time for reefer madness." (yee-ha! was the form of the laugh on this occasion)

We smoked, him furtive (the police), me wrapped up in new wonder – not intoxication as such, more the releasing of the monkey mind.

This was not my dream, and the wonder came from the humanity of him.

Had we been there all day? – no. (Watch still working!) Then he cracked the whip, despite my lingering wonder-cloud. "Must earn some money," he declared. "I'm properly hungry. Fancy burger and fries, milkshakes. I AM too proud to beg but you'd better not be too proud to busk. Can you sing?"

I sang him a bit of "Inchworm" and "Thumbelina."

12. Why do I keep seizin' up?

I said Tash was crazed, meaning only the joke-laugh axis. What came up next was hours of his mildly crazed. He knew the owner of a kind of rag-and-bone stall and got from him a pair of long lime-green socks, a big clownish polka-dot bow tie, two thick rubber bands and a flat cap. I'd told him (made the mistake of telling him) that I only remembered a few Danny Kaye songs, and he concocted the image of Danny as a prancing zany.

He did not persuade me to do this, he *told* me to do it, and I did. So this is what I'm like; not what Michael Griffin has become since some accident, it's what I am, happily am. I trusted him to get me to do what was just my cup of tea, as it turned out.

As the lime-green socks went on, after I'd peeled off the second skin of the sensible socks, he told me: "Keep them clean, they've got to go back." Two things then snapped on: the tie (elasticated), and the rubber bands, just above my calves, to hike up the trousers and expose the lime-green beauties. The cap he'd use to gather money in. Said Tash:

"Leap around when you sing – big steps, moon steps.

Pretend your feet are sticking to the pavement – then lift! Rise suddenly high! Big smile and never make eye contact. Be loose-limbed, like a puppet with slackened strings. Think puppet, Michael."

On a crowded street I kicked off with "Thumbelina," giving a double thumbs-up to display the faces he'd drawn on their pads, trying to keep the ridged-paper cake containers ("dresses," found in a bin) in place (my thumbs stuck through them). He'd been toying with the idea of a hair-do for the thumbs – pigeon feathers stuck on with chewing gum – but they stayed bald. (I think I'd put my foot down and he'd taken heed.) The idea was to continue the set with "I'm Hans Christian Anderson," "Wonderful, Wonderful Copenhagen," and "The Ugly Duckling."

The thing is, except for smirks and pitying looks, I was ignored. Maybe we needed a tambourine? Maracas? No, we needed to be in a calm spot, one of those cute little oases, with a statue or a fountain you find over there, where kids play while mum or the babyminder text and natter and smoke. We found one ...

Here; and now I was not singing at pedestrian faces side-on, I could be louder and leapier. Had to make up the lyrics I didn't know.

> *Wonderful wonderful Copenhagen*
> *Friendly old girl of the sea*
> *As I sail away from your moonlit bay*
> *Let us drink and drink to me*

I only knew the chorus of "Hans Christian Andersen" so had to make up the rest.

You ask me who I am
I'll tell you who I am
You tell me you're a native of the sea
You ask me who I am
I'm not your average man
My second name is started with a "C"

I'm ... etc. etc.

All went well on the first run. Recalling my emotional hiccup with Poor Jack singing "Inchworm," I decided to blast through, flatten the hurdle on "stop and see how beautiful they are" through extreme enunciation and a shouting project that was probably a shriek. Some children looked scared; some mothers were surely put in mind of a banana republic's mad dictator. Made it! No problem foreseen on "Ugly Duckling." And then ... then I reached the culminating point of the duckling-swan transformation.

But a glide and a whistle and a snowy white back
and a head so noble and high
Say who's an ugly duckling?
Not I!

Screeched to a halt. Squatted down, staring at the dust patterns on the paving slabs.

Ugly ugly ugly. The ugly contortion of Poor Jack. The ugly lies that hold lives together held Michael Griffin's together around an empty centre. Waking from my dream of Paris to ugly politics. Ugly, not evil. Evil might be romantic, might flip a conviction to its opposite. But ugly is small, pitiful, lacking all conviction. Lies? Knowing you cannot take a pneumatic drill to the bedrock of you; but doing it anyway, you judder away in an ugly dance. (All this in a second? Yes.)

I remained in the melodramatic crouch, saying once, "Not I?"

Tash came over and got down beside me and I saw we had a good crop of coins in the cap. "It's OK," he whispered. "We'll knock off. Was only a bit of fun."

I was paralysed.

"Think of something funny," he advised.

I did. It worked. A song to end the set instead of "Duckling." Even had a bit of French in it. The song stayed in; we made a handsome sum. Had to make some of it up, thank God.

> *Jennifer Juniper rides a dappled mare*
> *Jennifer Juniper bollocks in her hair*
> *Is she pretty?*
> *I don't think so*
> *Is she breathing?*
> *Yes ever so*
> *Watcha doin' Jennifer my love?*
>
> *Jennifer Juniper lives upon a hill*
> *Jennifer Juniper isn't on the pill*
> *Is she happy?*
> *I've forgotten*
> *Is she breathing?*
> *Something rotten*
>
> *Jennifer Juniper*
> *Lee soo lah canteen*
> *Jennifer Juniper*
> *Arsey tray trankeen*

Doorbell?
Chew neigh crow bar
Respree tell?
We may toot pah
Keskeh toofay Jenny mon amoor.

Childish? Yes, as it turns out.

We found a café that would serve us beers. My taste for yellow fizz was coming along nicely.

"You look healthy. Outdoor life," said Tash.

"Wish I *was* healthy," said I.

"What's up?"

"Docs say I've got dangerously high blood pressure."

"Well," he fixed me with a mock-serious look, "I'd say your blood pressure was ... um ... three pasty over four."

His laugh drew the wrong kind of attention.

Burger time!

13. Park life

After a visit to the rag-and-bone man, we wandered up and down. I gave up trying to make conversation as he clearly preferred his own thoughts to my wittering, half-cooked ones. He said we'd better get back to the park before they locked up. He seemed ... quiet beyond his usual quiet. Tense.

"What's up, Tash?"

"Could be trouble tonight. My mate from Sudan got into a scrap with an Afghan after one called the other's wife a whore and it wasn't properly settled. Word spread. Anyway, chin up: I'll take you to the British Embassy tomorrow. I've got some Metro tickets."

"Going home ..." I mused aloud.

"Well, showbiz's loss is your Food-and-Wine's gain."
(the laugh again)

Did I go on about my Food-and-Wine so much? Probably.

The park was the opposite of a Food-and-Wine, though
hooch was being passed around and a similar range of skin
tints were on offer. But: no abundance; paucity city. I wasn't
in the mood for sleep, though I could feel it creeping up. As
the sun set, we claimed our bench. Sleep kept being driven
back as Tash kept getting into conversations: low-voiced
confabs with allies, rapid-harsh backchat with non-allies.

It felt like what it was: the last day of the holiday. I stank
and still had scraps of *Tender is the Night* between shirt and
skin, damp and yellow. I picked some out like fortune cookies. One read:

For a moment he stood over him in savage triumph.

I'd been using my bag as a pillow, plumped out with wastepa-
per and grass cuttings, and in my ear there was a frantic beat.
Soundtrack fitting in. Had another dream but I won't tell you
about it for obvious reasons. (I admit, it was good.)

Distant street lights and the moon contributed to a glow of
sorts. After the dream, around 2.00 a.m., I heard raucous
sounds and could see through the bench slats that Tash
wasn't there. I also saw that on the other side of the little
lake two groups had formed, between which two guys were
fighting. Somebody said something after one was knocked
down, and then it was a free-for-all, like a broth come
straight to the boil.

The sight did not surprise me (it looked like dancing).
The sound did, however – it could have passed for the

screams of 100 animals being slaughtered. Lights went on in the apartment blocks round the park as the fighters moved unpredictably, with some falling in the lake.

Then, sirens ... The coppers turned up.

I crawled out from under our bench and went to spectate. Tash stood out because of his height. A copper picked him out because of this or his extreme commitment to fighting. This cop was not impressed by Tash's rapid backchat but let it go, running off after a guy who'd ripped out a bench plank to use as a weapon. Another copper did not let it go and attacked Tash.

This was a fight between a bamboo stalk and a bulked-out armadillo ... The police were dressed for terminal combat; batons wielded like medieval beef-sticks; their helmets gleamed in the aforementioned glow-of-sorts. They were methodical, silent, untouchable. Tash's copper laid into him with his stick and a vengeance, and "For a moment he stood over him in savage triumph."

The triumph-stance: legs planted apart, knees locked, which afforded me an invitation to act on playground memories of collapsed juniors in short trousers. I crept up behind him, matching my legs to his, then hard-and-quick I pushed my kneecaps into his knee-backs so he crumpled to the ground in a satisfying way. Now to kick him in the gob insofar as his helmet would afford.

Good plan, indeed! But another copper ran up, baton raised. The pain in my head was a whacking-thwacking-quaking pain that shuddered my entire self.

14. *Light dawns gradually over the whole*

It was one of those situations when a thing can be both inside and outside you. Inside, a pain that could also be the bright sun, shooting down into the park like a lightning strike. You shut your eyes but it's still there, inside. Because the shut-eye field is red, you know it's still getting in. No escape from this or from the other kind of pain: knowing the memory inside and the nasty fact in the world outside. I mean the nasty fact of what armadillo had been doing to Tash. I could remember it as the chopping of a cleaver on a sugar beet plant. I could still hear the absence of Tash's voice afterwards.

All is well (idiot me, thinking); Tash has moved off. He's not there anymore. He's gone to get us something for our breakfast.
    Oh yeah?
    I stand up, stare down at that dark red stain on the mud-grass where his head had been last night, and I know for certain there's no tall, thin, black man on a coffee and cake hunt with a running-red head. No, he's over there, beneath a shrub, a dark, unmoving lump. The guilty, evil armadillo had made a half-hearted attempt at hiding him.

Like a toddler or a lover I call out "Tash! Tash!" as I run up to him, hoping in a dumb chorus way to see a jerk of recognition from him even before I show myself. People say "My heart was in my mouth." My heart was there alright, blocking everything so I couldn't speak, and as I needed the speaking to think, I couldn't think, only feel the horror.

His face was uppermost to the air, and it maintained something of a grin, as if to say ... "Just look at me in this state with that deep dark lozenge bang across my left eye up to the top of my forehead and down to my no-more-there cheekbone."

Now I thanked the blaring sun for the illumination of this. This what? For one thing, proof that the evil armadillo must have looked into his face when he did it, looked at Tash's clever, kind, father's face; then BANG! Was he held by Tash's eyes to the last?

It was as if my heart had leapt from my mouth and into the world, to be with the concrete horror of this: dark-red crusted blood, and, below that, pink-flesh blood, and below THAT a creaminess, brain cream. This was our horror breakfast of strawberries and cream.

I ran – not away, but over the ruts made by the police tanks last night. I ran towards the nearest copper. My head pain? My mind had pushed it away from me, freeing me to deal with this fact, with urgency.

What I heard myself say – no, scream – in a hard voice, was "Vous avez tué mon ami!"

I kept repeating this over and over, even though it wasn't fair. Not only had he not killed Tash, he was not an armadillo but an everyday, strolling kind of Paris bobby. But he did come when I pulled at his sleeve, him saying "Oui. Oui."

"Regarde! Ils n'ont pas fait les choses à moité!" I said

I looked at his face and saw he was shocked. Upset, too, in his heart. He was a good man and, seeing the look on his face, I felt a reprise of Danny Kaye's tenderness. It made me cry, hard. Not the weeping of my sentimental singing out of childhood, but crying from the gut. For Tash, of course, but for the whole world too, because this kind of thing happens in it all the time.

I understood all he said, some of which was "I'm so sorry" and he'd fetch a colleague. At this point I pause.

This French-speaking by me? It's like this. You know when you go to the pictures and there's a film by a certain film company – I forget which one – where before the film starts there's a sort of grand cartoon with crashing classical music. Screen in shades of black, maybe less black at the top, and the outline of a blacker hill, a few jet-black trees, then just one shout of light at the seam of the hill, a single beam like a cry or a magic sliver of yellow crayon or a stab of joy. The sentence "Vous avez tué mon ami!" was that beam. You know that it's got to spread bit by bit over something that's already there.

It happened. It was not a torch in a dark room, not a turning on of a switch to the top light. It's like waking ... no, it's like *growing* up. I squatted on the ground and heard myself say from some recess being treated to light ... "Light dawns gradually over the whole." Then: "Petit à petit, la lumiére se fait sur toute chose."

Yes. Good.

It was.

But bad, too.

Do I want the light to dawn over *all* of Michael Griffin? Frankly, no thank you. The burning eyes and the wanting of Milly – let those stay in the dark, under the hill, please.

Meanwhile, the nice copper came back with his senior, a bearded guy who looked like he'd been pulled away from a crucial card game, snooty, having to torture himself to meet my eyes. He just glanced down and said:

"C'est pas nous. C'est ces cons d' Arabes qui ont fait ça!"

The other cop looked shrunken and full of shame.

"Pauvre con!" was my reaction to beardy, and I said – it came out as easy as a breath, or rather a stream of angry vomit, but *in French* – "I saw it happen. I saw the armed spaceman stand over him. That's the wound of a truncheon, and you know it!"

Then I punched beardy in the mouth and that's why they brought me here.

To all their questions I answer, "Petit à petit, la Lumiére se fait sur toute chose." Just to serve them. And this was what inspired them to bring in a psychologist or psychiatrist or therapist or whatever. I said it all in French like a dream, the whole story, just to serve him. Then the poor guy says to me he thinks the bang on my head may have been – "Sur le plan médical, c'est à la limite du possible" – the crack of dawn.

I laugh a good laugh with all the freedom of a prisoner and tell him, "You mean like in a Laurel and Hardy sketch? Not very good at this, are you?"

I did not tell him so (because it's none of his blinking business), but it was the death of Tash that was the crack of dawn. How can a death – I suspect it'll take years before I manage to think it out – be the mother of light, mother of dawning? Well, it just can, and that tells you how complicated life is.

I've thought it before and I'll think it again: light is dawning over the whole, but I don't want it to dawn over *all* of Michael Griffin, I mean the bit that would have me reaching for *The Audacity of Reasonable Force* instead of *The Blue Flower*. Some parts of a landscape must remain in darkness so I can live in sunlit meadows.

Nicole? I can't remember this wife of mine beyond a smile, her so-sillys, and little punctures of other facts. Let's put it this way: I can't remember the plot of a single one of those Penelope Fitzgerald novels I read, but I could never forget that I liked them a lot. Same goes for Nicole.

The two boys? If ever there were sunlit meadows, that's what they are. And I know their dad will never again stride down a corridor in a tight suit shouting into a mobile. Mark and Billy: that's them. Now, which one's which? Mark's the bossy one, I think.

Yes, that's it. That'll do for now.

Class War

"He looks like a man who has seen trouble." You can't say that about lads nowadays; about Beckham and Lampard. They look like they've just got ready for bed after polishing off their mam's supper on a Sunday night.

Mark E. Smith
(*Renegade*, 2008)

Auberon

June 8ᵗʰ

This is pleasant. The Fall coming through the headphones and the sun shining in from Jesus Green. I[1] should do some work, really, but the end-of-term feeling is on me now. Postgrads like me are washed up on a beach of tourists and, and … what? I'm not a natural diarist, but I'll give it a go. Maybe I should write to Judy.[2]

1 Auberon Steven Castle, aged 29, at that time known to all as Bron. Later he would style himself "Steve", as will emerge. He is in the first year of a postgraduate degree in Philosophy at Cambridge. He's from a good family and resident in Hampstead, with all that this connotes. Do enjoy the relative expansiveness of some of his sentences. It won't last; I can assure you.

2 Judith Morgan (*Morgan!*) Scott. Think of her as Violet Elizabeth Bott without the upper-crust lisp, the *character*, and with the accents and deportment of a checkout girl. She thinks of herself as a visual artist and indeed that is mostly if not necessarily a fact destined to remain within the mental realm! She is pretty, nay, *vigorously* attractive. A redhead. Her father is that tycoon of trash clothing George "Josh" Scott, a yacht-owner twice over. Egregious vulgarian.

My landlord wants me to call him Con, but I would say Rad suits him better.[3] I could try Sunshine or Skip.[4] Such a ponce;[5] though my dad reckons he's alright really.

Yes, pleasant enough. But I should have stuck out for Oxford. When I used to go there to see Jaydon,[6] you would walk up from the station and you were in a medieval campus – like being on a film set, or in New York. You've seen it on the screen, now walk in, my friends. Here it's distributed, watered down. Christ's is practically next door to Marks and Spencer. It lacks spice, depth of flavour.[7] King's Parade is a beach promenade with King's itself a marine pavilion and the chapel a grand pier. Floating out to sea are Selwyn, Newham, and a few Faculty buildings.[8] Too much air. You could land a plane on the Downing courts. I was on Parker's Piece[9] one day and two young American girls asked me if it was a college; with the University Arms Hotel as the college buildings, I assume. They must have just been in Downing. Maybe if they'd taken me at Caius or St John's I'd have been plugged in to the place. But Churchill? It's a logarithm of Cambridge itself. Where's the core, the heart? You walk past the Porter's Lodge and you're in a featureless maze of brick and glass.

Similar theme for the Sidgwick Site.[10]

3 This is me, myself, I: Sir Conrad Tartt, Fellow of Trinity College, Professor of Behavioural Economics. My Professorship straddles the Department of Psychology and the Judge Institute.

4 A kind of joke, apparently.

5 Well, really!

6 I have made no efforts to discover the identity. I mean, who would? Silly name, too.

7 I'll try to refrain from commenting on such sloppiness and self-indulgence of style. Mostly! We shall see.

8 This is getting silly!

9 "Piece" is the term for some common land in this part of the world. What is being referred to here is a large grassy area south of Downing College on which cricket and other games are played.

10 Literate readers will surely know of the man Henry Sidgwick and of the importance of this site within the University. I won't pander!

As for the Philosophy Faculty, you could be in Sussex, UEA, Keele. A sixties build, I suppose. And the faculty is so small, especially compared to Oxford. I hear the latter is full of male bitches who make a sport of putting you on the spot. Here they are "nice," suburban, and they offer you "support."

I'm a snob, I find, as I write this. Hole in one. If you talk to yourself it bloody talks back.

June 10th

No, I am NOT a snob. Not a conventional one, at least. I'm fine with *nouveau riche* like Josh[11] and I bloody detest *academic nouveau riche* like Rad. When Josh talks or moves or selects from a menu, it's B.O.F. B.O.F. B.O.F.[12] like in a superhero comic. But B.O.F. is cool. When you come to Rad, it's more a spiritual phoniness. He's more FOB – a fobber off.[13] You require knowledge, reasoned judgement, intellect, and he fobs you off with the persona of a Tom Stoppardly-imagined "Oxbridge Fellow," one with squeaky circumlocutions, name-dropping, and arch jokes; bullshitting effetely about things he semi-understands. "He must have *some* talent!" Yes, for collaboration, for incubussing the brains of clever naïves, for claiming credit where no credit is due. And, of course, for that word I cannot spell that

11 See footnote 2; and do try to keep up.

12 This French term stands for *beurre, oeufs, fromage*. Originally it referred to a black marketer, now a term for a *nouveau riche*. He is no French scholar. This must have been gleaned from his father, who worked in Paris early in his career.

13 It's best to regard the following as the splutterings of a 6-year-old who's been sent to bed. Utterly pathetic. You see, I bettered him over dinner and in front of Judy the day before. The poor boy was stung. So, yes – pathetic.

rhymes with foot-spa.[14]

"Behavioural Economics."[15] What? It's a pretty good rule that intellectual frauds[16] live *between* disciplines. (What a pity I missed little George Steiner at Churchill.) How about Chemical Linguistics, Historical Low-Temperature Physics, Engineering Latin? And we all know where the Knighthood came from. He chaired a sub-committee of "behavioural scientists" which thoroughly whitewashed the fucking uselessness of Johnson and Co. during the pandemic. Actually, chaps, it's a jolly good thing to avoid telling people what they should do, then telling them ambiguously and too late. If you do it at all, and clearly, and on time, they will only get fatigued and turn bolshie-peevish. Certain phrases in the report leapt out, like saying that something "nurtures the

14 Chutzpah! You ignoramus.

15 The foolishnesses nesting in the next few sentences are so blatant, they require no illumination. Yes, behavioural economics. I'll merely say this: every lawful generalisation in economics reduces to a lawful generalisation in psychology. What else is the neo-classical concept of *marginal utility* but the *perceived* increase in hedonic outcome, on a parallel with the just-noticeable difference in psychophysics? Eh? It's Weber-Fechner, of course! Marshall's Cross, or the law of supply and demand (to civilians), is a psychological law. Try it for yourselves. Prices on the vertical axis; quantity of goods bought or provided on the horizontal axis; the demand curve moving down from the top left to the bottom right; the supply curve moving down from the top right to the bottom left. This is about what "rational" agents will do or not do in response to a state of the world. The same goes for more arcane graphs, such as the determination of real interest rates (vertical axis) in relation to savings-plus-investment (horizontal), with the investment schedule moving from top left to bottom right and savings being a vertical line on the horizontal axis. And, by extension, this explains the phenomenon of *crowding out,* which tells us – oh yes! – that investment by the state must crowd out private investment and thus cripple the economy. That laissez-faire is good is profound psychology. (*En passant*, this was what I bettered him on at dinner, flooding his leaky leftie little boat.) I scare-quoted "rational" of course. Need I add that I side with the man I'm proud to call a friend – Dan Kahneman – in *denying* our essential rationality, all of which makes my field so exciting, so fruitful.

16 You've guessed it. The handwriting is large and wayward. One can almost smell the ethanol rising from the pages.

wrong narrative." While on T-shirts worn ironically or not you would see "COMPULSION FOSTERS ALIENATION." It's a joke, but jokes can succeed. No need to add "like Johnson himself." And he's a Fellow of *Trinity*. I'll stop calling him Rad for now and move to calling him The False Positive.

How did he ever come to marry Gwen,[17] who is so nice. OK, she's a God-botherer who dresses like and is built like a sofa, but she's lovely.

June 14th

Well that was a long weekend in Heaven!

Staying at Judy's in Primrose Hill and bombing around London in her little VW soft-top in the sun is good enough; but *this*. It will become my talisman of the soul, my visual image of bliss.

Saturday morning, and Judy is standing with her back to me, naked, looking out of that long window with the Juliet balcony. The strong sun flares up her long curly hair in a cloud of fire. Her legs are together. She has a perfect female form (at least below the waist).[18] There is a triangle formed – I think of it as a spandrel[19] – at the crotch, where the

17 This, of course, is Gwendolyn Barlow, my ex-wife. Readers must know that she published these diaries with an extensive commentary a year ago under the title *A Soul Lost in the Class War*. Notoriously, and with heroic futility, she attempted to fit Bron Castle's sad story onto the Procrustean bed of Christian doctrine. Oh dear. Oh very dear. I hope my present efforts will redress the balance "even unto" (a locution of hers) psychological realism.

18 It is evident that the breasts are of a modest size.

19 The educated reader will know that this is a term in architecture used to describe a space formed epiphenomenally by the confluence of two elements. Say, the two triangular areas formed by the top of an arch and its stone frame. It's also a term in evolutionary biology to describe the non-functional offshoot of beneficial features. Notoriously, Chomsky argued that human language is a spandrel. I mean, of course, "argued!"

thighs touch at the top. The sun shone through it. Call me a berk, but I imagine this as spandrel starring in medieval myths. The beam, if it falls upon a bible, brings into being an angel;[20] the motes in the beam – there is no actual beam, of course, I think like a cartoonist – are the to-be-born souls of fertile, ravening, believer-princesses. More likely, if the beam happens to fall onto the groin of an impotent man then his "nobler part" stands in its former "warmth and vigour,"[21] causing him to put it to the test at his earlier convenience.

Yes, of course, she's a flake, too. Try as I may, I can't wean her off astrology. During this visit she produced a tome by one Alan Leo, published at the turn of the previous century. Having worked out from another book which sign my Moon resided in (Scorpio), she reads in Leo what colours you get when you mix Sun Pisces with Moon Scorpio, having first read at least twice about her own combination of both Sun and Moon in Cancer. In the latter, certain things stayed behind with me: "fancy," much changeableness, good parental influence, inheritance. She was delighted with "psychic abilities," though much disappointed that no mention was made of artistic talent.

My Pisces-Scorpio pairing was longer, perhaps because it's an inharmonious combination, so she limited herself to only four readings of it. Here we go ... jealousy; morbid inclinations; the native will tend to find himself in a job that does not match his "real" nature; too much possessiveness and self-assertion will mislead him into doing and saying things he cannot justify. One of the jobs he will be a fish out of water in is ... AERATED WATER DEALER. Soda jerk, here I come – for a bit. It's probably all I'll get with a PhD

20 Sugar rush evidence? Many a time I saw him with Mars Bars around this period.

21 Ms Barlow informs the reader in her earlier edition of these diaries that these phrases derive from a poem by the Earl of Rochester.

thesis on constitutive moral luck. "You CAN be a tortured soul, you sexy Scorpio," she said. As I say, not a bad weekend at all at all at all.

But it sucks you in, this stuff.[22] I asked about Mark E. Smith. Does he have Moon in Scorpio? After all, we share a birthday (March 5th). "It-does-not-work-like-that, silly!" was her reaction. It was Aries. Christ, though, it's spot on for him.

I wrote a mainly-"found" poem based on it when she was doing her lengthy ablutions and makings up. When she was dousing her lovely feet in aqueous cream, this happened:

Fish-Ram Shout Out

Straight up *some force and energy* to the Fish
considerable wilfulness starts making sense.
This is my clutch-bog of speciality Maltesers Geordie —
positiveness, force, energy, activity, "rather ..."
("rather"?? fuck off!)
restless and unsettled.

The native is boiling you in the bag so busy and brisk
prolific (prole-if-dick) *in ideas*/words/enthus-
iasms. Coping stone copious workier for sure.
Wha u wan wiv yr chips?
Want *ardour/active fancy / a many-sided nature* and
mushy peas.

New causes taken up eagerly (come on a my house)
then – I shit you not – *"incontinently dropped
again"*
Get off the banquet and own up
to Your Royal Heart?

22 I'm still here, quietly laughing my socks off.

WHAT to?
"Overmuch tendency to change, novelty, variety"
You jokin' me Moira!
*"too little steady persistency and
sober self-control."*

What you do at Christmastime?
Gonna laugh at home at "a little" in
*"a little danger of the personal desires and passions
getting out of control."*[23]

And now I'm back in this pleasantly dead set-up. Opened one of my Fall books, I came across these lines from Mr Smith himself:

> *Down pokey quaint streets in Cambridge
> cycles our distant spastic heritage.*

"Pokey quaint streets" is more Oxford. Let's say "plein-air spectacles," "cold-water cottage industries," "corporate low-rise" ... No, let's not bother.

I miss Judy in every way possible right now. Do I love her? You'd see her and say, "Well, who wouldn't love her?" It's more than that. We connect. We talk a lot, because with her I don't filter, feel-think-speak. Never a fear of being boring – the Great Oxbridge Evil. The downside is that she herself – how to put this? – never slants her talk towards the interesting. But I love her speaking as sound-and-vision. Bit like that old punk Siouxsie Sioux, when in her prime.

I want to be on a beach with her, counting the waves to see who can come up with the more interesting number. Why must we wait for the honeymoon, the marriage? Only a few weeks to go now. Do I see myself in these clothes I've

---

23 Out of kindness I will refrain from comment on this 6th-Form mess.

just made myself buy, standing in All Saints Church W1. The clothes have drama. *Ridiculous* drama.

June 16th

Some good news. The nice chaps and nurturing chapesses of the Philosophy Faculty have deemed my essays good enough for me to upgrade registration from MPhil to PhD. Title of proposed thesis: "The Real Ethical Consequences of the Notion of Constitutive Moral Luck." What's more, I've been chosen to be a graduate rep on the Faculty Board.

I know the thesis will begin with those famous lines of Blake's that go something like: "Every night and every morn / some to misery are born / every morn and every night / some are born to sweet delight."

For me, the burden of Bernard Williams' concept of moral luck is that the sweet-delight merchants are more inclined to do good things. So where's the moral standard in generalisations across "all agents"?[24] It's temperament that interests me, not being born with the sweet delight of a silver spoon. I think of Peter,[25] as a kid, so happy and easygoing, generous too – a good egg from the off. Responsibility here?

Then there's the whole question of being *born good*. I could construct a thought-experiment along the lines of all humans being born good. Would the category of "good act" retain a foothold here? Does not, as I suspect, doing good

24 Oh dear. And into the miasma of subjectivity and logic-chopping we go. Wrongheaded, I'm afraid. One needs, of course, an externalist perspective on moral luck, affording operationalizations both neuro-scientific and behavioral. Which is the more reprehensible, a driver who shoots a red light when late but luckily misses the child in a pushchair, or the driver who *accidentally* runs the light, tries to avoid the child but kills it? One can scan the brain of the respondents. One can correlate responses with performance on the O.C.E.A.N. personality test.
25 His younger brother.

require resistance against the pull to do wrong, the pull to be selfish? Is doing good conceptually tied to doing so against the wind of temptation? Cf., Jesus. I'm looking forward to tucking into this.

I love reading Bernard Williams. *Problems of the Self* is my bedtime reading just now. I mentioned this to The False Positive. He leans back in his pomp and languor and tells of some other False Positive who managed to get her feet under the table at King's[26] and who described Williams as an intellectual bully. This is just how FPs operate: struggling, through personal bollocky rumour, to pull down successful agents to their own sad level. FPs just *hate* True Positives. I'd pay good money to be intellectually bullied by Williams.

June 18th

I need purple ink for this entry, or dark red, or black paper with high pink ink. Something or everything changed yesterday.

I was walking across Parker's Piece in the early evening, on my way to the Arts Cinema. Just in front of me was a group of undergrads in black-and-white, making their merry way to, I assume, a Ball. I think it would have been the Emma Ball. About six of them, including two girls. Coming from the direction of Mill Road.

Just to their left, some guys were playing football. Dark-skinned, mostly, and young. It was pretty certain they were a mix of Deliveroo and Virgin-*Manger* peddlers who'd chained their bikes under a tree. Accidentally, the ball landed right in front of the undergrads. One of them – not a natural instigator, but rather desperate to please, I think

26 She had a perfectly respectable Research Fellowship, albeit non-stipendiary. As for what he says, he falls beneath his own "sad level."

– trapped the ball, dribbled, and passed it back to the group. The black-tie brigade then had their own little go at Premier League football.

Cries of "OK, that's enough!" "Come on mate!" Ignored.

Suddenly the tallest and most sporty of the undergrads shouted, "Have your ball then, fellas!" He kicked it as high as he could – and it stuck in a tree. Irretrievable. Inatreevable! The girls began to apologise. Then one of the undergrads got out his wallet, removed a £20 and a £10 note and offered them to the peddlers. Without a second's hesitation, one of them took the notes, tore them into as many pieces as he could, tossed the pieces in the air, then spat in the face of the walleteer.

No come-back from the black-tie brigade, just comments like "Well, *really!*" from the girls.

Off they went muttering – pathetic.

The footballers took out their cigarettes.

Just a nasty vignette? No, here was the gulf dramatized between the poor and the pampered parasitic crust. That it was the *brown-skinned* poor is relevant; though some of the undergrad group were pretty brown too.[27] (Why do I return to the word "pretty" for something so ugly?) THAT is how angry it makes you to be placed as they are placed. They would be nice when they deliver your din-dins or speciality socks but they are angry. The poor are passive dissemblers – no choice, really. Their anger travelled to me[28] and I abandoned my cinema plans and went "home."

Given how I am, I turned to writing and music for ways to assimilate this. Not just the grand and solid in this case but now-obscure '60s British Poetry Revival guy, Scottish,

27 This is hardly a vivid account, is it? It's not unlike a police report.
28 Is this restraint or is he really so inarticulate about his feelings? According to him, this was a mentally cataclysmic event . . . "Their anger travelled to me." Oh how interesting! Rage, rage and read a book, crack open a CD is about the size of it.

called Alan Jackson; new-wave jazz, too. I'd picked up a book of Jackson's from a charity shop a few months ago. His poem "Labour" had stuck in my mind. I remembered it as going, "The working man's heart is black black." After, all – or rather "for me" – the scene was about labour, the kind and the amount of work some people have to do to get by. It wasn't about accents, entitlement, education, even privilege: it was about working your guts out for fuck all. That they were making the most of a precious break from modern slavery.

I checked. It starts

> *the black makes the black black*
> *the black makes the black black*
> *the black makes the black black*

goes on to say that the world's

> *smithereens are held together*
> *by toil and care*
> *sweat of the ox*

and ends

> *the labouring man is black*
> *at heart.*

The guy's spit in the face? When metaphor is made concrete. A concrete poem.

I didn't really know what I was doing and why. Surely you don't turn to screaming, slicing, endlessly recursive John Coltrane for resolution, or whatever it was I felt I needed. Well, I was impotently in my pleasant room wanting to feel the anger I'd just seen "for myself" … Yes, and why? Coltrane playing "One Up, One Down" at Newport. Here comes "the master of them all, Mr John Coltrane" (the announcer), then the basic tune, but one you could imagine setting about a punchbag to.

I think it sometimes helps to ignore what Coltrane said about what he was doing. You can park the "spiritual" the "questioning" and all the transcendence-truffling and just allow yourself to hear the pure anger. As pure as the anger on the streets of the US now. The anger of the fully-human assumed to be sub-human by the white-skinned blessed. I didn't play it over headphones.[29] Wanted to fill my space with it. So, yes, I think I actually agree with LeRoi Jones[30] here: the music is racial anger stripped bare. Not just the anger of the dispossessed, the marginalised. It's anger at the assumption *of their sub-human nature*: that actually they were *well-fitted* for slavery. Though half a century before Richard Spencer and co. would say, they should be grateful for their "rescue" from Africa.

Direct relevance to the Parker's Piece incident? None. Indirect/inverted? Immense. I mean for me. The problem of racism is a problem in the mind of the racist. It's not a problem that can be set right in the object of contempt. Race is unchangeable, happily innate. Poverty and the fate of "low social quality" are not, however, innate. So back to Blake. The sweet delight can be lifted away, in this case, and spread around; the endless night ended, in this case.

I know the way I think myself from here to there to my frictionless satisfaction is not impressive; but seeing the ball-tree-spit event has cured my obsession with the *inher-*

29 Gwen said to me, "Does he have a kettle in his room?" Yes, it sounded like a kettle coming to the boil with one of these oojahs on its spout. Ten minutes of torture, following by some talking to himself.

30 Poet, playwright, racist (speciality: anti-Semitism), gay homophobe. Changed his name to Amiri Baraka. Implicated Israel in 9/11. This is the kind of person our lodger aligned himself with.

ent/innate reading of "constitutive" in "constitutive moral luck." I have just caught myself in the act of writing this. I have just read it aloud in The False Positive's lisping, faux-precise little voice. Yes, I'm stuck there. It would be funny were it not so not-remotely funny.

I've touched this base before. When the Queen died last year, not so long after that energetic boor Prince Take-Me-As-I-Am-or-Let-Me-Go Philip, it was sad. We all loved the Queen as our supreme granny. But these self-delighted worms in the upper-crust filling the airwaves with their polished sentences from their fine living rooms: wry, dry, crisp and spry, warming their hands on their own closeness to The Quality Fleet[31] ... I was filled, as I am now, with a desire to shave off Johnson's hair and fix immovable clothes-pegs to his tongue, to build a slide by the Thames and push down it every titled tit.[32] No, better: a bottomless tank of molasses with dog turds and razor blades well implicated in the mix. That they should assume superiority over *anybody* beggar's belief.

June 23rd

"If I hear that name Bernard Walliams" [sic] "again ... Oh, I'll ask you to shoot me in the head." Judy was joking, but "Walliams" was not a joke – a genuine false belief. She was joking; but she does dislike my talking about work. And I didn't have the energy to roll out the obvious jokes myself: Bernard Williams cross-dressing, writing children's books, and the like.

No, the weekend was not one of our best. I don't do what

31 Need I point out: lazy and misfiring.
32 The inarticulacy is staggering, isn't it. No turns of phrase, no punchiness, zero originality. It's hardly Voltaire. Pure playground. Stilted, too.

one has to do to aim for the best, not since the Parker's Piece day. Much tongue-biting too, because I actually dislike her paintings. Josh paid a fortune for her to be taught by the best, but she lacks the patience to learn. She's only up for shortcuts. She sees a Munch or a Leger, whatever, and immediately she does her version of it, with what she thinks of as brilliant originality. Her walls are adorned with these little triumphs over modesty.

And then there was our feast of astrology. I had to rack my brains to remember how old the FP is and when his birthday was. Sun Taurus, moon Libra, it turns out. "Terrible to have those two together," said Mystic Jude. "Look at Thatcher and Hitler." Again, I have to admit: some things rang true. There should be surface affability and polish masking an earthy determination to get what you want, by intellectual force if necessary. "Much vindictiveness towards opponents." She concluded that knowing this should help me to be more "understanding" towards him ... "I always find him very nice."[33]

Dreading the grandeur of our wedding day. Longing for the wedded state.

I want us to buy a house in Chesterton that's on the market right now. Perfect for us. I can escape the FP. What about the Primrose Hill house? She's determined to keep it and daddums thinks she really must "because London's the centre of the aaaahrt world." Funny how no matter how rough in speech people are, if they live in or revere the art world they give the word this long posh "a" – all such BOLLOCKS.

33 Yes, I'm still here, laughing off my socks.

July 13th[34]

I'm determined to be ridiculous and call this my Wyatt Day, as it began and ended with (two different) Wyatts. They bookended a day when I risked saying goodbye to big-brained books. Perhaps I have. We'll see.

People are going off me. I'm not invited. I suggest a drink; they say they're busy. I've changed. This morning, cleaning my teeth, that line of Wyatt's kept running through my head: "They fly from me that sometime did me seek." And God how free that made me feel. All I need is for her to catch *me in her arms long and small.* Who could ever need the types that this place is peopled with?

It was as this kind of black free-spirit that I went along to the Raised Faculty Building for my first Philosophy Faculty meeting in a cramped, over-windowed room near the Faculty Library. Before things got underway, they chatted like members of the little family they are. Lots of half-jokes converging on the question of why The Laughing Policeman[35] is always late.

Then he turned up; then we plodded off, jokingly. The LP set the tone, but I don't think he needed to. The undercurrent of "this isn't serious, we jess gotta get to the end" was what he had to work with. (They had welcomed me nicely; and I had smiled nicely.) Much of it I couldn't follow until, towards the end of the period before they discussed the progress of individual students and I would have to

---

34 There were quite a few intervening entries, but far too dull and miserabilist to bother with.

35 This is the Chairman of the Faculty. I have not taken the trouble to find out his name, or rather to recall it. I understand the nickname derives from (a) his being a joker, and (b) his manner of speech being reminiscent of a policeman giving evidence: "I was proceeding in a easterly direction ..." etc.

leave, The LP opened a discussion on how to fill two new posts, one at the Professorial level, one at the Reader level. Now he becomes more Policeman than Laughing. He has an idea: that they earmark these posts for "Nick" and "Trace." Everybody seemed to know who these folks were. He took out his little moleskin notebook, wetted the tip of his pencil and recorded our reaction for the jury. He explained, for the ignoramuses such as myself: "Professor Nicolas McLeod, currently at Rutgers, New Jersey, and his Australian wife Tracey Burns-Goonhall, also there." Apparently he's a philosopher of mind and she's a sort of free-stylist, mainly writes on Feminism. He and McLeod were undergraduates together at Pembroke; and the thought of feisty funky Trace coming on board seemed to be just too much for some of the gals. You see, they're FAMILY. No need to break them in. They won't shit on your bed.

"But surely we have to advertise."

"That's fine, we will."

"But the jobs will already be taken."

"Err, yes. And ...?"

The trumping assumption was how "good" they would be for us, for our suburban family fortunes.

"But what if somebody of extreme brilliance applied?"

"Well," goes the LP, "if Wittgenstein were to apply we might think again."

They laughed, dutifully.

No point in trying to describe how I felt at this point. I said, "That's not funny."

These were the first words I'd spoken – croaky and too loud.

"Please note that remark for the record," the LP said to Diane, the secretary, grinning.

"Ha-bloody-ha. I mean, you're happy, all of you, for applicants and their families, the referees, the admin people, to waste their time and hopes because of a non-existent job!"

"Well, put like that ..." (smiling)

"But that's not the main point. The point is you are lying. Lying through your teeth. Not one of you fucking[36] sniggering sheep has even commented on the moral dubiousness here. Institutionalised lying doesn't matter to you."

"You crossed a line with that language, Brian. I suggest you–"

"My name is Bron! You can't even get that right. I'm doing a PhD in moral philosophy. Some of you around this table are moral philosophers. Bernard Walliams ..."

At this point I nearly lost them. I could see the LP preparing a joke.

"Sorry, that's what my girlfriend calls him."

"Oh, so you *can* say sorry, then." (someone else)

"Bernard WILLIAMS used to chair this committee as Knightbridge Professor. Can you imagine his position on this?" I was back on solid ground now. "Doesn't this bring home that what you call philosophy is just a glass bead game. A game. Nothing to do with real life."

"So you know better than do we what philosophy is – as a *student?*" (spake Jeff Watkins, formal epistemologist hod-carrier)

"I know this: it's not a subject at all, it's empty. Philosophers know nothing worth knowing. Scientists and people in the arts know things; they have expertise. You lot are experts in ideas other people have had *and what's wrong with them* and in making a bit of elbow room for your own little ideas. Imagine an academic subject (I'd been thinking about this) called 'Intelligence.' Being intelligent is what we aspire to. This subject cuts out the middle man of stuff to be intelligent ABOUT and boils down to no more than being intelligent about whatever comes to hand. Taking a philosophical view on things is what we aspire to. You don't bother with the

36 One of our Junior Research Fellows relayed this to us over lunch. Actually, he is toning down the swearing and the violence of what he said. He had turned red, eyes staring wide, apparently.

'about' and just colonise what we all aspire to."

"Well, thanks for the meta-philosophy lecture," said The LP. "So that's all we are then?"

"No, you are also a bunch of cunts. A privileged, simpering, lightweight, lying load of cunts, living off the labour of real workers, real intellectuals."

My aim had been to walk out at that point, but when they told me to get out I decided to stay put till it was Student Business. After which, I blew them a kiss and left.

While I was talking I believed what I was saying. I believed in who I was at that moment. When I was silent, and especially when I silently left the meeting alone, I returned to the rather shy and delicately pompous me. In fact, I hate bolshie people, hate loudmouths and people who swear like that. I went for a coffee at the place on the Sidgwick Site just outside. Drank it in the sun with a bunch of normal people, feeling a freak beside them.

What I said about philosophy was not just wrong but silly. There's no parallel with intelligence. Doesn't work. It works as a flavour, as a whiff of something in the distance; but it doesn't work. (Maybe a version of it works for poetry?) This is the kind of thing tutors would put on my undergrad essays: "You have in mind something bold and original, but when you get closer to it you will see it doesn't stand up. I hope you will see this." If this kind of thing *did* work, philosophy would be easy; but it's not.

Though in my defence, the sliver-of or flavour-of or whiff-of was all I needed for the purposes I had (though these are beyond me right now). The emotion was spot on, while the thought that this emotional spasm was probably enough to scupper not just my PhD but any future in academia was kept waiting in the anteroom.

I wandered along the Backs to and fro, over the bridge that leads to the passage by Caius, then back to the Backs, feeling I should say goodbye to it. Enough!

I texted Gwen to say sorry but I couldn't make dinner, followed by an excuse that would have been plausible if I still had a social life. Then I wandered lonely as a clod down Mill Road, aiming for a few pints and a pub meal. I tried a few backstreet boozers and ended up at *The White Swan*, just before the railway bridge. Chose it because it was the sort of place in which I wasn't likely to encounter people I knew.

My modus op. is to down the beer first (four pints) then eat ravenously. I ordered meat pie and chips, three pints down, glowingly. The place had resisted the lure of a bourgeois makeover, and so it still had a jukebox, on which was playing "Shipbuilding" – Robert Wyatt singing. What I heard though was "Bridge Burning." I sang along what-I thought-was-quietly in a falsetto version of Wyatt's voice.

Now, if this were a novel, one of the people who'd been at the Faculty meeting that afternoon would have walked in and said "I see you've found your level then, BRIAN." Instead, people heard me singing "Is it worth it?" numerous times as I finished the rest of my fourth pint. There was sniggering. Or I fancy there was. Embarrassedly pissed, having already paid for the food, I got up and left. Bought two kebabs in *Fagito* and ate them on Parker's Piece.

The Deliveroo ball was still up the tree.

Crept in very quietly about an hour later.[37]

---

37 We heard him crashing in. We heard the squeaked-out repetitions of "Is it worth it?" However, his "Bridge Burning" sounded to us like "Fudge Churning." "Another sugar rush, perhaps?" I jested to Gwen.

July 16th

Maybe other people have anger glands. I know I don't. I must have a fixed innate quantum of anger in me, like libido; and it went for a burton at the Faculty Board meeting. We all need a pinch of anger to get by, to add a bit of feist. I've squandered mine – well, that's how it feels – like people are supposed to "spend" libido.

The upshot is a raging embarrassment; and it's tenderised me. I'm actually nice to Conrad;[38] and look, I've called him by his name. I deferred to the corner-shop guy who said I'd underpaid him, though I knew I hadn't. All of which sets me for my treatment – yes, that's the word – not so much *by* as *within* the Cambridge system.

The Laughing Policeman reported me to Churchill as a suitable case for punishment or banishment. Accordingly, I was told to see the Senior Tutor, a scientist like most Churchillians, and a good guy in this case.

First thing he says is, "Well, to be honest, I agree with you about philosophy. Treading water is what it is. And the airs they give themselves ..." Then he put on his serious face while suppressing a chortle and said, "But you really can't be allowed to call people 'a bunch of cunts' at a Faculty Board meeting, even if that's what a subset of them actually are." (chortle fighting its way out) "The college must take some kind of action, otherwise the Faculty will have an excuse to chuck you out. Only thing I can do is to say you're a decent chap really who's clearly suffering at the moment from mental health ISSUES, and refer you to the DRC.[39] Then the car-

---

38 He would call it that. I would call it "slyly, watchfully polite."

39 No, not the Democratic Republic of Congo. I jest, of course. This is the Disabilities Resource Centre. This is a fearsomely powerful body. (I hear Queens' made the DRC Director a Fellow Commoner. Good politics.) If the DRC says that a student should be able to audio-record supervisions or use a computer and have extra time in the exams, or be given six weeks to write his weekly essay, then you'd better agree with them. Otherwise ... I don't know what they do but we assume they would be the terrors of the earth.

ing-sharing ones will interview you to decide which of the many newly-invented mental pathologies you have fallen victim to, then crochet a report with roses sewn in at the corners (well, this was the flavour of what he said) and we can forget all about it. But DO you want to finish your PhD, Bron?"

"Yes, I do."

July 21ˢᵗ

"I put it down to wedding nerves. I know there's only a week to go, but what'll you be like on the day if this is you now?" Thus Judy over the weekend. Since when have nerves made people subservient and dull? Weirdly, this alteration has turned up my love for her. Never needed her more. Never hated the privilege that surrounds us more.

July 23ʳᵈ

I shot awake at 4.00 a.m. Never really went back to sleep. I was consumed by this thought: What's eating away at me is not only moral revulsion at social injustice, it's revulsion at Auberon Steven Castle. He's got to go. Just as, so I've decided, doing good needs the headwind of temptation-to-the-bad to make it good, so being yourself needs the headwind of practical struggle.[40] The fucking EASE of my life! The ease I'll enjoy when we're married. I won't even need to work. My dad's loaded too. What a doddle. For people like Conrad this ease is their natural element.[41] Of course, "entitlement" is a massive cliché, but we need, all of us, to be dis-entitled.

40 Top marks to anyone who can find a connective thread of logic in the last four sentences. The school of free-associative philosophy?

41 Quoting Bob Dylan can be the dipstick indicator of a moronic nature. Notwithstanding this: "You'll never know the hurt I suffer / and all the pain I rise above." I think I'll leave it at that.

It's another hot sunny day. My nose detects that Gwen is making one of her excellent fried breakfasts for us. Morning at 8.15. All's unwell with the world, but well with me now. The weakness has gone and I'm starting to line up the pricks like skittles, ready to kick them all down.

August 4th

I knew what I had to do as soon as I received the guest list. And now, on my wedding day, I'm sitting up in bed with my diary and looking at the rig I should be wearing at the altar around now: high-collared dress shirt with white tie and white waistcoat, black tailcoat, sponge-bag trousers, not forgetting the individuating touch of my own, which is a thin red silk scarf for the more open-air posturings. They hang on my wardrobe door and will continue to do so.

The logistics were a pain:[42] finding a courier to hand-deliver the letter to the Reverend Bayes,[43] plus a note from me saying "Please read it out to the congregation." The courier firm just emailed to say it's been delivered safely. I see-saw between Gulliver-in-Lilliput elation and terror. Terror for what I could have done to the heart of Judy. "OK, babe, I've left you standing at the altar, humiliated you; but hey, can't we just carry on as we were? It's US against THEM now, babe. Luv ya, babe!" I "could" have done? *Could!!!* Who am I kidding?

---

42 I should add that he is "speaking" now from my home. Gwen and I had travelled to London the night before. He said he could not and would catch the 06:45 train because he had an "important meeting" the day before. No doubt an important meeting with a cheeseburger and some strong lager in *The Tram Depot*. Honestly!

43 The poor chap's face betokened that he was calculating the probability of causing a riot. (To be explicit, I am referencing here both the Reverend Bayes' famous theorem of probability and the pop song "I predict a riot," owning to The Kaiser Chiefs. Feeling somewhat giddy today!)

I find it difficult to write. Like wading through seaweed. Can't do it. And my hands are shaking.

THERE! I made a mess of it, but I've managed to Pritt-Stick the letter into the diary. Not happy with the glue job, but it's too late now.

My darling Judy,[44]

You mean everything to me. We must be married soon. But not like this.[45] *This repulsive display of wealth and golden connections has nothing to do with us. In recent weeks I've been filling up with shame at the privilege that surrounds me – I cannot respect myself within it – while at the same time my future happiness depends upon a married life with you, living with you in dignity. By "dignity" I mean being able to hold our heads up as people who deserve what they have, and leading a morally defensible life.*[46]

    Look at the people gathered here. Thanks to your father, we have a crop of nicely corruptible Tory politicians, including new-boy Lawrence Fox, MP. You don't know that it took all my strength to dissuade Josh from having this creature do one of the readings. "He's a trained actor," said Josh. "Reading out is what

44 Such a relief not to be forced to decipher his scratchy italic hand. Yes, I am working from the original diary. My ex-wife asserts – I say "asserts" – that she did too; though I see no sign of her cough-drops and lavender-water on the pages!

45 Just prior to the absurd letter being read out, I had turned to Gwen and joked that this will be like the Archers storyline where Justin, at this stage, announces that he cannot marry Lilian because he loves her too much. Oh dear, oh very dear. Reviewers of the first edition of this diary mentioned similarities here to *Aurora Leigh*, a verse-novel I am far too busy into which to dip.

46 At this point there were some groans and sniggers. I merely grimaced at the awkwardness of the expression and the bathos.

he's good at."[47] These people are the principal agents of the misery we all drive past on the way to our treats and fine terraces.

Thanks to my dad, we also have The Great and the Good from old Universities and new Medicine. These are the Rolls Royces, The Excellents, The Immured-from-Social-Reality,[48] and above all The Self-Delighteds. They are The Nothing to do with Us.

From my mum we have the free-floating, beautiful people of the Arts. These sweeties must go and be beautiful elsewhere. They are very easily forgettable, in fact.

From Elaine[49] we have the beautifully untalented of the pop world. Just how much thought did they lavish on their clothes for today? Irrelevant to us, is what they are.

They all have one thing in common. They want to retain their fat resources while keeping an eye open for ways to get more – money, fame, cachet, power. They are parasites. Beneath them – by which I mean morally superior to them – are those who service their glorious state.

When we are properly married, my darling, we'll do it in the company of those we love and respect, not with this embarrassment of wretches.[50]

Things cannot go on as they are. With public relations operatives and actor-politicians nudging the slaves to vote for their own enslavement.

Josh has taken over the ICA for the day, as you know. What foods and wines, what distractions, await you there. GO THERE NOW! Get out of God's house.

---

47 I have to admit that the laughter was *with* him at this point.
48 Cliché lolls over cliché over cliché.
49 Wife of Josh.
50 Oh, house point to that boy!

That you should be gated here in the house of our supreme moralist Jesus Christ[51] is horrible to contemplate.

Darling, "sorry" is such a puny word. But I am so sorry to do this to you. Can you forgive me? I'm crying as I type this. I love you. I was going to add "abjectly," given what I have not done today. I'm ashamed. But we can go our own way now[52] and triumph.

From this point forward, I cease to be Auberon or Bron. My middle name is Steven, so I shall answer only to "Steve."

But you will always be Judy and the light of my life.

Steve[53]

---

51 Oh, it's not Bernard "Walliams" then. This was surely the passage that led one senior primate idiot to call his letter "wholly admirable, in my view."

52 Two little pop persons in front of us broke into the Fleetwood Mac song at this point.

53 George Scott made a sort of speech. "Lays ayn gens. Despite the inaush ...inawspish ... bad turn of events" we were still invited to the ICA bean feast. Gwen and I went. In the church all eyes were on Judy. Would she collapse? Oh no. Erect and composed, pushing away proffered arms, almost rudely. She did turn pale. However, bearing in mind that she already had the pale skin of the typical ginger nut, this was hard to detect. Please see footnote 16 on the principle of the just-noticeable difference and its relation to marginal utility. At the ICA she was still fiercely composed, drank much champagne, and danced copiously with slavering men. Strange to some perhaps, but not to a behavioural scientist. I have to report that the event had more than an element of debauch, that, I venture, it would not have had if the wedding had gone ahead. Sex in the toilets (obvious to those with alert eyes); though Gwen and I did not partake. I jest. (I mean the whole idea of our doing so is jestable, not the *negation*!) Much sniffing among the younger contingent post solo visits to the toilets. No prizes for diagnosis here.

Steve

*August 6*th

"Come. Shall we pray together?"

Gwen cannot grasp that the things I said in the letter were just little boats I'd pushed out into the pond to let gusts of wind take where it would. Communications, not. No, I'm not really a member of the Jesus-and-God Chain. My religion is the Church of Judy Scott of the Latter Day Gingers. The mind is over-stuffed with Judy-thoughts; splitting open wiv 'em, squire. I phone and text, phone and text, email, landline and mobile, night and day, every hour at least, and nothing is delivered in return.

> *Cease and Desist*
> *Cease and Desist*

I've been expecting such a letter any day now from Josh's lawyers.

The job of MY letter was, dear Gwen, to set out my emotions, fan them out in all their negation, framed around a great big Fuck You! But sentence-by-sentence ... forget it.

Yes, I care about inequality and all that stuff, but more than that I care about her.

There had been *behaviour* here: Gwen tapped on my door, crept in, head down, sat across from me, took my hands within her bigger ones – she's a big-boned "girl"⁵⁴ – fixed me

---

54 While earlier, you may recall, she was described as being built like a sofa. "This is my ex-wife you are talking about?" do I hear myself object. No, she was a not a superlative editor (biased, sentimental, over-forgiving) but was the wife of myself notwithstanding.

with her watery eyes[55] and said, "Let us talk about pain and faith. The pain of life and love and faith in a deeper love."

Having done my praying duty, I thought I'd earned the right to pose some earthly questions.

"Did Judy go to the ICA?"

"She did."

"How was she?"

"Serious and composed."

Cease and Desist
Cease and Desist

Gwen let slip she'd danced. I did not dance on 4/8. She, however, did.

"Who did she dance with?"

"Didn't recognise them."

THEM!!!

"All male? Young?"[56]

Don't torture yourself, Bron."

"Steve," I said. "*Steve.*"

"That's one sentence that was not a little boat. It was a bolt fired into your crowd. Steve is me."

Cease and Desist
Cease and Desist

August 8ᵗʰ

The Railway and Naturalist

What story lies behind that name? Lying in front of the name is a serviceable boozer in Prestwich, North Manches-

---

55 What next? Bad breath? Goodness!
56 I suspect I saw only the half of it.

ter, the domain of Mark E. Smith[57] in his living years. It was where I had lunch yesterday, having set off for London in the early morning for a day of danger, in which I planned to knock on Judy's door, and/or wait outside until ...

I would have done this but for the engineering ructions at Euston, causing Manchester trains to leave from Kings Cross. I arrived full of fear and trembling on the KX concourse to see Manchester on offer – took the offer.

I liked it in *The Railway and Naturalist*. Industrial suburbia, would you call it? Liked the voices, liked the rubbing along a difficult grain happily (more or less). Liked the lunch of two pork pies and two bags of crisps, two pints of fizzy beer. Did not like steeling myself to approach drinkers who looked like they at least knew what Mark Smith had been. They would start a low laugh, glancing sideways before the first sentence was out of my mouth.

But I did strike gold:

"Did Mark drink in *this* pub?"

"Can't think of a pub in Prestwich he didn't drink in, mate. (Fuck me, d'you hear that, Len?) Played snooker in *The White Horse* just down the road, if that helps."

He looked like a Californian hippie circa 1969 but with bad teeth and swathed in man-made fabrics brightly coloured. I thanked him profusely and finished reading my paper.

Then he came back:

"Tell you where he liked to drink on sunny days like this.

---

57 Mercifully, one cannot hear his shouted, slurred lyrics. He has become a pet of the Guardian-reading classes. Incoherent, alcoholic troublemaker does sum it up.

The Church. Down by the clough."[58] (he gave directions) "About fifteen minutes away. And you can walk past *Bargain Booze*. He kept the place going did Mark."

Then Len joins in:
   "*The Woolthorpe* on Bury Old Road was his pub. Don't listen to this twat. This is Bury NEW Road, guvnor."

The Railway and Naturalist. I rolled it round my tongue. Decided to go to *The Church*.

The first guy added:
   "He liked the actual church next to *The Church* 'cos it's where Corrie film their weddings."

I knew he liked Coronation Street. What did he say again? "The things I like are Scottish people, cats, Coronation Street, and CAN."[59]

Walked past *Bargain Booze*. Saw they gave out their own bags blazoned with BARGAIN BOOZE in red and black. I bought a bottle of water for one.

Like a country pub, *The Church* nestled, in a rough-and-ready Manchester way, next to a big sandstone church. The clough backed them. In no way a park; not a hint of Hampstead Heath. The countryside had just been left to get on with it.

---

58 Clough is northern word for wooded river valley. My researcher, Stephanie Frame, discovered these lines in an obscure poem about Prestwich Clough: "*ravine, steep valley, usu with torrent bed.* / There is no torrent bed. A red-earth throat / Buried in trees befits the locked-up church / Above, its hillside paved with ancient graves. / There is no high heroic crest; no coat / of sense." No, not much sense here! But at least it carries some descriptive colour that the diary account does signally lack.
59 According to Stephanie, a German noise-rock or "Krautrock" band.

Had another beer and wandered through the church grounds, down the steep valley to the dry river bed, darker, cooler, quiet and unreal. Sat there on a log while checking my phone. The plan had been to shock her by my silence, then turn up. Christ! A message from her:

> *How do you make spag boll your way? I fancy*
> *some tonight. J*

I replied, hardly thinking:

> *Ham jam, and bah-lamb. Sling it in a pot*
> *for an hour. Cheers, Mr Universe.*

And waited. A long wait. Then ...

> *Idiot!!!*

That was the old tone. Was it? Sent a long message with detailed instructions, ending with *or better still I could get a train back from Manchester* (be mysterious!) *and make it for you. Steve, XXXX*

Ignored! Then some low-level toing and froing, with her giving cold little thank-yous and queries, such as *How do you "dice" a carrot?* Then, after a very long gap, I was already on the train home, with:

> *I'm sorry but I must try to keep some*
> *PEACE OF MIND so we certainly cannot*
> *meet up. Dad says if you want to see me*
> *at all then a condition is you must see a*
> *psychiatrist who he chooses. I'm writing*
> *you an email about this.*
> *J*

I waited all evening for her email. Calmed myself with the writings and speech of M.E.S. The relevance to my day (lack of):

"I remember being in *The Church* on acid. Like a Hammer Horror pub. Everybody turns round as you walk in. Log fire. It's that sort of mentality."

Also, "the old Labour Club headquarters in Prestwich above what is now the great and wonderful *Bargain Booze*."

An email came but not from her. This is a job for Pritt-Stick Man.

Dear Bron Castle,[60]

I hope you don't mind my contacting you like this, "out of the blue." I am somebody you do not know. I am the son of Mrs Diane Brasher, a senior administrator in the Philosophy Faculty Office who also serves as Secretary to the Faculty Board.

My name is John but I am known as "Jack." My mum told me all about your wonderful outburst at the Board a few days ago. If what they did had been done by a middle manager in John Lewis, he or she would have been sacked forthwith. But to my mind there is one law above a certain line and another law below it.

Second, along with many other people, I saw in the newspapers about the fantastic statement you made when not turning up for your society wedding.

I have put these two things together and doing so

---

60 I have nothing to say about this beyond the observation that at least he did not begin "Dear Bron (if I may?)" *If I may!* Doesn't that kind of thing irritate you? It certainly does me.

*has emboldened me to contact you with regard to
your joining what I will call for now a "by-
invitation-only club" in Cambridge made up of
people who feel strongly about the existence of an
over-powerful ELITE that makes us all jump to its
tune. We recognise that conventional politics cannot
address this cancer and that it needs ablation as
soon as humanly possible.*

*If you would like to hear more about this club
and about what we do, I suggest we meet on Friday
at 6.00 p.m. in* The Free Press.[61] *I will be wearing a
red T-shirt and carrying a copy of the* TLS.

Best wishes,

Jack Brasher

Hardly thinking about it (my mind on Judy, what else) I
said yes, I'd come. I liked Diane. We all did. She worked in
the office at an angle to us all. Pretty, a bit cheeky. Of course,
I disliked the limping way the email was written and the
awful forced tone, but on the strength of his mum (good
phrase!) I decided to go. And also on the strength of now
being a social outcast and having nobody else to drink with.
How good it would be to sit outside *The Press* – forecast
good for Friday – actually chatting rather than reading an
article in *The Proceedings of the Aristotelian Society,* about
which my second pint persuades me to care sod all.

Texted Judy to ask her how the bolognaise went. Nothing.
Followed by more of the same. Then followed by the fearful
thought of her cooking *for someone she met at the ICA.*

61 This is rather a bijou watering hole between the East Road and
Parker's Piece. Frankly, the kind of place I myself might be seen in. Small,
bare, stylish, has restrained itself from stinking itself out with oven chips.

Then a cool draft of reason: that she would need to impress a man by her *cooking?*

August 11th

Obviously him, immediate, a tomato-red T-shirt and *TLS* for display purposes only. Young and good-looking, jet-black hair in a sort of scruffy-short Beatle cut. But toss? I could give not one at that time.

As I was approaching *The Press,* a text from Judy came through, finally telling me how the bolognaise has turned out:

> *It was quite good, thanks for asking. Have to admit*
> *I couldn't be bothered dicing the carrots so I greated*
> *(sic) them.*
> *Best wishes, Judy*

GREATED. It melted my heart. She can spell so it must have been a speed error. In that moment, this non-word seemed to catch her purity and set it beside my knowing, mechanically intelligent, dishonourable adolescent posturing.

Enough!

I use all these bloody adjectives but the real words are:

Innocence. (her)

Cruelty. (me)

It melted my heart, and my brain followed. It's still in a semi-solid state, telling me about cruelty, saying "Screw your principles, you big *boy.*" Bad enough to leave her standing; but to make her a news item and an almost-joke. The latter was this ... On *Have I Got News for You* there was a press cutting about a stranded ginger cat. Ian Hislop offered, "Was the cat called Judith Scott, by any chance?" (grin grin grin) That she should reply at all. Germaine Greer once said men are more magnanimous than women. Huh? A male Judy would be plotting murder now. I'm cruel at heart.[62]

And Cruel-at-Heart was in no state at that moment to meet Jack. I would have cancelled if I'd had his mobile number. Well-spoken he was too, with no hint of the email stiffness. He insisted we stay inside as it was "quieter."

At once he told me about himself. No curiosity about me at all. Unblinking hard stare. Turns out he'd gone to Bristol to do a photography course. *Of course,* this was a photographer's stare, not an artist's. No shred of humility and, again, no curiosity. He had to *capture* you, effectively.

While in Bristol he drifted towards the Class War[63] bunch and did layout and some photos for their newspaper, when it was an actual paper, not a zine, and well before it was a political party.

> He had me at "Class War"
> He had me at "Class War"

The powerful wave of the phrase nearly smashed down "greated" ... nearly. Magnificently to the point. Isn't it a spondee? Not quite: second word stressed a bit more. Some of the power comes from that. Nothing if not direct. I love directness. I'd love to live in a world where sex shops announce "Your Wanking Needs Met," toilets are "Shit Houses," off-licences "Alcohol Shops," and pubs have signs outside declaring "Get Pissed Here." (My *Bargain Booze* bag is Sellotaped to the side of my desk; now *there's* a direct shop name.)

---

62 Silly at heart, of course.

63 I have to say that I used to find these half-baked yahoos almost endearing. There were moves to order their tabloid *Class War* for the SCR for humorous purposes. I SUPPORTED these. After all, we take *The Guardian* (I jest; I don't mean about our taking it. We do.)

Apparently, he didn't get on with Ian Bone[64] either person-ally (no details) or ideologically. (Details galore to be given now. I had to ask permission to fetch myself a pint before he really got underway.)

"Anarchy is not-at-all a socialist option," he said. "It's the opposite of one." Much vitriol directed at Chomsky here. "People may be innately moral and rational, but rotten apples rot them easily, hence the need for CLASS WAR." Yes, surely a spondee.

His black eyes "pinned me to the wall," i.e. the wooden wall of the Press. "First, anarchism is a stupid political system." But for him and countless others, countless *hidden* others, "*Experimental Anarchism or EXAN* is the best route towards smashing the class system." (Yes-yes, I know anar-chy is from the Greek, meaning "without a head." He saw me wince at his telling me so and toned it down.) "The idea is to 'cut off the heads' of the politico-economic aristocracy as an experiment."

An experiment!? I bit my tongue.

"The hypothesis – nothing more – is that doing this will destroy faith in the naturalness and inevitability of these people lording over us, and given" (tick-tick to Noam C. here) "our innate good sense, and indeed goodness, a fairer system will emerge."

I unbit my tongue:

"Can you unpack 'cut off the heads,' please? You surely don't mean cause-to-die?" (Little philosophical joke here;

64 This unfortunate little man is the founder and leader of the silly movement. If you wish to know more, go online. As I said before: I won't pander.

no, not a joke.)[65]

Now he toned it up, roughly like this, and with cold anger:

"A hundred and seventy-three thousand dead from Covid, the huge majority of whom were poor or, if not dirt-poor, struggling members of the working class – the dregs and drones (as thought of by the happy minority). Look, mate, life was cheap to them and now it's cheap to the victim class as well. Killing Jacob Rees-Mogg – rejoice! Killing Prince Edward – OK, then. Killing little Prince George – too bad, but life's tough."

"Well, he had a good innings." (feeble joke – angrily ignored)

"Basically, these deaths would mean little to most people. EXAN believes in biological reality. It's easy to kill those on top of the heap; and they stay dead; then you can think again. Death is the mother of justice."

Me again:

"You say this new order 'will emerge' – without leaders?"

"WITH leaders, of course, ones with socialist principles. We have a plan."

And here's his plan, the gist of it:

"The Tories have got to call an election within three months. The assassinations will begin in a month and be conducted over a period of three days."

(And my mind drove past the thought of Knights of the Realm being on the hit list: goodbye Professor Sir False Positive Tartt.)

---

65 According to my former wife's notes on her previous edition of this diary, the philosopher Jerry Fodor wrote an influential paper called "Three Reasons for Not Deriving 'Kill' from 'Cause to Die.'" I mean: as if anybody cared! Or is this "Fodor's Guide" to making a name for yourself as a purveyor of untruths? (If you catch my drift.) Does anybody read these guides in this digital era? I did ask Stephanie to check. But *did* she?! (No.)

"EXAN is democratic. They will put up candidates. Sooooo many people ready to stand!

"The party will *hint* that it can end the killings. And that's a strength, not something to be unearthed by enemies. After all, the best man to stop the East-End killings was Jack the Ripper. People would be happy with that."

I, however, was not happy being skewered by his Ripper eyes.

"What will you call the party?"

"Class War, of course. The name was registered with the Electoral Commission by old Bone."

"Why that?"

"Two strong words of equal weight. Sounds strong and means strong."

He accepted, of course, that they couldn't win. The next stage of the plan was to form a ruling alliance with Labour, on condition that proportional representation would be introduced. And he assured me that EXANers were embedded now in the police, armed forces, universities, civil service.

"It's primed, primed in the shadows. Covid spurred this on. Plenty of scientists ready to lend a hand. They could fast-track vaccines. They can and have fast-tracked ways of killing on the quiet. They are part of the biological reality programme."

Death is the mother of justice.

He stopped suddenly, told me I had exactly two weeks to decide if I was joining them. He then warmed up, grew chatty, told me for instance that he used to play bass in a punk band called *Rich Trendies*. Asked me about shallow stuff. Gave me his card with his personal mobile number. It read *Brasher Studios*, London, NW3. He was, as I averred, a photographer.

August 13th

Hi Bron (I will not call you Steve if you don't mind, sorry!)[66]

As I said I would, I'm sending you this email to explain what the business of Dad and the Psychiatrist is all about. I hope you are well.

Dad did not have to be talked round by me that what you did on that day was sincere. I mean not something like "cold feet" or just suddenly "going off" me. He does not think you are a bad person deep down. I don't think that either. But that's not to say that I can get back together with you as if what happened did not happen.

I told Dad that I felt I should at least meet you "face to face" to hear what you have to say and for me to tell you "straight from the top" what all this has done to me. It was terrible for me as somebody as intelligent as you can work out for yourself.

I come back now to the business of the Psychiatrist. Dad is worried that you could be mentally dangerous for me. You may be "unbalanced." He said to me that people who are unbalanced grab on to others when they fall over and bring them down with them!!! So because of this he has made the condition that you cannot meet up with me unless you have had some sessions with a Psychiatrist who writes a report after to say you are not unbalanced. He has chosen the famous Joel Wiessler and Joel has already agreed to do it! His mobile number is 07565027166.

Finally, you asked how my painting is

---

66 Here we go again! By which I mean here was another job for Pritt-Stick Man, as he put it.

progressing. Well I had not been painting at all until one day somebody[67] showed me some of the so-called Black Paintings of Goya in a book. I did two of these last Tuesday and they turned out very well. They fitted my mood but I'm cheering up a bit now.

Take care!
Judy

This arrived suddenly into the vacuum. It was after meeting Brasher, which had been as if I were a forced compliant in a bit of immersive theatre in Shoreditch or somewhere, where the line between audience and actor is blurred. Yes, he touched some spots in me, but did so as a kind of accident, as if a three-year-old just happened to crayon $E=MC^2$. Onto the back burner with him, stranded there after he said he had to go. He pissed off and left me to my pint.

First, there was my speciality anger at her growing happier. By the agency of a "somebody." But which "somebody" would that be? Could not *not* imagine she had (as she would put it) "moved on." But maybe not – and the door is, seems, slightly ajar now.

Spark of optimism dampened by ... Joel Wiessler, an intellectual poseur-cum-author on whatever takes his feverish fancy, with Freud put near for the sake of form like the meat in a workhouse soup. Can't recall a single title, but mainly in this vein:

On Gossip and the Dishonesty Mandate
On Why we should Refuse to Learn from our Mistakes

67 Note the clever insertion of this word. She knows Castle's potential for jealously. But one must strive to be generous.

Loving as an Aggressive Move
Strong Poets and Weakling Heroes
On Masturbation

Skittish tilts at received ideas – check.
Sprightly *belles lettres* – check.
Lorry-loads of dotty resonance – check.
Background music of Sigmund spinning in his grave – check.

THAT SAID (why?), he's clever alright, good taste in literature, amazingly fluent media performer, has charm. (And,
the above said, he was probably at the wedding.)

Lay on my bed, shut my eyes the better to imagine Judy's
spandrel as dinner-party noises filtered up to me. Played
Iggy Pop[68] to drown the braying and fluting, and relished:

> *Lay right down in my favourite place.*

Men should never live without women. New book idea for
Joel Wiessler – *On why the Sexes should never Meet.*

August 14ᵗʰ

Pregnant in the Park

Not[69] something you can cure
by the wearing of perfumed gloves
this crowding with other snow ghosts
at Heaven's Gate[70]

---

68 We jested below: But why does he want to be someone's dog? To avoid
being sectioned? I think it was myself who said this, in fact.
69 He's back in the failed poetic mode, God help us.
70 Oh dear. All I can say is "Oh dear."

while balancing Jack the Ripper
against the comic potential of her "black paintings."

No I don't want her barefoot and pregnant
No it's not enough for the light to shine
through her onto me.
I want to be joined with her, simply.

But I'm back in the plague summer now:
swimming through sunshine with poisoned spores my
plankton.
It's a sun freezing me to the bone.
Here I am, pottering to get ready to take a train
to London then the tube to Ladbroke Grove.
Could he not just take my temperature over the phone?
Yes, it's within the normal range of ice.
If we were to meet, heads across tables,
she'd melt this snow ghost to a humble pool.

*August 18*th

Well, whaddahu know? A three-day oasis converting me to
the very idea of the listening cure: *Die Deutsche Biskuit*
mandate, the curate revealed. (All will be.)

There he was in his scruffy-funky dark house (dark
wood, all walls were bookcases, all tables book-stacked, all
chairs beaten-up brown leather props – old gym-horse
leather); his Dylanesque grey frizz and distracted sly attention. Some excellent coffee and those little dark-chocolate
German biscuits plus football chat. (Like me, a follower of
"The Arse.")

Then, without my noticing it, he slips in some questions
about my work and interests and Judy, and before I could
realise it I was telling him about my anti-wedding day. Then

some poetry chat, and suddenly a hard turn to very direct queries about myself, to which I stuttered out answers that left me frustrated and him thinking hard. A generous glass of a super malt and home time. Next day the same, and the day after that.

At the end of which he tells me he's ready to write the report for Josh. I'll reconstruct what he said as best I can, cutting the little verbal curlicues and ironies and probably-false modesty spasms. And yes, I did like the guy and was sad it had to end.

"Weighing up all against everything, you're not a raving loony and I'll tell Josh Scott so." Pronounced safe to meet his lovely daughter. (No, he did not go to the wedding, though he had been invited.) "But I have to tell you that you are NOTHING[71] like any of the countless philosophers that have been in this room.

"A hundred and fifty years ago you would have been a priest – a vicar tortured by the demands of sexual continence and Darwinian theory. Much of you, if not the core, believes in the Soul – an agent minus a personality who by an act of pure will can locate itself somewhere along the continuum from Good to Evil. But where the real self-torture comes in – torturing also the auditors of your long, opinionated sermons – is the idea that Good and Evil could, even by a little, be reduced to chance settings of a biological or social kind. These facts are out of the Soul's hands. And as I say this I'm reminded of Frank O'Hara's lines about the Soul holding the ribbons of a life. So that's one thing. And there are two others: immaturity and aggression.

"First, like many children, you don't listen to what you do in fact know about the differences between yourself and others and stamp people as versions of yourself. You breed false beliefs about others like a child would breed his white

71 Hello, I'm still here, fighting back tears of boredom.

mice. You actually *believed* that Judy would see your point of view and side with you. You think that if people understand what you are saying then necessarily they will agree with you. Not a great starting-state for a philosopher: to think 'Understanding me is much the same as agreeing with me.'

"Relatedly, there is something of the child lost in an adult world – wide-eyed and bruised already. You stand in a deserted supermarket aisle in a wet nappy.

"Listen: this is dangerous. You are easily led by people whose bad ideas seem to promise what you think you need, promise to complete your picture and nurture whatever theory rules you at any one time. Don't let the strange stranger take your hand even though he says he can bring you back to mummy and daddy.

"Of course you wouldn't hurt a fly, but destruction *especially of what is dear to you* can give you orgasmic joy. As you know, I tend to dance around Freud; but one thing in his theory that's far more to me than a theme to improvise on is the notion of Thanatos – the will to destroy.

"I can imagine you playing with Lego figures as a child – these two are mummy and daddy. You play at their dying when your toy jeep runs them over. Or you put them on a hot radiator face down to see their melting: how delicious your tears. Then, as an adult, the moment of destruction and loss is delicious – promising freedom and the strength of an adult.

"I think you like a drink. Be careful. And don't go near serious drugs. This is one – only one! – route to addiction: the joy of carrying on doing what you know is destroying you – for the above reasons: a pretty paradoxical kind of freedom and adult strength."

He then gave me a top-up, and we joked about and rejoiced in nuggets from the report (here at long last) of the Government's handling of Covid. I complimented him on his Frank O'Hara knowledge and he complimented me on my Archie Shepp knowledge. Then, goodbye.

I have no ironical postscript to this. Just "OK, then."

August 21st

I've spoken to her. But has she spoken to me? I mean, does setting your "peripheral systems" (or whatever Chomsky or Fodor calls them) to "respond appropriately" actually count as speaking?

And God, the long frustrating text ping-pong to set up the call!

I suppose I should be pleased: a meeting has been arranged. I wanted it to be in London, but no, it must be Cambridge, given all the "free-lance paps" still hanging around –

> *free-lance paps*
> *free-lance paps*
> *Free-lance paps with their black-and-white caps*

And "it would be bad publicity for Dad." *WHAT!*

Her voice tiny and distant.

"Where are you speaking from?"

"The study."

But she doesn't have a study, unless she means the cubbyhole where she keeps her laptop and all her shoes. This was silly. I couldn't help it:

"What are you wearing?"

Long pause, then almost angrily: "Leggings and a T-shirt, if you must know."

"Sorry."

Stuck in the apologetic mode and level. To show I'm sorry
for one enormous thing, even the tiniest thing, must be
"sorried."

"We can go punting."

"That would be nice."

"Maybe dinner in Hotel du Vin."

"That would be nice."

Felt like saying, "We can dress up as cops and push little
kids in the river."

"That would be nice."

"Good luck with the paps."

"Thank you."

"Really can't wait to see you again."

"Thank you."

The Free-Lance Paps[72]

"Whoever answers the door, ask them
if their mother's in."

"What, even if it's an old man?"

"That's like asking if a temperature reading will be different
if you do it because you're worried about high
or low temperature."

"No it isn't."

The Free-Lance Paps debate in the teaming rain.
The shunable ones amongst them drop the phrases
"perfectly marvellous" and "ready for the off."
while her face at the window appears like a single shoe
left on a carpet. Will a matching shoe
come knocking with its face set as if told to phone

72 "Here comes art," I yawn.

its ancient cousin or slavering
like an undervalued butcher?

Catch as catch can for the free-lance paps
in dog-eared weather with low-grade lunch pails
of frozen blancmange or month-old sloppy joe.

I walk past them with their crowding
glottal stops sounding like one long gargle.
Reminds me of those seagulls flocking over
the Atocha Station –
Just how near the sea is Madrid, again?
No chips for them to steal
just hard-skinned bread from La Casita.
Was I ever even there?
I'm even here now as the free-lance paps
try the air (grey air, afternoon stuff, suburban.)

The free-lance paps' attention flickers
free-lance paps downloading apps
with their old winkle-pickers
and their aerodynamic hips
diving for your chips.[73]

August 25th

The first glance on the station fixed the day: Is *that* her?
　My eyes caught by the bustling figure with scraped-back hair (it used to fall free) with two exasperated strands falling over her face; and by the failed irony of her flared blue

73 When I took my first degree in psychology – I admit, at a provincial university – we were obliged to read a book called *Language in the Crib* which documented the pre-sleep soliloquies of toddlers. This "poem" reminds me of them. The toddlers soliloquies are much better, however. I jest you not!

jeans.

Knew it was her by the time I clocked the stars, moons, suns on the velvet of her black blouson.

But what really hooked my peepers was the huge leather zip-round folder, surely for the transportation of artworks. So all-in-all the display was "Look, man, I'm an upper-echelon arty type."

She permitted a cheek-peck as I tried to confirm that these were paint specks on the flared bottoms – yes.

"Can we nip to Conrad's first?" (her first words)

I said I'd planned a snack lunch near the station, to which: "Oh, it's fine, I ate something on the train."

I'd have to lump my hunger, then.

Cab rank. If I hadn't been speaking free-associatively about whatever came to mind, then and for the rest of the day we would have been in perfect silence.

In reply to my strained query, she explained that "on August 4th" the FP had told her that she should exhibit at the College's FFF art event (Find 'em, Fuck 'em and Forget 'em? No: Fellows' Family and Friends), and casually added that she would be back "soon" for the closing wine reception AND that the FP had invited her to lunch in college to meet the art-farty Fellow who might – be still, my beating heart! – arrange for a solo exhibition of her "work" (aka, inept mimickings, as I must in bitch-mode add) in one of the College houses.

Mainly to stimulate her into telling me off for eating in the street, like old times, I gobbled a baguette in the queue. Indifference.

Jesus! The False Positive. Unction Unction and Unction: the long unavuncular hug, his cheeky face on her shoulder, locking eyes with me.[74] Her pouring herself into his silly-arse ears. I hovered, now and then reminding her when the punt was booked for. I don't much like punting on the Grantchester side; fewer tourist yobs but the water's deeper, current stronger, and what's worse is that the pole keeps sticking. There could have been comic moments to share, if she had paid any attention. I wanted to moor the thing and sit with her on the grass and talk.

Trails her hands in the water as she admires the strong resolve of the punter? Err, no. "Punter," though, yes. Taking a punt on her and nothing more. And punter as consumer, civilian, foot-soldier-passive. I think I'll shut up! And a rest from description, please God.

I wanted the promised setting-me-to-rights, and the ... what did she call it? Giving me "something from the top." And I wanted it now, in this square yard of the meadow. I had my case prepared, my quotations, my confessions and gulped-back endearments, all teed up for prostration. Prepared, too, for this being the final end.

"Can we talk about what happened?"

"Happened?" (half to herself) "About what you *did,* you mean?" (in a bored tone) "Why spoil the lovely weather. Isn't the sun just fantastic?"

Things improved over dinner, the wine helping. Also, she released her wonderful hair. I told her about the Parker's Piece incident and my Faculty Board explosion that was hardly an "incident." I added in my true position on the FP. My case that made itself was that, of course, I should not have done that on August 4th, but something decent spurred it, something big and *above us.* Then, channelling Joel W:

74 And his shuffling, like a caught-out schoolboy, charmless and needy. What a blessing for him to be tongue-tied.

"My enormous folly was to assume that you'd say 'Yes, of course, I see what you mean, that had never occurred to me till now' and join me in the worthy struggle."

I added, welling up, "I've missed you so much, Judy."

She'd been listening with her head tilted like certain GPs do after their empathy training. Then, at my final sentence, she lifted herself from her seat. Was he going to kiss me across the table? She placed a hand on each of my flushed cheeks as if framing a child's face, to deliver, "I'm sure your friends just forgot to call for you. Why not go up the park and see who's around. Aaawh."

In fact, she said nothing and returned to her starter.

But there were flashes of the old Judy; and in the cab to the station she sat close to me as I silently missed the way she dressed up always to go anywhere, made up well, not with these kohl-panda eyes which hardened her face.

Indeed, things had warmed so much, I fancied a farewell kiss on the lips and a proper hug were on the horizon, and I manoeuvred my imagination towards them.

Then I caught sight of Jack Brasher just to the side. A curt nod from him. He saw Judy and up he came all smiles.

"Hi there, Steve!" (He knew I was that now.) I introduced them; we chatted blandly; and he went to work:

"Chasing the 9.45? Let's travel together, then."

All I got from her was a "Ciao."

They walked towards the barrier. He said something. She turned towards him, looking up, laughing. Laughing for the first time that day. I sang the latter fact with mechanical grim irony to the tune of that yellow polka-dot bikini song.

> *OK! EXAN is on!*
> *I'm keeping him NEAR.*

Actually, I'm not remotely clear why I decided this, but it will stay decided.

"Not much to lose now," was one thought.

I really must buck up.

August 31ˢᵗ

Little ol' whine-harbinger me imagined them sitting up in bed together typing away in a post-coital fug. (Their emails had arrived together.)

His expressing delight and telling me to come and meet *the rest of the cell* in a few days time. Now, either the following should make me happy or he is a good politician (sounds like a formal logic example):

> *I have to admit that Judy and I did talk about*
> *"things." Frankly, Steve, just keep on doing*
> *what you're doing and she'll come round.*
> *That's my strong advice, mate.*

(MATE!)

As for her, as if from a slight acquaintance:

> *Nice to catch up. Thanks for the delicious meal*
> *and the punt ride. Jack's fun, isn't he?*
> (no)
> *He's only over the hill, in Gospel Oak.*
> (oh goody)
> *He gave me his card. I think I'll have some photos*
> *done.*

(fantabulosa!)
Could be handy for exhibitions, catalogues, etc. Or
am I getting ahead of myself?
(yes)

She added that the FFF reception was in two days time and that we could perhaps meet up before it.

When the day came we had afternoon tea in Fitzbillies. She was different, but only a chatty version of the same new absence; telling me about people I had never heard of, and her "work." But she said that a London visit could be on: an exhibition at Tate Britain we might go to. Well, that's good.

Then the next day it was off to Romsey Town for EXAN funtime.

I cycled over the Mill Road Railway Bridge – boringly enough. Well, it's no Prestwich Village, but it's not Cambridge either. It had what's demanded in my desired new normal: a hardware store, a chip shop, a Co-op, a cycle repair shop run by an old smoker with Brylcreemed hair.

First left past the Hertz car rental. OK. Looked like a place he'd rented for the purpose.

He explained that each cell had five members plus a Jack figure, that there were thousands of these across the country, that he ran ten of the many in Cambridge but he ran only five in London.

Here are the other four members, with the names Jack has given us. I'm Rex, by the way, the dog in the band.

Sheena
She's a cockroach, a scorpion.
Black clad, black fringe, hair shaved up at the back. Vituperation is the name of her game. Seething is what she excels at,

during which her jaw protrudes Habsburg-style; her lower teeth scrape her upper lip. She disguises her surely upper-middle-class nature with clumsily-dropped hs and ts, glottal stops galore, "sort-a-likes," "know-whaddeye-means," and the like. But she's no monkey; knows her stuff. Lots of imaginative swearing. (If only she could northernise her vituperative Habsburg spasms – "Ooooh, I could croosh a grape.")

Marlon

Exterior – Byronic, laconic, heroic.

Interior: dope.

This apparition was vaping outside when I turned up, blowing out great roosters of steam in his floor-length leather coat, leather-look trousers, romantically billowing white linen shirt. He languorously speaks:

"Oh, hi! You here for the experienced anarchism meeting?"

Everything had to be explained at least twice for his benefit. He was proudly, plumily posh. And so positive:

"Why, that's absolutely marvellous!"

Likeable, it has to be said.

Petroc

I know him, though not by name, and I'm sure he does not know me. A constant in the Churchill bar, eyes peeled for powerful or attractive people to impress, constantly looking over his shoulder for better people to talk to.

I think a post-doc or junior lecturer in social sciences.

The face – it's Elon Musk's; it's Bear Grylls' – it's in bad need of a smack.

He showers us with little half-jokes and clever-dick stupidities, forcing the thought: What the fuck is he doing here?

Hill

Guy in his mid 60s. Spruce in an old-fashioned way. Cavalry twills! Can you still get them? No need: he's got what's needed. Probably had them since 1974. Sports jacket with half-football buttons. Rarely spoke, and when he did it was to be sceptical in a measured, ironic way.

He too is a seether, but *innerly,* with, I think, some personal wound, not Sheena's social fury. I think he tries for a kind of Orwellian decency but he carries some grudge in him like a tapeworm.[75]

I could manage a drink with Petroc (till he spotted someone better at the bar) but not with this chap.

They all knew, and I was due to know, that on September 29th all of the cells are due, over a two/three-day period, to organise the killing of (a) royalty (b) aristocrats (c) egregiously Tory Tories. Details of how and where to be given at the next meeting.

Jack was impressive. He told us he knew that on that day he would be travelling up to Chester for the killing of the Duke of Westminster. So ... all in all a lorra lorra laughs. I'm hooked, bothered and engendered.

Was für ein Tag, mein Freund!

Why the 29th? King Charles III and Camilla are visiting Cambridge with Wills and Kate. Good pickin's there, me hearties.

75 Surely you, like me, must be tiring of this overwrought stuff.

September 3rd

Bronsteve Rex – a dinosaur, a living statue of one weeping with damp, fails to think with its tiny prehistoric brain what yesterday meant. Would have been easier to dally with, in the words of M. E. Smith, "girls in tikka masala tans totalled on White Lightning." Simpler, anyway.

I love Tate Britain as much as I do not love Tate Modern, that bombastic leisure centre. And here was my friend with her friendly smile and air-kiss. My plan was a late lunch at the gallery's Whistler Restaurant after the exhibition, then a wander of some kind, finally a meal in Chinatown. Then the train back.

The exhibition was a conceptually-driven exercise that engaged neither of us,[76] though she dispensed rough random judgements and her sad decision that she could not see it "influencing my work." I like to revisit paintings,[77] but she would swiftly decide "I've seen these, thanks" and march off somewhere else.[78]

Hard work![79]

Roy Hattersley.[80] How often has he been used as an argument against republicanism! "So you would be happy for somebody like Roy Hattersley to be President, eh? – eh? – *eh?*" (I only really know of him through dad, tbh.) Well, he was at the next table along, in the company of two faces who

76 Those of you looking for a chink of light in this remorseless negativity will look in vain.

77 Is this it?

78 No, it's not.

79 That cannot be gainsaid.

80 Venerable Labour politician. No chink of light he! Google him. As I said, I will not pander.

looked familiar from political documentaries on TV – experienced ("lived in," in old money), lean, ironic faces. And my, were they all tucking into the best wines on the card. Then a face I recognised turned up – William Keegan,[81] looking like a veteran jazz drummer: the moustache, the compact cool, the poiseful shedding of his raincoat, moving smoothly to read bottle labels and approve ... and the bollocks I do write, supposedly of my *Judy* day!

Only so much space in my dinosaur brain yesterday, not enough to listen to Judy's empty narratives, frame some sentences, and eavesdrop *successfully*. After their gossip and febrile jolly, soon settled by food arriving, they darkened towards How We Live Now. What a joy to hear "Johnson" and never "Boris." What a fact: that these two words, when preceded by "Prime Minister," are not in fact the punchline of a joke. Anyway, I couldn't really hear, just caught the flavour of intelligent despair.

Nothing to see here.

Well, I'd be perfectly happy for he who was so often called "Fattersley" to be our figurehead Pres, flying round the world, eating and drinking of the best – he's earned it, for fuck's sake – and handing out copies of his latest book to guys on baked savannahs.

"Penny for them?" she said at one point. I'd been imagining joining their table – Sheena would! – and saying, "My solution, chaps, is swift, selective killing. It's only an experiment *but it just might work*. Now, my photographer mate Jack ..."

I'd wanted to linger after pudding to catch any straws of new fact and new viewpoint in the old-Labour wind, but she said:

"I've always wanted to go up the London Eye."

So we did. Then killed time, walking through uncom-

---

81 Still allowed to pen an economically illiterate column in *The Observer*.

panionable silences, interspersed by adrenaline shots for me from her references to Jack and their photo-shoot plans and his being "handy." I tried my previous tactic of free-associative witter as we sat over our Chinese meal. Then I just gave up. I didn't have to bite my tongue; it had crawled into the cave of my midbrain. What was she playing at? This was precisely what "making nice" means. Then she too grew quiet, till eventually I said I'd better catch my train.

In a small voice, her:
"You don't want to stay over?"
Did I?
I did and I did.

The usual things happened before sleep. She wasn't passive: she was pensive. Her mind was elsewhere, in a poker-faced reverie, as I half-enjoyed my usual sequence alone – or so it felt.

No sunny spandrel morning. I woke in an empty bed. Her note:

> *Gone for a run and breakfast at Demitri's caff.*
> *Can you sort yourself out, please. Do make sure*
> *the front door is slammed in. Thanks for yesterday.*

Signed with a J. No XXXs.

I have become extinct.

That is the meaning of yesterday.

September 7ᵗʰ

Lady of the Pritt-Stick[82]

Deeper by night lighter by degrees
joy-shock by day.
Dawn of those mauve streaks
curling about my heart *(tired poeticism. Ed.)*
I can recite it whole and who couldn't
all in the inner speech of her own mauve voice.

In every home a heartbeat
and this is mine
beats with the small hard torch tattoo
    (avoid facile alliteration. Ed.)
of the Pritt torch, the beacon of rebirth.

I carry The Lady of Pritt all the way
from my handle-less mug blazoned YOU ROCK!
cheek-by-cheek with scissors pens thin flotsam varia
across the choppy channel
    (avoid facile alliteration. Ed.)
of the worn carpet
to my desk, offering a prayer:
"Thank you, Sir Bernard,[83] for having her write
on one side of the paper only. This creamy art-paper
bared for its smearing
as my diary awaits on its back with opened limbs."

O Torch of Pritt!
O Glory of Impossible Truths!

82 Auberon Castle – not noted for his sense of humour. How dreadful to
have a sense of humour, if such it can be called, trapped inside occasional,
ill-judged pseudo-poems.
83 "Williams" one assumes. Po-faced, sham self-knowledge? Posing as
jouissance, in any event.

Here is the secret flag of mutual adhesion
crossed and squared
as the Union Flag it is
a flag of sticky invisible ink
clapped down
on receptive pages
    (prolixity muddies a decent figure. Ed.)

Express!
Flare your tacky bald grey head!
Welcome the Trinity –
– Judy
– Bronsteve Rex
– The ghost of their future unity.
    (frankly, a weak culmination. Ed.)

Dear Bron,[84]

> *I have to say sorry. I should have been there ~~for~~
> when you woke up. I came back home after my
> breakfast alone to the empty house, of course. Your
> not being there all of a sudden seemed very
> important and it made me sad. I missed you a lot to
> tell you the truth. When I saw what was left of your
> toast and Marmite and your tea mug I did cry a bit.*
>   *The point is that try as I might I cannot get back
> to "being myself" with you ~~yet~~. Don't forget that I
> not only have the Sun in Cancer but also the Moon
> in it. I have a very sensitive centre that I have to
> protect with a hard shell. You only saw the shell
> yesterday you see, even I think "between the sheets."*
>   *Being in my house without you in it as if your not*

---

84 As adumbrated in the "poem." She had written the letter in mauve ink,
with a fine roller-ball pen, I imagine. The hand was large and loopy
(ambiguity intended!), all in a girlish fashion.

*being there was a kind of "presence" (I hope this
makes some sense!) changed something in me. Lets
have another day soon when the Crab welcomes you
into her ~~soft~~ tender heart.*

*This Friday is the day arranged for me to come
up to have lunch in Trinity with Conrad so I can
meet Dr Jocasta Eilan the keeper of the pictures (or
whatever she's called). I have already emailed her
photos of a lot of them that Jack helped me with,
though that may be a bit "forward."*

*If you are going to be free that afternoon we can
have a drink outside* The Mill *pub in the sun as the
forecast is good. Then we can have a ~~nice~~ very
"early night."*

*Love from
Judy
XXXX*

Yes-yes, of course, *that Jack helped me with* is the crack in
the perfect specimen of a letter. But who cares. Her words
exclude him.

September 10th

I was sitting on the low wall overlooking the weir outside
The Mill pub in the glorious sunshine, knowing – yes, knowing – there was a glorious day ahead of me with Judy.

This primed me for the irritation of seeing the long streak of
piss himself[85] emerge from Laundress Lane with Judy,

85 Yes, indeed, I am tall and slim, just as he is under the average height,
with a furtive demeanor and the promise of a pot belly (the beer-drinking,
you see).

point me out to her, face her, place one proprietorial hand on each shoulder and kiss her left, right, left cheek. (He calls this "Gallic," I call it daylight robbery.)

She skipped over to me. I was glad of the need to fetch drinks to deep breathe away from that vision. "I was squeezed between two Simons," she said in something like her old way.

This was the basics of her day ... When the FP met her in the lodge, all smiles, he broke the bad news that, worse luck, Jocasta was "stuck in London," but that she'd reported to him being "bowled over by your friend's paintings." She congratulated the FP on "finding such a fresh young talent with its eclectic verve," adding, "Hold on to her, Con – don't let another College snap her up for an exhibition." I snorted beer onto the famous low wall. ("Sorry, frog in my throat, please go on ...")

Aaaaanyeeewayyyy, they went to lunch and sat *vis-à-vis* at the end of a table in a quiet spot. Were joined suddenly by Simon Baron-Cohen (another Sir!),[86] who asked her, gently, warmly, if she was the new JRF[87] in Psychology. He ignored the FP.

Judy explained about her art and Jocasta and he continued to ask her questions sympathetically, "just like his cousin Sasha," drawing her out, just like the cousin, giving nothing away, while she felt she'd given quite a lot away.

The FP tried to bracket off Simon and failed.

86 Perhaps it is worth noting that his knighthood was awarded for services to a *minority* of the population (autists) whereas mine was awarded for services to the population as a whole. Also, I am not stymied by a reductive, brain-enamoured ideology.

87 Junior Research Fellow.

Then another Simon turned up, Simon Blackburn,[88] to sit on the other side of her and ask, with a breezy authority, so it seemed – yes – was she the new Psychology JRF? He too ignored the FP, but this time, so it seemed, with distinct animus.

She explained again about her work and Dr Eilan, at which he threw back his head "for a good old laugh," pulling back from which he wished her all the best and apologized nicely, blaming a sleepless night and age.

"I knew," he said, "you couldn't be a psychologist because you dress too well. Look at Simon over there: day after day, dark-blue jacket and slacks, light-blue open-necked shirt; never changes. I doubt you always wear that, Miss Scott."

She did look magnificent. But Her Magnificence managed to note how his gaze shot from the FP to her and back, sharply, and how he cut off the FP's interjections almost angrily ... All of which made her think he was jealous of the FP's being a Knight.

She liked the Simons until the FP was able to take her off for coffee in the SCR. ("Like a departure lounge," she added.) The FP told her on the way to *The Mill* that Jocasta had suggested dinner for the three of them in one of the College's bookable rooms to "hammer out the next stage."

We drank, then wandered around Coe Fen. I showed her the spot where – according to dad, who was a medical student at the time – Syd Barrett and two other Floyds had a photo taken in 1965. But she was more interested in her "sketching" in a reporter's notebook: me (a generic male), a cow (a

88 Distinguished philosopher, Life Fellow. No, he is not brain-enamoured, but he is Hume-enamoured. In her previous attempt to edit this diary, my ex-wife notes: "Simon's book *Spreading the Word* marked the first stage in my shuffling off my Wittgenstinean chains." I'm sure it would mark the first stage in my shuffling off my insomnia chains!

very large pig), the river (the M4 with shrubbery).

Yes, she'd changed from last time, but not quite changed back to pre 4/8 Judy. There was warmth but it was – that word again– generic.

The "early night" that she mentioned was at 5.30 p.m. Enthusiasm – yes, no poker face, no hint of duty, but I felt again "the generic male" – not quite *me*.

More important – yes, really – was that I felt I could bore her and that she could bore me. For the first time ever, this, her enthusiasm for engagement, was treacherous, and so I pre-edited and so I'm sure did she. Thoughts were not floated out to share.

She told me that in a couple of weekends' time (near EXAN D-Day) she'd be going down to Brighton to see her friend Kaaren; so I thought I'd nip down then to see dad (mum still in the US).

I'm happier, without actually being happy, O logicians. I'm confused. EXAN meeting tomorrow, to have the modus (or is it modi?) operandi (or is it baloney?) set before us. I *am* confused, yup.

September 12th

Jack set a large cardboard box down on the floor and said, "Here we are, ladies and gents."
Sheena: an impatient Habsburg seethe.
Petroc: eyes flickering, probably dredging for a witticism or to-the-point remark; abandoned.
Marlon: the face of a four-year-old on Christmas morning.

Hill: ironic smile, masking real excitement?

Jack opened the box and pulled out what looked like an asthma inhaler emblazoned: DuoResp.

"You'll each receive seven of these little efforts."

Sheena: "Pissing hell!"

Petroc: "I'd bet good money these monkeys are fatal to the max."

Jack: "Yup."

Marlon: "So we give them to people we want to kill and they inhale them and it kills them, right?"

Jack: "Nope."

Hill: "I'm intrigued."

Jack: "Yes, they're supposed to look like inhalers – Ventolin – for people with acute asthma. You pretend you need a puff. Watch."

He put one to his lips and squeezed the side. It became an inch or so longer at the top, to reveal a small window. So, more like a periscope now.

"People won't notice this, but the top can be expanded to give you a viewfinder. You get the target in the cross-hairs then you press the bottom button very smartly as if you're taking a puff. At the speed of a bullet a small dart – it's got to be heavy in case of strong wind – will shoot out. Each one contains four shots, so you have twenty-eight shots. A poisoned dart that will kill say King Charlie or Wills or Kate instantly. We've had top scientists and engineers working on this, Porton Down, North Cambridge, all over."

Hill: "Nice piece of kit."

Marlon: "But what if you breathe in accidentally? Do you get poisoned arrows in your throat?"

Petroc: "It would cure your asthma for sure, ha ha ha."

Marlon, puzzled: "I don't have it."

Jack: "There will be multiple agents working each target and you won't know who the other ones are. They will be following walkabouts or lingering outside, but ideally it should be done inside because of the wind. It's good to gain entry to the buildings.

"Now, Rex, I had you in mind for Charlie, as you, I believe, have an entré to Trinity."

"Well ..."

"The King is going to give an address in the dining hall of his old college. D'you think you could wangle a ticket to that through your landlord?"

"Well ..."

"Sheena will go up to Woodland's Care Home off Milton Road to join a blow-pipe convergence on William. Petroc will go to St Paul's Infants near Panton Road where Kate is visiting to shoot poisoned arrows to her heart, all being well. Hill will travel up to Ely where a cousin of the King is opening a community centre. Marlon will join the throng on King's Parade for the walkabout, if Charlie is still able to walk after his address in Trinity."

Then Jack suggested that we should at least try to practise on living but non-human creatures.

Marlon: "Like kids, you mean?"

Jack: "No, Jim – sorry, I mean Marlon. Children are human, aren't they?"

Marlon: "Like animals, then."

Jack: "Got it. But if it means there being a lot of dead moggies and doggies around the place, that will arouse suspicion, so be restrained, yeah?"

Marlon: "I know! I'll go to a pet shop and buy some snakes. I don't like them at all. Not keen on gerbils either. Or those tall rats that say 'Simples' on the TV ad. Them!"

Hill: "Ducks on the river, could be."

Marlon: "Or swans. But I like swans."

Exaggerate? I do not.

There were lots of routine jokes about people they could practise on (Sheena – her godson). But generally we were subdued. The final meeting will be in a week, then it's all systems pseudo-puff. And I'm subdued now; subdued alone, here.

The FP says Gwen will be away on a "retreat" during the royal visit and, yes, I can have her ticket for the King's address. He's not going himself. He would certainly *not* be going if *per impossibile* (as I've never heard anybody say) I could try out my "piece of kit" on him ...

Imagine the scene of the FP's demise: "... and he expressed *amazement* that I was not an FRS. I said, 'In fact, Lord Man ...'"

"What's up, Con?" says Gwen with satisfaction as I pocket my piece of kit.

September, 20th

"Invisible Lady" – the Mingus track dad plays a lot: trombone curves out the blue regretful theme of an attic ghost, invisible as skylight light.

Invisible girlfriend – we talk on the phone, text, add upper-case crosses at the end of messages; but she's invisible when I see her. Body visible, pliant, smilingly available, and invisible in herself.

Two goodish London visits under my belt or not? Not knowing really if they were good or not; all benchmarks being absent. Where there'd been morning spandrels there are now the upshots of photoshoots on Primrose Hill set before me cornily, making much of hair; done for themselves, of course. Functionless: "for catalogues?" – "for exhibitions?" – for God's sake! But with benchmarks gone, the sap dries from all possible jealousy.

Daah Daaah Dah-Dah, Dah-Dah Daaaah Dah, the theme goes ... as if you could capture it in ink! It's in my head when we're in one of the boisterous restaurants she chooses, after one of those minimalist mini-exhibitions she takes us to. The theme's in my head at her response to my "I love you!"

"And so you should, young man."

"Do *you*, though, love *me?*"

"Please! My peace of mind. Please respect my need for this, Bron dear."

I would prefer a visible, audible, tangible rebuff. And I know it won't come – would take too much from her.

September, 24th

I suppose this was the final EXAN knees-up, certainly the last before puff-day. We were all a bit ratty and defensive – nerves. Except for Marlon, of course, who delighted us with his account of his mostly missing white mice running around in a box, of how sad it made him when he hit one, of his buying some goldfish instead ("not keen on them"). How his eyes gleamed to describe the "plip" sound the darts made on the water's surface and the tiny dents in it "like pimples," then his sadness when they floated to the surface.

There was one more killing story. Hill: "Bumped off next door's cat. Used to piss on the lavender."

When the various practicalities were ironed out (too boring

to describe), there was general chat. Only Jack was self-revealing, telling us about his Class War experience in Bristol. This caused high febrile laughter in Petroc.

Sheena: "What's so funny?"

Petroc: "The name, so *out there* ... It's, I don't know, so *camp*. A newspaper called that – Christ!"

Sheena: "You don't believe in class war, then?"

Petroc: "I believe in class divisions caused by economic decisions."

He then tied himself in knots, saying the idea of class war was "childish," adding a few pompous expressions like "some economic intelligence is required."

That's when Sheena forgot about all the t- and h-dropping and the sorta-likes. She was furious. "You really are a stupid little tit, Mr Intelligence. You make Marlon sound like Noam Chomsky ..."

Marlon: "Oh, thanks!" (obviously delighted)

Sheena: "Do you really think capitalists believe in all that neo-classical stuff about the benign equilibria that are bound to come about if we leave the markets alone? That the market knows best, even when it comes to delivering public services? Do you really think fiscal sustainability is an apolitical goal? Do you think capitalists really want *full employment?* As Kalecki[89] said, capitalists' 'class instinct' (makes quote signs in the air) tells them to keep a healthy level of unemployment and so keep wages down. Their class instinct tells them to make the less-well-off pay for government borrowing.

"So yes, Petroc, there *is* a class war, *and they fucking started it!*

"As even PaulfuckingKrugman – once so friendly to the

---

89 Well this gives the game away. Michal Kalecki (1899–1970) was a Polish economist and Marxist. Some people might wish to call him a left Keynesian or – I kid you not – the bridge between Keynes and Marx. But this is a self-avowed Marxman. He peeps out from time to time from the dustbin of history. As now.

so-called 'neo-classical-Keynesian synthesis' (quote marks again) and rampant globalisation – finally worked out in his 2012 book, Republicans prioritising so-called fiscal sustainability was a stealthy act of class war. And in the UK, don't capitalists like the well-upholstered ideas of Edmund Burke and dear old Michael Oakeshot? But they're only finding excuses to hang on to what they've got. Their class instinct comes first, and *they fit the social and economic theories around that*. You think they go in for dispassionate fucking *analysis!?*

"OK, we're all nervous about killing. But that's what you do in a war. *They kill the poor and ill by stealth*. OK, none of us particularly likes the idea of killing sort-of drifty people like Kate Middleton. Here's a comparison: Peasants might revolt when the Lord of the Manor oppressed them. They might crucify his favourite dog. They may like dogs–"

Marlon: "I Iike dogs!"

"But what they are doing is saying 'That's how serious we are. This is what you've reduced us to. This can't go on.'"

Then she became self-conscious and re-adopted her faux-prole speech; started to talk about Rees-Mogg's drawl, how it was like a womanly knight posturing over the body of a dangerous peasant. We all happily joined in re the Mogg, chastened Petroc and all.

I was impressed, certainly. Was I energised? Didn't somehow feel like it.

I hadn't brought my bike (puncture), so I happened to walk back along Mill Road with Hill, mostly in silence. I wanted to get away but as we passed his road (Stockwell Street, just before the bridge) he invited me in for a cuppa.

Why not?

Overwhelming smell of Dettol inside. Some houses lack

a woman's touch. This one lacked an inhabitant's touch. Bare floors – not stripped and varnished, just bare. No pictures. Few easy chairs, and these with thin wooden arms. No plants or lamps.

"Just moved in?"

"Been here twenty-five years."

He went for the tea.

"How do you know Jack?" I asked.

"Taught him French at Hills Road."

"That why he calls you Hill?"

"It's my name – John Hill – would not stand for all that fancy-fanny Petroc and Marlon crap."

"Oh."

"I radicalised him. I was a firebrand in those days. Told him first about Charles Fourier, the *soixante-huitards*. He was all mixed up, needed an ideology to cling to, struggling with his sexuality, you see."

"He's *gay*?"

"Queer as a coot, mate."

(An insane shot of pure joy jabbed me.)

But while I was puzzling out why a gay guy would latch on to Judy at the station, and slowly deciding he wanted a fabulous model, Hill was telling me about his own change of fortune. How he was once a happily married man living in "a lovely house" in De Freville Avenue,[90] then came the divorce because he had "a roving eye" that "did for him" (his eyes are grey and fishy).

He suddenly asked me if I fancied some "sweetmeats." I did, as the weak tea had a dusty taste; and I was *celebrating*. He opened a cupboard by his side. Empty apart from a row of "sweetmeats" – Mars, Twix, Kit-Kat, Smarties, etc. Then

90 Pleasant suburbia just north of the river, Chesterton area. Pricey, yes, but *pas chic*.

he gave me their prices! I had no mental space to reflect on this and went for a pack of Revels at £4.50. Offered him one. He took three. When it was time to go, I tried a joke:

"Not charging me for the tea, then."

"No. Re-used a bag."

I felt like giving him a tenner.

And a hug.

Friday September 26th

Written at home, or should I say "at mum and dad's?" Or "at dad's?" (Mum, as mentioned, still in New York with Peter[91] and Sylvia.) Would I rather be at Judy's? Can't honestly say yes to that. (Would love to pop over there for a couple of hours, though, if she were in town).

She texts from Brighton to say she and Kaaren are planning an (ironically) touristy weekend: the pier, buying trinkets in The Lanes, fish and chips, drop of beer, candy floss. How droll, how very droll ... Why not some vomiting on the prom? Why not some kind of Patrick Hamilton experience to balance things out? Go to a boarding house, meet a seedy Captain Truscott with Mock Tudor speech who promises them modelling work that turns out to be the first step downwards to the life of drink-sodden hookerdom. Yer godda larf, incha?

It's idyllic here. I love it, especially after days alone in the house with the FP. Stop your retreating, Gwen, and cook for us. Shut your husband up. Smother him with religion.

One thing that the blessed M.E. Smith got wrong: that mid-

91 See footnote 26. I won't pander.

dle-class kids hate their parents and rebel, while working-class kids, seeing their struggles, love their parents.

It's bollocks, Mark. Sorry.

I love dad's company. We share tastes in literature, music, people, humour. Went to the pub before supper – his aubergine-free moussaka. (There! We do differ. I like aubergines. I'm sounding like Marlon.)

Asked him why he rates the FP, despite it all. He said they'd met on one of those Covid committees. The FP was "deferential, eager to please, a bit of a dogsbody, really," though with some weird ideas about statistics. He could be "effete and dull … soppy-stern"[92] but he was "solid." So dad thought he might integrate me into Cambridge academic life, given how I'm a bit mature to be a graduate student.

Mum and dad seem not to care too much about my directionless path, especially compared to whizz-kid Pete. Pleasantly pissed. I'll finish this now and read dad's *Private Eye* in bed.

10 minutes later –

A text from Jack to say there's a fault with our batch of puffers. (The little poison chamber sometimes leaks into the plastic, eroding it. Fatal.) Can I meet him at 8.00 a.m. outside M&S in the Market Square to collect replacements from him? Told him where I was and he settled for 10.30.

Not looking forward to telling dad. We were going to Ronnie Scott's (what's left of it). It's Puff D-Day on Monday. Puff Daddy? I really am struggling now.

92 And this from Professor Stonewall, Professor If-I-could-just-finish-my-point, Professor You-lack-the knowledge-base-to-understand-my position. As for these abusive adjectives … pots and kettles, friend, pots and kettles.

God knows when I'll see dad again – standing in the dock? In a hospital bed having been beaten to a pulp by security guards? Or never, because this bloody batch leaks, too?

It's all crazy. It's Keystone Cops. We're turning revolt not into style but into sit-com. I mean, Charles is exactly the same age as dad. I quite like him, in fact. They both have that face of the non-vulnerable worrier. Wilful. Over-careful dressers. Both have sharp corners (Judy and all that "both Scorpio" malarkey).

I wouldn't mind a spot of righteous anger right now. Though when I wake up would be better.

Saturday September 27th

I'll get this on the record. So *this* is why she wanted me to be so precise about which train I would get down and back.

I can't stay here.

I picked the weapons up from Jack, half-thought I'd try the "periscope" on an angry dog as I was sitting on a bench by the Town Hall. But I was feeling hung-over and lazy, so I went back. Let myself in. Thought he was out as it was quiet ... But then I heard his voice coming from the attic room ("guest room," though never any guests). Decided to tell him I'd come back. The room door was open, as I could see, as I ascended the steep, awkward stairs. Sun streaming through the dormer window and streaming through the red hair of Judy, standing naked at the window with her back to the door.

I'll get this on the record. So *this* is why she wanted me to be so precise about which train I would get down and back.

I can't stay here.

From the bed, Tartt's voice:[93] "Can you push the door to, darling? I think I can hear Magda[94] bustling around."

I ducked down fast, stepped backwards down the stairs to here. Here I am again. How useless introspection is. It tells you what you already know, not what you need to know.

Clothes unmaketh the man. On my wardrobe door, my wedding togs. They'll be just the ticket. The rain that's been threatening all day has started. Let's wash it all away now. BUT LET THE RECORD STAND! The sun shines through her, the rain falls on me – because I walk in it. Can't help it, "mate."

I'll get this on the record. So *this* is why she wanted me to be so precise about which train I would get down and back.

I can't stay here.

93 How can I not own up, given that Ms Scott has already given her account endless times on various media. Our dalliance budded during the ICA event and blossomed later. I could tell that her response to what he did was, "Well in that case I'll do what I like; it's what I've always wanted." And what she likes above all is the prospect of people displaying her impoverished paintings. I think she rather relished the whorish arrangement: her body for my "help." Yes, I add the scare-quotes – one of her many false beliefs! The whorishness of it excited her. Maybe I was exciting for her, too, despite my relative age; I don't think I flatter myself. Of course, it was a piece of rabid incompetence on my part. My initial thought had been to take her to a country hotel; but she is – as indeed am I myself! – vividly recognizable. So we grabbed the window afforded by Gwen being on her retreat and Auberon being with Mike Castle. As I say, I don't pander, and so I will not "defend myself." In any event there's little to "defend." He caused great damage, defecating in his own nest. I was (am) a red-blooded male in a failing marriage (was) and he was collateral damage. Damage of another kind was inexcusably on his mind, after all.
94 Our cleaner.

Afterword

It is not known whether Dr Tartt intended to tell his readers what occurred subsequent to the final diary entry, both nationally and locally. This will have been because events intervened which impacted directly upon him. As he was writing his final footnotes, the long-delayed report on the quality of the scientific advice received by the government during the Covid 19 crisis was published. Among other things, it revealed that the "data" which underpinned the "behavioural phenomena" on which his advice to SAGE depended had been fabricated by him and two paid helpers (who later confessed). (Consequently, he was short of money, which is why he'd had to take in ASC as a lodger.) Phenomena such as "regulatory nihilism," "Injunction dis-attention," "the bulwark effect" and others were based on invented digital surveys and online experiments. Indeed, his profitable little book *Nudge not "No!"* was essentially a work of fiction. He was stripped of his Knighthood, Fellow-ship, Professorship, and University post.

We now describe the subsequent national and personal his-tories. What became known as The September Killings or Inhaler Eruption resulted in 243 deaths in England. Twenty-two of these were of innocent citizens undergoing asthma attacks, shot by police in the early days of October. Eighty-four deaths were of major and minor members of the royal family and the aristocracy and some righter-than-right-wing Conservative politicians. The remainder were of bystanders. This was because of the high winds on the 29th and 30th of September. The "inhaler" darts were insuffi-ciently heavy and fast to prevent many shots being blown off course.

All this certainly rattled the "Johnson-Redux" Govern-ment. And as one commentator put it, "This stimulated a different, darker facet of his mock-Churchillian persona: the facet of vicious, summary repression."

The reaction was draconian and, by common consent, it was the main factor in their losing the general election.

The King and Camilla were unhurt. As his address was winding up, word came through that eleven individuals – all North America tourists – had been killed in Kings Parade, causing the walkabout to be abandoned. James Fitzgerald (aka Marlon) was held responsible. It is not known whether this was because he was confusing use of the deadly (what he called) "exhalers" with vaping or because, as he later admitted: "I don't like American Tourists. I like EU ones though, and some Canadians, actually."

Dr Rachel Posner (aka Sheena) had long planned to travel, not to the Woodlands Care Home but to East Somerset to attend the Tuesday morning surgery of Jacob Rees-Mogg, posing as one of his constituents. This is indeed what she did. She killed him and his son who was beside his father taking notes. She stood over them in triumph, shouting "LOWER-THAN-VERMIN ONE, LOWER-THAN-VERMIN TWO!"

Dr Brian Troon (aka Petroc) had no intention of targeting Kate. His intention all along was to write a book about his "undercover tracking" of EXAN. The book, *Pooters of the Mass Mind,* was published to much derision.

John Hill had taken insufficient cash to buy a return ticket to Ely, and so was unable to travel there. Furious, he caught a bus up to De Freville Avenue and killed his ex-wife and her husband with an "inhaler."

Jack Brasher drowned in the river Dee while being pursued by police after killing the Duke of Westminster outside Chester Cathedral.

As for Auberon/Steve, he donned his wedding clothes and set out in the rain for the station. On arriving there, he attracted much attention. For instance: "Look at that posh wet ponce!" and the like from Cambridge United fans travelling to an away game. He bought a ticket for London and stood on Platform 1. He let two trains go by until he heard the announcement that the next train, an express, did not stop there and that "customers" should stand well clear of the platform edge.

He was seen to remove his dress jacket and unbutton his shirt to the waist before jumping to his death in front of the train. One bystander, Dr Ron Mitchum, Reader in English and Curator of Works of Art at Jesus College, described the scene in the following terms:

"It was unforgettable, horrible, and yet somehow magnificent. For me it was an enactment of Goya's painting *May 3rd, 1808* in which a Spaniard with wild hair and bulging eyes thrusts his chest forward, arms flung up, toward the guns of the Napoleonic firing squad. He stood on the line. Yes, his eyes were crazed but also derisive, as if saying to the approaching prow of the express, 'Is that the *best* you can do!'"

Maude Manzini and Mahmoud O'Higgins, Editors

June 2024

Sweet Marie

1. Ask Edgar

The tears were there and ready to fall but they'd stay put until she'd wound up school for the day and sent the little devils home. Eventually they would fall in at the outhouse WC, maybe with one or two of the bigger boys hammering on the door asking and giggling:

"You alright, Mrs Sewell, mam?"

"You wan eneh help in theyur, Miss?"

It happened often. It was a routine.

One of them (usually Ned Pinker, from Pinker's ranch) would steal one of her crib books. This time it had been the mathematics one – *Professor Hindley E. Cropper's Elementary Mathematics for Teachers with Fully Worked Solutions and Figures.* Without the worked solutions she was nowhere. She knew only English and French literature, and a bit of history. No science at all but a lot of dressmaking.

The Pinker boy or a buddy of his would say, "We think we can find your book, Miss, so long as you would ..."

Once, Ned Pinker had said, "Would you give me a kiss, Miss?"

But that was going too far.

The girls shrieked, and images of the sheriff rose up before the big boys' eyes.

Today it had been the more usual, "Would you read us from Mister Poe?" Absolutely. The only way she could hold them, not just hold but spellbind, was by reading an E. A. Poe story.

"Scuse me, Miss," said Polly Jarvis, "but could you ask Mister Poe to come along here to speak with us?"

"He's been dead these fifty years," she replied.

"Nobody told me. That's real sad." (from the Pinker boy, of course)

Yes, she read wonderfully well today, *The Pit and the Pendulum,* and at the end Josh Palfrey said he would look for the book under Penny Trotter's desk.

Hey presto!

"But please, no more arithmetic till Friday, Miss."

She'd entranced them with Poe. She could even entrance them by reciting (not reading, *reciting from memory*) Baudelaire. ("We like it Miss. What does it mean? It's in Foreign.")

They liked her but despised her too on account of her never fighting back; of having no authority about her in manner or speech; not the slightest knack for imposing herself on others. She might begin hotly and might have a spark in her eyes ...

"How *dare* you ..."; but it was a feather in a gale. Her voice would grow small and splutter like a failing engine, her word-bank would suddenly be spent, and she could not go on.

Then, with a kind of squeak, phrases such as, "if you please" would emerge as tiny creatures from a cave, and then, pitifully, the word "please."

There would be a groan from the whole class, even from her handful of allies, then sharp laughter from the boys at the back. The only time she could manage a complete reprimand was one when one of the boys called her Marie.

"Do *not* use my Christian name!" Only to spoil it with "...

if you don't mind."

"Sorry, Miss, I was calling on Barry, but I do suffer from these slips of the tongue, Miss."

This was the wound, and wounds like this do heal. But this wound could never heal as long as her son Teddy was a member of the Pinker boy's posse; as long as he was the posse's most subservient and snivelling member. He never spoke in class even when Marie asked him a direct question to which she knew he knew the answer. It was always:

"Don't know... *Miss*."

And there could be no healing-time at the end of the school day, as Teddy would relate his mother's humiliations over dinner to his father, Markus ...

"And guess what Josh Palfrey said then, paw?"

"You tell me, son."

"Why, he ..."

She really wanted to hit her son hard across his fat chops. She dreamt of starting to do it but her hand would flutter away like a wounded bird. She felt guilt at the dream and told her husband about it the next day.

"You don't really want to hurt him, honey. It's just that you're ineffectual even when you're asleep."

"I guess you're right, Markus."

2. Counterfactually Sweet Marie

It's my peaceful hour, with Markus snoring upstairs, and I bet with Teddy snoring in synchrony. The Boys, I call them. Boys. When I meet with other mothers and wives (not often, because I always feel I'm the youngest there, a greenhorn), they talk about "the menfolk" even if one of the "men" is a babe in arms. I don't have menfolk, I have boyfolk. Markus swaggers and bullies and, of course, anybody can bully me who's strong enough to draw a breath. But his actions are those of a boy; boy enthusiasms; boy bragging; boy brains; bushfire boys' lusts suddenly flaring amid his general sterility. Above all, a boy's confidence, talking as if in a dream with such solid certainty about things leagues away from his knowledge. They both do it.

The Ultracrepidarians – what a lovely old ugly old word for those who pontificate from total ignorance. I also call them The Ultracreps. And at this point in my meditations I ask myself: How was it that Markus and I ever got together? A vacuum was there to be filled after my folks had gone back to Donegal and I'd graduated from Leland Stanford University up in Palo Alto with my fine degree and absolutely no money at all.

At that time they wanted me to follow them back, and Markus Sewell was a good excuse to stay. Solid. And of course they'd wanted me to return with them in the first place (before Leland). But what education could a girl acquire in Old Ireland! Leland Stanford was co-educational.

I had been trying to catch the right train to get me back from San Francisco to Salinas, and was in a flurry and muddle over a lost ticket and a book.

There he was (he'd just been up for the reading of his uncle's will), so cool in himself, addressing the stationmaster as if he were his butler. A big gentleman. He was indeed big; though like a big pear. Not bear, *pear*.

Oh dear Lord, I'd even thought he was a literary man because he could talk about *Oliver Twist* – the only book he'd ever read, or, rather, followed the story of in pictures.

He said he lived in Salinas. But he lived and we live in this nest of shacks south of Salinas, a staging post between here and there called Higson's Draw.

There I stopped being Marie Gallagher.

But none of that is an excuse for my being the way I am. Most people have a spirit threaded with wire and bone (like a corset!), while mine is of spider-web and smoke. When the sun shines through it, it might catch a rainbow; but as my husband would say, "There ain't no sun round here, honey bun."

He'd told me he "managed" a big ranch. But he's an odd-job man: castrating pigs, digging wells, clearing couch grass, driving a rig that rattles like a skeleton.

No, I don't stay down here to avoid his embraces, of which there are few enough, Lord knows; I stay here to read or to push my poems a little farther up the hill.

I'd published one or two at Leland – conventional, pious, willed, clustered around a single image. How did one of them go now? Can't recall, except I had the image of a swan's neck "questioning the lake" and probably there were some "golden orbs" and some "o'ers" in there.

I'd been caught between sugarplums and Baudelaire (who scared and addicted me) till I discovered Emily Dickinson. I adapted her to my domestic pains and fancies, but could never catch her universal note.

I keep returning to the question again and again of why I am the way I am. Let's imagine, against the facts, that I had been adopted by a warm fun-seeking couple. It's so droll to think that people expect the Irish to be of twinkling eye, fanciful and with a word for everyone, yarn-spinners and drinkers, agents of social ease. Though maybe a little "away with the fairies."

Well, my folks were about as fey as pharmacists. I was their homebound project and nucleus. We never had visitors. They were too busy inspecting me for rectifiable faults and blaming me for failing to bring (here we go again) some sunshine into their lives. Other people were a kind of benign enemy, to be kow-towed to sometimes, or to be the targets of poison spat at them in private, never trusted. Who's to know what could have been before the fact.

3. Sunday's unbright hours

Sunday morning in the Sewell kitchen. Silence broken only by the fast munching of Teddy and the frequent clink of his knife on the butter dish.

"Sweetie," says Marie, "do you think you could wipe the jam from your knife before putting it in the butter? The butter's getting all jammy."

"Sorry, ma. But then again" – shooting a glance at his father – "it means folks can get their butter 'n' jam together. Save themselves a journey." A snigger rounds it off.

But I don't take jam, Teddy, as you well know."

"You see," says Markus, "your mother is sweet enough alreadeh."

Teddy laughs long and hard to this very familiar remark.

"Tell you what, Marie." Markus is a little buoyed up by his witticism. "It's that some mornings it would be fine if the breakfast kitchen could be filled with the warm aroma of ... what do you call them? Those batter cakes ..."

"SWEETBREADS!" says Teddy.

"Sweetbreads," says Marie, "are an offal dish, darling."

"An awful dish? Wass wrong with 'em?"

"No, *offal* ... Inner organs, like kidney or liver."

"Well thass juss plain dumb! The words are 'sweet' and 'bread'. Sure ain't no kinda meat if it's bread and sweet and all."

"I wouldn't have said meat." (Markus)

Teddy is so exercised he has actually stopped eating.

"OK, Miss Clever: What kind of 'inner organ' are they?"

"I don't rightly know, sweetie."

Then, in a surprisingly grown-up response (imitated from somewhere): "Now where have I heard that before, ma!"

At this point the classroom has just invaded her kitchen as Marie says, in one of her smaller small voices:

"Anyway, I don't know how to make them, Markus."

"Pretty simple. You get the skillet good and hot, mix a batter of milk, flour, eggs and uh ..."

"MOLASSES!"

"Don't think so, Ted."

"Sugar, I guess," says Marie. "Maybe you could show me how to make them someday?"

"Paw's too busy fur that. Anyways, Josh Palfrey's Sunday breakfast is fried salt pork and fried eggs. So whadya think of THAT?"

"Sounds damned good to me." (Markus)

"Maybe one day," says Marie.

"Yup. Maybe one day," says Markus, "when you find time away from writing your poems."

She looked at her son's chewing, laughing face.

Big Pear and Little Pear (as she called them) received top-class entertainment from the very idea of Marie's poems. A few weeks ago, Marie had opened her bureau to find at the bottom of the copper-plated fair copy of her latest composition, the words

ASS (ANUS)

in Teddy's rough hand.

"Boy's jess got a lively sense of humour, honey. Cut him

some slack," Markus said.

She'd given a reply with wryness wasted: "At least he's mastered the principle of disambiguation."

"Sure ... He's got a good head on him, that boy."

As the laughter faded, a familiar Sunday routine began. Marie would suggest going to church, as there was "still time." She was not a firm believer but loved the singing and the Bible readings.

"Paw's too busy fur that!"

Markus would put on his serious face: "Weeeell, I got chores that jess won't wait any longer. Got to mortar up the lean-to before the weather breaks. And, yes, I'd better refresh the axle grease on the rig."

Then, while she was cleaning the house and fixing a pot roast of beef, she would hear pistol shots. Father and son would be shooting tin cans off a wall. Then Markus would shuffle into the kitchen and give some reason why he and the boy had to attend to something well away from there.

This Sunday:

"God damn it, we're fresh out of mortar and axle grease. But you know that crazy grizzly I was telling you about?"

"The crazy grizzly, of course." (Teddy, stifling a laugh)

"The one that's been causing trouble in the woods up by the Hinkley place ... Well, I kinda promised I'd go up and see how close I can git to blowing the critter's brains out. Be an education for Ted."

There is, of course, no bear. The two of them would sit in the sun drinking apple juice and eating crackers. They rode out on horseback, Teddy on his pony like a cartoon of vulnerability. She sighed deeply for relief.

"Take care, the pair of you!" she called after them and

thought, "The pear of you."

As soon as it was time to serve the midday meal, they were back and ready. Father and son were fully engrossed in the food and seemed to be racing towards a finishing line. After the pot roast, a blueberry pie.

With a full belly, Markus said:

"You know, Marie, I would admire to have at some period in the future a pork roast turning before the fire."

"Yeah, with apple sauce, paw. With *apple sauce*."

"Of course," (he puts on his serious face) "with pig meat you gotta be real careful about freshness. If not ... parasites, worms in your gut and rising up to your voice box."

Smoothly then, from literal parasites he expanded on to the figurative kind and "the Injun problem."

There was no "Injun problem."

"Now this is jess my idea, jess a suggestion, though worth a second thought maybe. Maybe try an experiment. Can't do no harm. Like the folks in the South with their Nigras used to do ... we should maybe work Injuns as slaves. Cut down their laziness and wastrel ways and drinkin'." He'd just poured himself a big tumbler of whisky.

This inspired Teddy to his own field of expansion: on the failings of character, and the root causes of them, among the boys in his class whom he trailed after and flattered, till it hit his mother hard that here was living proof of there being such a thing as a loveable parasite.

Without a second's thought, she said:

"I'd say a little prayer for somebody who is *not* a parasite."

The "boys" looked at her, shocked, and then at each other ...

"You'd better git started on the washing up, Marie, if you're to reach the Bright Hour before three o'clock."

More than the usual amount of disgust was rising in her. But at least the Bright Hour was a blessing, though mixed: an escape from Camp Pear. It was a church offshoot, a discussion group cum half-hearted prayer meeting whose centrepiece was usually an address by a Bright Houerer or guest. Marie also attended because her only friend in town, Suzie Ancona, did so too. Suzie was an outsider, like her.

For this Bright Hour address by Mrs Baxter, a banker's wife, there was no polite, sweet smile, but the agape of wonderment and a brightness of eye she'd never shown before. Usually, if the speaker had returned from travels, there was uplift (the Grand Canyon as exemplifying the glory of God's creation). This time, though, the speaker was reporting back from a circle of Hell. Its main points:

"My husband and I stayed some nights on Manhattan Island, preparatory to meeting His Cousin The Senator, fresh off the boat from Europe ––– chose to stay in a part of town whose name suggested it was homely, called Greenwich (rhymes with Queen Witch) Village ––– a cesspit of moral laxity ––– bars open all hours with jingly-jangling music reminiscent of the Nigra and the mountain man ––– raucous rhythms ––– women uncorsetted, with hair down their backs ––– at least in Salinas the whores know their place and stay there, upstairs ––– women smoking in the street, arm-in-arm with scruffy youths, I believe the word is bo-heem-ee-un ––– We saw a couple check in to our hotel under DIFFERENT NAMES ––– sound of their love-making arrested our slumber ––– a veritable cornucopia of bars and chop houses, some down cellar steps, where people, even women, might scribble or sketch in a corner over a whole bottle of French wine ——— and the poets that declaim there: one big-bearded but oh-so feminine who did neither rhyme nor scan and ranted about bodies and the pleasures of them and universal love and just plain nonsense ——— surely in this newly-dawning century, in this age of scientific and industrial advance, we do not want to indulge those wallowing in ART and in rough public and rough private pleasures ——— self-loving youth poking its tongue out at the striving of honest tourists."

The audience was struck dumb ... till one brazen lady enquired as to how she knew these women in the street were whores. Mrs Baxter flushed ...

"Well, my husband was told, he was TOLD, that if some of them were approached, um, for business, they could be offended. But then, as Michael put it, 'As sure as shootin' some of them WERE pro-fessional wenches.'"

"Well," said Marie, as she and Suzie began their walk home beside the dry river, "that place sounds like a very Heaven."

"You're right there, my dear. And I bet nobody mistook old Baxter for one of those 'whores.'"

"EXCUSE ME!" (Female voice from behind.) She barged between them.

"A word with you, Mrs Sewell. My husband and I will be visiting after school on Tuesday and would admire to have an interview with you. Indeed, we insist it be so!"

"Do you have a concern, Mrs Toole?"

"Indeed I do – *we* do! We are concerned that our son knew more about geography and arithmetic *before* you arrived at the school. Marked correct: the square root of 7 is 49; Lemur is the capital city of Peru."

"Hey-Ho, the wind and the rain," said Suzie after the barger-in had gone. Marie explained how she's been marking without proper attention and half-thinking that poor Aaron Toole needed a boost.

"Chin up, chest out, girl," laughed Suzie skipping on ahead.

4. Supernaturally Sweet Marie

Somewhere in "The Prelude" Wordsworth talks about the "shy and the meek" being "unpractised in the strife of phrase." Compared to the fluent phrase-mongers, whom fools think to possess elevated souls, the tongue-tied are supposed to have "the language of the heavens." Their (or our) words, you see, are only "the under-agents of their souls."

Bliss it would have been to see William taking notes in the classroom today. Respectfully, my soul (if I have one) is not meek and I thirst after, with all my aggression, words to achieve some parity. My spoken sentences are made of tissue paper prone to burning up in my emotions, to being blown off course by others' huffing breaths. Or, as today, they melt like ice in sun as my unmeek soul makes an importunate and foolish display.

Today, inspired by Markus' thoughtful thesis about "Nigras," I'd decided to tell them how the slave trade worked, the Civil War, and all the rest of it. Apart from the usual pigtail pulling, burping and needling questions, they were attentive, even interested. But their attention was so new to me that I became coldly self-aware and fearful, like one learning to swim whose feet for the first time don't reach the bottom. My voice became that of a woman talking to herself, and this gave confidence to the lower, dimmer tier of revolutionaries such as Jordy Peterson, a fairly unpopular, lanky child, always eager to impress. When I asked for questions, he said something like:

"Well, I reckon they ain't a thing wrong with slavery. Seems a good way of USING UP Nigras cus they better off here than in Africay. They get work here and whisky and get to play the banjos here and sing lots of hymns."

I won't pause to think of what I could have said to this. What I actually said, in a sour tone, with I'm sure a sour face, was:

"What a disgusting thing to say ... In fact, you are a disgusting little boy."

I heard myself say it and then heard the echo of it and the deep silence that followed.

I think, or thought: they basically liked me, as a harmless thing sharing a lot of their own fears, but now fewer if any of them liked me. The rest of the day was punctuated by rioting. I sent them home early with the triumphant grin of Jordy seared onto my retinas. And that's why I'm home so early. Teddy is out, following his leaders, and I'm here marooned on book island.

Well, at least I have a chance to look at my poems or even start one in the light of day. This one. It's OK but it's marmorial in the wrong way. I meant to go on, but it finished itself as a single quatrain.

> The orioles above my roof
> Are sacred feathers in a dance?
> Are thought-streams from my bricky jail?
> They're flambeaux in the night of Truth.

And here's one where my Emily-reading shouts out. With me, you can see what I want to say, and you see the images that reach towards it almost independently from one another, whereas in Emily, what she's saying and how she says it fuse magically. Plus, I prop myself up with alliteration and simile, in the way that she does not ...

Something is coming like a tardy train
Beyond below our clean horizon.
Visible only to the Mind
Its upshot will not blazon.

Peaceful campfires on the plane
Are flattened by its windy wash.
Peaceful presents slick with words
Will falter like a preacher's gush.

You think your world's a tale concluded
A finite phrase of *mise en scène*.
The train drags us a landscape with
Less a backcloth than a darkling dream.

The dream of finding potent drugs
To melt the bullet of perdition
To make us safe in modern light
To still the pain of Crucifixion?

The Future is a spry conceit
A wishful thought within a brain
Empty as an empty reticule
Miles of unlaid track remain.

Now this one ... hmm. It's not bad as far as it goes. I take a phrase from Emily – "confident despair" – and go on from there as an autobiographical complaint.

I've striven for your "confident despair."
The streets ran rivers with my striving tears.
He me touches like a twig the air
His mimic offspring is alert with ears
Attuning to my weakness as overt as skin –
As whole battalions of a novel strength
Unconfidently wait within.

Maybe I should save Teddy the trouble; find a red crayon and scribble FART at the bottom of it. Now that's the door. I knew this peace was too good to last.

Later ... That was the most frightening yet heartening experience of my life. He was dressed so strangely, in a kind of suit, but a basic version of the proper suiting that gentlemen wear, as if the tailor could not be troubled to add the usual furnishings of lapel and waisting. The kind of suit a man might wear to cut down wind-resistance – ha-ha. His hair was unbrilliantined and unkempt though cleaner than most; and he was indeed clean and crisp in his strange speech too. From the East? As far East as England? He said he was selling brooms and could he please come in.

It looked as though he'd just been handed the brooms and the briefcase with brushes and cleaning stuff. Not a speck of dust on them. I invited him in, and when he was in he looked stranger still. Most people are of a type or they remind you of others.

Not him.

He was so undistinctive, so lacking in features – a first draft of a person, before you filled in the details. You noted his eye- and hair-colour and his height and immediately forgot them. He was disguised as nobody in particular.

I offered him a glass of water, which he gratefully

accepted, and let him sit to drink it.

"Another hot day," I said.

"I'm not selling anything," he said, cutting off small-talk. "I have come to give you help and a tool, or rather a weapon, in the battle of social life."

Yet another new religion, I thought, strangely unsurprised and calm. Excited, though, too.

"You are oppressed by people, aren't you, Miss Gallagher?"

Gallagher!!!!

"Most people express their selves through speech. Their souls leak from their mouths. What they are stands in what they say and how they say it. Not you! I will not insult you by telling you what you already know. I believe you have long wanted to give some of your oppressors what I might call 'a taste of their own medicine.' How would THEY deal with the tied tongue, the loss of faith in their own expression, the drooping of intent, the locutionary impotence? I will give you a simple weapon or assay.

"You say the following to them as they tell you what's what.

"Tell them: 'GO FIGURE!'

"This is a phrase from the near future of America."

I just asked him who he was and where he was from.

"I'll be frank. I'm from the far future and you can call me Jocelyn."

My laugh was one of nervousness and a kind of happy terror. Nothing was funny.

"If you say to them, 'Go figure!' they will lose the will to go on with their mouth-music." (he laughs to himself) "And they may indeed" (here his bright demeanour darkens) "lose the will more generally."

Then he was gone. I have been sitting here, frozen, for Lord knows how long.

Oh, here's Teddy back.

5. What in the world's gonna happen to the whole town now?

It's natural to wonder how Marie ever came to be a teacher in Higson's Draw, or anywhere else. Her predecessor was a fine teacher, authoritative in manner, with wide knowledge across domains and a ready wit. A sportsman, too. But a ferocious drinker. Also the most loyal client of Jayne's brothel, upstairs at the East-Town Saloon. There he paid over the odds ($10) for his masochistic treatments. "Well, that's not so bad," you might say. But to balance the books of pain, he practised a sadism on his pupils as ferocious as his drinking. It's good to have a son or daughter brilliant at simultaneous equations, but not so good when he cries or she quivers and wails every schoolday morning and has che-root burns on the upper arm.

He left suddenly for God-knows-where. Marie was local, with a good degree, a mild aura, and the least sadistic eyes in the known universe. Teddy was eleven and the family was hard-up.

She hated teaching from the very first, despite the occasional good days. This Tuesday had been one of those days. Something about Jocelyn's visit had brought a serenity to her, and the children could see she'd been humbled by her anger-spasm. (And nobody liked Jordy Peterson anyway.) Now they were gone, though the classroom remembered their electric presence.

"Mrs Sewell!!!" (a stentorian voice from the back of the room)

Strange how Joshua Toole's voice could come from such a mini-man, a voice tending to linger over verbalisations like "the disadvantages are LEGION" and "these propositions I DEPLORE." Somebody must once have told him he looked like Abe Lincoln, because he wore a too-thin ear-to-ear moustacheless beard and struck orator poses (necessarily viewed by his listeners from above). He was accompanied by his barging wife. They sat before Marie on little class-room chairs which fitted Joshua's behind just fine. He held his fire and silently handed her one of Aaron's essays, at the end of which Marie had written "9/10 – good work!"

She read:
The Merican War of Dependence tock plaice in 776 when Napoleane or Bonnie of france was replussed by the British Invayderers. King Gordy the Tird wanted to tax em a lot so they pourded all the tee away to swerve him Rite ...

There was much more of this kind of thing.

"WELL!!! Good work???"

The fact was that Aaron was a natively untalented boy and that this was indeed good by his standards. The mark Marie had given him was to boost the confidence eroded by the couple now before her. She pointed out that "See me" was also at the bottom of the work and that during this "seeing" she had tried to put Aaron right in facts and spelling. But the Tooles could not accept their son's mental situation. Male Toole began: "This abominable screed you call good work."

"Good? *By all that's righteous*." (female Toole)

"It's good *for him*. Aaron is not a natural scholar."

"Please tell me," he thundered, "what is a Natural Scholar? Explain now, young lady!"

"Go figure!"

"Go ... *figure*. What excrescence of jargon is this? A shameful evasion. Why, I've a good mind to ..."

It was not a problem of articulation or the lack of what-to-say. He seemed simply to lose the desire to say it. He lapsed into a glassy-eyed reverie, as if he had partaken of a hashish pipe.

His wife stepped in. "And moreover ..."

"Oh, go figure!"

"My husband is weak of heart. What have you done to him, you incompetent hussy! Why I ..."

Like her husband, she gave up and began to pick threads from her skirt.

"Now off you pop, Tooles," I said. And off they dutifully popped, slowly, dreamily.

If only Jocelyn could be here now to receive a thank-you kiss.

The next candidate for go-figuring was a physical contrast – sky-scrapingly tall Mr Peterson of "Peterson and Cousin, ironmongers."

"So you think my son is a disgusting little boy, do you!"

"Well, not so little, but certainly disgusting. Go figure!"

With blazing eyes: "Your days are numbered here, woman. The sheriff is a good friend o'mine. Prepare yourself ..."

He removed his hat, examined it, ran a finger round the brim rather as Oliver Hardy would, years later, be seen to do, while poking out the tip of his tongue like a cat. He then acquired a satisfied grin.

Next, Marie called in at the cobblers to collect her best boots, left for repair. The heel still wobbled and the charge was absurd. When she protested, the roughneck replied, "We did our best, Missus. Take your custom elsewhere if you ain't best pleased."

"Go figure!"

"You *what!* Vacate these premis–"

Toddlerlike, he made little towers of shoes, then proceeded to push them gently over.

All this mischief took up time, so Marie found herself walking just behind her son on the way home. Her heart melted as she watched him run a hawthorn twig along a fence, his shoulders drooping and his pace a shuffle.

She came up behind him at their gate. Ruffling his hair, she said:

"Buck up, Ted. Let's see if I can make some of these hot cakes your pa was talking about ... What you call sweetbreads."

He laughed along with her.

She'd seen pictures of sweetbreads in cookbooks and so tried to reproduce the moundy form of them.

"Your sweetbreads, sir."

They smelled delicious.

"Gee, thanks, ma."

Teddy merrily gobbled. The two of them chatted just as merrily. She prepared the evening stew. The afternoon faded into evening and still no Markus.

Till he burst into the kitchen, his face overshadowed, his mood foul.

"Been ruinin' the boy's appetite, so I see. By all that's holy, Marie!"

Eventually, the reason for his mood unfolded. He'd been directing two Chinamen and a Mexican in the digging of a well, to the specifications given by his boss, Beecham. Beecham turned up late afternoon. He laughed in the face of Markus. "Too narrow, you fool."

Markus produced the specifications he'd followed to the letter.

"They was just approxee-mations. Should-uh used yr common sense, man."

"The well's usable," Markus offered.

"Sure, usable to piss in."

The workers laughed like drains, repeating "Good for pissing, sir. Very good, sir."

That it was easy to humiliate Markus did not mean he was habituated to it, that he could withstand it. He was defeated.

"What did you say to him, honey? It was his fault, after all. You had a defence ..."

At this, he became truly mad. There was danger. He was never violent with her but he was given to smashing things up.

"What business is it of yours, woman!"

"I hate to see you like this, Markus. All you can do is keep your dignity. He knows in his heart you are the injured party."

"What the hell do you know! What the hell do you know about *anything*. You can cook and sew, you can grow flowers, but you cannot UNDERSTAND MY PAIN!"

This shouted, full volume, in her face.

"Go figure!"

"Go *what*! Why, for two bits I'd ..."

Markus fell back onto a kitchen chair. He tidied his hair with his earthy hands and sighed: "Ahhh, Weeelll."

He tried again:

"The point is ..."

He held up a spoon and examined his inverted face in it, poked out his tongue to it and smiled broadly.

Teddy examined his dad through angry tears.

"Look what you done to paw."

"Teddy, please."

"Back off, ma. *This is man's business.*"

"Oh ... go figure!"

The boy collapsed like a happy drunk, pursing his lips.

They sat side by side in chairs like stuffed animals. The stew was put before them. They were silent and still; would not reply. Without reflection, she put the eating irons in their hands to get them started. Food reached their mouths. One slight chew. Spat or dribbled out. "Maybe I put too much sage in," she explained. "Kind of bitter."

But the apple tart suffered the same fate. Markus had no will to walk or act at all. She undressed him, and as she did he tried harder to finish sentences. "... not to forget to ... the breaths so far ... if I don't remember ... remind myself ..."

He was more resigned than scared, as phrases fell well short of clauses.

"breathing in ... need to ... air in here ..."

She then helped Teddy to bed.

This illness or spell, it later emerged, messed with volition. Will was lost "across the board" and not just that: automatic actions such as breathing needed acts of will. The sufferer had to remember to breathe. And this could not happen in sleep.

It was a gentle, quiet end. Waking beside her stone-cold husband, her first thought was of Teddy. Stone cold too. Numbly, she noted how his pear-stalk hair formed a question mark from his night-time tossing and turning.

The tears only came – and they came in torrents – when, on going down to the kitchen, she saw the plate with a crust of hot-cake, and on the back of a chair the jacket she'd had made for Markus, padded out at the shoulders and cut long so as to cover his wide hips.

6. Solipsistically Sweet Marie

So what do I think of myself now? Yes, I caused six people to die, but who would say I *killed* them? Yet it's not as if it had been inadvertent, nor that it was free of venom, and it sure wasn't like mistakenly giving them a poisoned cake "all in good faith."

Yes, these were darts aimed at my husband and son, and now I'm alone, alone in our kitchen as summer shows promise of autumn. And this loneliness overwhelms any guilt I do feel, and any feelings about the guilt I feel I ought to feel. Now I actually want to go to the school and see the children, hear the human noises and face living human dangers. Also the children have been easier since the deaths. Ned Pinker organised a sympathy card and its signing by the whole class – except Jordy Peterson, of course.

I've decided to teach them a bit of French. They call it hong-hong-hong. They enjoy it now, but this will wear off as my new sourness begins to settle in. Now that I have all this time to write my poems, I write nothing and read little. What I feel is that poems should half-write themselves, then urge you to complete and expel them – which, for me, never happens.

Maybe I used to write them *against* Camp Pear, to build a bulwark of fancy and – let's be honest – solipsistic strivings against them. I live in darkness now. Death darkness, of course, but also the dark power. I mean Jocelyn, who is as far from the unfathomable Christianity of Emily as you can get. It's plain I've lost my taste for her devotional mysteries. What I used to do was prettify my gestures. But why prettify at all? Why cover over reality with tropes and curlicues, express solipsistic misery in sugar-coated rhymes?

But I must get on and prepare a pie for Suzie's visit tomorrow. Now where did I put those apples? Must add plenty of sugar. She has such a sweet tooth. Never puts on weight except in those quarters men appreciate. You could say she is voluptuous – voluptuous, intelligent, gay. Gay as a raree show. I'm hardly voluptuous and my intelligence can only scratch traces through my pencil; and as for being gay! Maybe she figures that she has enough gaiety for the two of us, for at least two. She's my life-giver; but it's not simple. We agree on so much. We agree about people, but the gaiety spills over sometimes to a careless, not carefree, levity. I used to sometimes call husband and son "The Pears" to her, and she still does, *even now*. A failure of what? Taste? True sympathy? Lack of niceness?

Men and her. Markus would try a version of the formulaic charm that helped to win me whenever we met her on the street, or he would get all tongue-tied, and if she did not show the right warm appreciation of this fine example of manhood he would give her the bad word to me. His impoverished venom – poor man.

Her romantic life is a story in itself. Her folks wanted her to marry a banker's son called Rooney, but as she felt no spark for the well-heeled bore she gave a solid no and that was the end of it. She "sees" a farmhand from the Stawlker ranch where "see" means long walks to reach secret places, venturing home late, dishevelled and not caring a hoot. Her folks wait up for her but her return overwhelms them and they simply cannot scold her.

7. Is horse-riding Hebrew?

"Well, I guess that brings my total up to seven," said Marie to herself as she sat before a cooling apple pie and the letter she'd picked up on the way home from school. Though Markus's dad was long gone, his mother lived on in Salinas. Lived? Alas, no more. She'd heard the news of her son's and grandson's deaths and her heart stopped. The mode of death was inked at the bottom of the lawyer's letter, telling her that the mother had left all her estate to Markus and because, as he too had passed on, it passed down to her. That is: $14,000 and a house in Salinas.

To protect herself from further thinking she was composing a reply, saying, "Yes, she would be happy for the firm to arrange the house sale for 5% of the final price." With the draft done, she was waiting for Suzie, who was usually late; till Suzie dawdled in saying:

"What's up, girl? You look strange. Have 'The Pears' come back to life? ... Sorry, dear."

Marie explained about the legacy and this brought a rare seriousness to Suzie's face.

"Well," said she, "I know what I would do with it: I'd go to New York, enjoy the raucous Godless music and befriend two or three of these uncorsetted whores."

"So would I ..."

"*Would?* There's no *would*, girl. It's *can*. It's *will*."

"Yes, I really think I will."

And that was how the plan came about.

Marie stared into space with a half-smile while Suzie tucked into the pie.

"Some tea would not go amiss, darling." (Suzie)

"You got it!"

"What? I haven't got it."

"What I meant was, you *will* have it ..."

It was difficult to achieve chit-chat after that. On Marie's side all now seemed provisional. Suzie could tell her funny anecdotes about the Higson's Draw folks; but these people were now as real to her as creatures that lived under the sea.

She recalled how she and Suzie became friends. At a meeting of the Bright Hour they'd happened to catch each other's eye as they grimaced to stifle guffaws at the day's speaker (who'd been reading a story of her own composition based on King Lear, but with a happy ending, and nobody dying, and Gloucester's blinding being replaced by his being deprived of a beloved jerkin, at the end of which the whole cast prayed and said God Bless America in unison), until, meeting outside, they'd collapsed laughing into each other's arms.

It took Suzie not long to find out what a serious little body Marie really was.

"Hey!" (Suzie) "Who's that tying up his horse outside? – with a *stetson* on."

A knock at the door.

"Mrs Sewell?" (he was holding the stetson now) "May I come in? I'm Robert Carpenter, Deputy Sheriff at Salinas." He flashed his badge by flipping a lapel.

He was only a little taller, if taller at all, than the two ladies; but not a mini-man. Broad of shoulder, narrow of hip, and the whole dominated by a mass of curly too-long hair that was clearly a stranger to the comb.

While exchanging pleasantries with Marie, and accepting a cup of tea, his attention lingered on Suzie.

"And this is my friend, Miss Suzie Webster," Marie said, as to imply:"Unglue your impertinent eyes, mister."

"Actually, I was just about to go home." (she wasn't) "So I'll leave you to your ... interrogation. Please be gentle with her, Mr Carpenter." (said with a coquettish grin)

Robert sat disappointedly down and Marie regarded him. Could he be a Hebrew? she wondered. The nose, the unAmerican shrugs, the slight over-articulation, the slightly insinuating prosody ... Oh, this is nonsense, she wisely decided. So is curly hair Hebrew? Horse-riding, no? Being a lawman, no-no? Feverish thoughts sped by, as right then she felt not uncriminal.

"I called in the hope that you might be able to shed a little light on a mystery, Mrs Sewell. Six people dead: Jeff Peterson, the Tooles, Hogue Prentice the cobbler's assistant, and of course your poor son and your beloved husband Markus. I'm so sorry."

"Thank you. A difficult time."

"They all died in their sleep, after falling ill, and you were the last person they saw before falling ill."

He said this as if it were an abstract proposition to be discussed at leisure and with proper nuance.

"I've given it a lot of thought."

She'd given it none. But now, under pressure she had to come up with something.

"My husband had inherited a weak heart on his mother's side. Indeed, I have just received the sad news that his mom fell dead of a heart attack on hearing the news about Markus and Teddy."

She must keep the letter away from him ... financial motive? But how could she have known the news would kill her?

"A lovely old lady."

In fact, a domineering bitch who nagged and undermined her son ... Marie sniffs, wiping away a non-existent tear.

"Yes indeed, a very difficult time for you. I'm sorry."

"That day, Markus – you can check this – had been

aggressively and unfairly used by his boss. He came home fuming smoke through his nostrils." (she told herself not to overdo it) "More to the point, a vein was throbbing on his left temple. I made an anodyne ..." (she felt he would understand this word, even be flattered that she thought he would know it) "... comment that made him explode in rage. He fell suddenly silent, became – how shall I put this? – paralyzed of will and, I assume, had a heart attack in his sleep."

"And Teddy?"

"He was deeply shocked by what he saw happen to his father and suffered a similar fate. I assume he too had a weak heart, poor lamb."

"And the other four? All weak hearts?" (that ironic smile, the seminar disinterestedness).

"All I know is that for three of them there was again an explosion of anger. The Tooles had visited my classroom to harangue me, quite unfairly, about how I had marked their son's homework. Well, for once I stood my ground." (she watched the progress of a thought steal across his eyes) "And I fought back."

"Peterson?"

"Same story. He fumed about how I'd spoken to his son ... But it's funny, isn't it, that while one explanation of an event can seem plausible by itself, if the same explanation is applied to a set of near-simultaneous events it all of a sudden becomes implausible. People seem to think that rare events must be spaced, when really they are just as likely to appear in clusters."

"I'm not a philosopher, Mrs Sewell. There was no report of anger in the case of Hogue Prentice."

"No, indeed. Hogue ..." (she was treading water till she had an idea to cover the death of the cobbler) "Ah yes, Hogue." (she hadn't even known his name till his death day, just the name, evidently not his, on the sign above the shop door) "An *infamous* drinker! Red of face. How many times" (none) "had Markus and I seen him stagger from the tavern to cool himself in the horse trough. After so many years of hard drinking, his heart must have been fit to burst."

This all served to draw a sceptical, searching look from Robert. Not least because nobody had said Prentice was a drinker. She'd let her tongue run loose.

"That's all very interesting, Mrs Sewell, but, forgive me, I'm not convinced. And why are you making out a case for heart attacks as if, forgive me, you feel *it falls to you* to mount a defence?"

Marie was bored and annoyed. The instinct to go-figure him had to be suppressed. In a fit of something, she offered him a piece of pie. He associated the pie with Suzie and would have dearly loved to lick the spoon from her plate. But he accepted from hunger.

They ate together in silence.

Marie: "I'll tell you why. It's the product of pondering. I feel an overwhelming guilt. I feel I have actually KILLED people and yet I did nothing. And what COULD I have done? Poisoned darts? I clutch at straws to avoid these thoughts – the heart-attack straw. What next? A magic-spell straw? The straw of my being a spore of the Devil sent here with a verbal virus to obliterate Californians. Guilt is bad enough, Robert." (she had planned the use of his name) "But guilt for something *you never did*. It's unBEARable!"

She clutched a napkin to her face, buried her face in it, convulsed her torso by an act of will, while noting how hungry he seemed and that more food might soften him.

Robert clearly *was* moved. "Maybe I should go now. I think I've made a mistake, Mrs Sewell."

"Marie, please. If you've really got to go, go now, Mr Carpenter, but I cannot fail to see you are very *hungry*. Can I rustle up some bread and cheese? The tomatoes are very fine right now ..."

Her intention was to say this through sobs, but they came out sounding more like hiccups. He really did like the way she'd breathed *hungry*. She let him eat. Pretending to tidy the kitchen, she furiously searched for Markus' bottle of whisky. Found it up by the pots.

"Oh, I say, I've just unearthed Markus' whisky on the top shelf. I don't suppose you would care for a tumbler to wash down your supper ..."

Robert's first expression was greedy delight. His second, wariness. His third, a politic acceptance: "If," he said, "you would join me." Maybe it would loosen her tongue. Something wasn't right here.

"I'm no drinker, but, yes, I do think I might. It is Saturday tomorrow, after all."

It wasn't Marie's tongue that was loosened: it was Robert's. But she went first. She told him about her Irish parents, told some practised anecdotes from her Leland Stanford days, described (playing it for laughs) how she'd met Markus, and soft-peddled on her hatred of teaching. And all the while she was monitoring the delicious effect of the whisky, as a surfer would monitor the strength and direction of his wave. Care had to be taken. There *were* rocks, and he *was* a lawman.

Meanwhile, there was a cheeky euphoria coming over him. He pounced on her casual remark that she wrote poems "for a hobby" and insisted she read one of them.

(poem duly recited)

"Well that was truly fine, Marie! I sure would love to set that to music."

"You're a musician, Robert?"

"Well, I aspire to being one …" And he was off. He delighted in telling her between refills that he played the Spanish guitar, that he had formed a duo with a half-breed buddy called Chad, or more correctly Little Feet.

"And *does* he have little feet, Robert?"

"Not really … Anyways, we're called *The Sacramento Eagle Catchers.*"

Apparently they took Mexican indigenous songs and Indian chants and songs and blended them with English lyrics of his own composition. To give an example, he launched into what he called "A Tolowa Eagle Song …"

> *Hyo Hooah Heya Ho*
> *Whoah Chapwhah Kay*
> *Hoya Ho WhaaaHa Ha!*
> *Taka Tow Whowhah Hey*

and so on, and on.

He vocalised with a rapt passion that put her in mind not of an Indian brave but of a wayward cantor. She rather liked this, but the English version less so:

> *Way up hold up there's the bear*
> *Can you see her by the tree?*
> *Way up hold up I don't care*
> *If she comes dancing down to me.*
> *Way up hold up …*

His voice was reedy, rough and almost cutting, but pleasant enough for all that. His delivery: laconic, despite the drink. Seductive, too, and meant to be. But the music was all nonsense to her. Thank the Lord, she thought, he didn't bring his guitar. When she glanced to one side she saw deep darkness on her window.

"Why, that is truly original, Robert. I've never heard a thing like it. But I say, it's real dark outside. How are you for riding back to Salinas tonight?"

"Oh, Mercy!" (he looked at the clock) "I would not trust myself riding over Chappaquak Ridge in the dark, especially after your fine hospitality. I'll get down to the hotel, they'll probably have a room."

"No, please. I can make you up a bed in Teddy's room." Her whisky "wave" pulled her towards adding: "His bed will be big enough for you." But this and so many other impulses were inhibited that night.

8. Matutinally Sweet Marie

What was Suzie's expression? "Jump on his bones." Yes, that's it. Was it the whisky or him? As I lay down and heard him undressing and singing to himself (Whoah Heyah ...), I wanted to leave my bed and go to him and jump on his bones. Or maybe I could have wandered there in my shift and led him like a half-dead Poe-waif into my "chamber" so he could "kill a rat" for me; then I would let the shift fall from my shoulders. Well, Heyup Whoah and begora ... So he left just after sun-up and here I am at the kitchen table turning over this trace of him, written on a page torn from his Sheriff's Office pad:

Dearest Marie,

Thank you for the lovely evening that could never have been predicted. My line of questioning was impertinent and caused you pain. For that I am more than sorry. Please forgive me.

I would dearly love to make it up to you. It would be a rare treat for me to see you again in

a situation when I am not behind a metal star.
Then I will make it up to you.
Yours in hope,

Robert A. Carpenter

Then, a scribbled afterthought:

There are many fine ~~eating-houses~~ restaurants in
Salinas and I would dearly love to accompany you
to one such at some time in the future. Here is my
address for correspondence.

So he wants to make it up to me by giving himself a treat ...
But he knows and I admit that it would be a rare treat for me
too. Fact is, though, whether he's behind a star or in front of
a hand-pump, or squinting down from his horse or spreading marmalade, he's suspicious of me. Who wouldn't be!
He's just an attractive, imp-like, vocalising deputy sheriff,
embodiment of all the strange looks I get in the street. Soon
these suspicions will filter down to child level. Imagine their
classroom routines ... "Hey, don't make Miss angry, you'll
breathe your last before you can say ..." (and here they'll
shout their favourite rude words).

It's like I'm sheltering in a doorway out of a raging storm. I
cannot wait for it to ease up. I'll have to pull up my skirts
and run. I'm going to have to move quickly. Maybe I'm still
drunk ... Some hot cakes "would not go amiss." Now where
does Suzie get these expressions from? Too tired to make
them now; it's back to bed for me. I can please myself.
"Behind a metal star" is a good phrase, too. When you wish
upon a star and a wish you didn't know you had comes true.
Who can tell what'll be behind it.

9. A non-transcendental aesthetic

It kept running through her head, the sentence: "She has gone out into the jungle and come back with another bunch of bananas." Out to the jungle of the school-board director's office to resign as from the end of the week, citing her recent trauma and the unspecified need to get to her folks in Ireland at once, bringing back their dismay echoing in her ears as a huffing-puffing sound. Out to the jungle of Salinas, to the lawyer's office, then a bank, and back with a fat check and $300 in cash ($200 of which would be sewn into her drawers). Out to the meagre town stores in a dim jungle clearing for a travelling bag, whisky, travelling clothes. Out to the jungle of the house-rental agency and back home with her $85 deposit. Out to the benign jungle of the Wells Fargo office and home with tickets to San Francisco, from where she would catch the cross-continental train to New York City.

Then out to Suzie's – hardly a jungle; and this was her first outward task, done on Sunday morning, to plead with her not to breathe a word about the legacy and to further her story that she was going to New York to catch the boat to Europe.

She brought back the banana of a dim unease squatting on her chest.

"Let me tell you about our curly-haired deputy ..." She began her account of Friday evening's events in the certainty that this would be a sure-fire delight for Suzie.

"Ah yes, ravening Robert," Suzie smiled initially, following it up with "The Concupiscent Kid."

But when she was told of the whisky intimacy, the come-hither Whoah Heyahing, and the letter on the kitchen table, a sourness came over Suzie and he was "Tiny Tim" or "Little Boots" or finally and with force, "The Old Dwarf."

What Marie had thought would bond them with giggles pulled them apart with Suzie's sneering. All for no reason Marie could fathom. Then, suddenly, Suzie altered, gripped Marie's arms so hard it hurt, and hugged her close ...

"I'm going to miss you, girl. You're the only friend I care to have in this Hellish place. But I'll be out to visit ..." (then, cowboy style) "... as shurr as shurr cayne be."

The unease continued to squat until her last day at the schoolhouse. She read *The Masque of the Red Death* and had them draw pictures of scenes in it, pinning all of them on the walls. She didn't try to teach them a thing and ended the day with lemonade and *Anabelle Lee*. Some giggled, fewer yawned; some were quietly amazed. Nearly all were sad to see her go.

The whole process took less than ten days, then she was on the struggling stagecoach to Salinas, packed against silent women and a couple of men who at every jolt and hiccup decided aloud, "The future's in internal combustion." Then the train to Frisco, buying a train ticket to New York City, and a hotel room in Frisco for the night, just off Union Square.

Her ticket seemed to be for an all-women carriage. Fine. Maybe that was better (maybe not). But as far as she cared, the carriage could have been stuffed with aardvarks and druids. The immediate reality was that she would steam through a pass between the Rockies, roll across broad plains unknown, and end up on Manhattan Island, God knows when. She had ceased her scorpion backward-loops of brooding, ceased to be set back from the now, and felt ready for any happening.

She had planned to luxuriate in *The Wings of a Dove,* but it was impossible. Why live falsely with those taking tea near Hyde Park when you are crossing a continent with real people various and garrulous! She even found herself joining in the chatter, which stopped almost of a sudden as excitement led to slumber. She was alone enough to take a substantial meal from her bag and enjoy it among snores.

> *As I was travelling on a train going east*
> *They fell asleep. I had my feast.*

Maybe Robert could set that to music, adding a few Whoah Heyahs.

Wake up and smell the whisky is another nice phrase, she decided. The moment she fished out her half-pint and uncorked it, eyes popped open and the bottle was finished collectively. Changing engines, many stops for this and that. Endless, endless plains. This was less travel than temporarily living somewhere new.

She had drunk just enough to linger in that early phase of inebriation when an imagined insight, which by good luck may be a real insight, swallowed her up. She had warmed to one or two of the women, was irritated by many, found some aloof and sharp, but now she thought she knew that reality was a social affair. The only kind of reality she wanted, in fact.

American individualism. The free generic-man, the single soul sorting everything out from his fine instincts set against Nature, brave shining solitude against the corruptions of "society." She didn't actually know what Transcendentalism was, but she hated the *word* – and that was enough. Nutrition comes from bumping up against others, from the doings and thoughts of others in relation to one's own. The play of your own consciousness, its snaking and detours and nonsenses, was all very fine, but the play is only as it is from what others put you in the way of, whether you like these "whats" or not.

A thinker on top of a mountain alone? In a room alone! Anything that can be achieved by the so-called (the drink may be turning bad at this point) imagination and so-called reason; even that kind of room-poetry ... ("sorry, Emily," she thought) ... now meant nothing to her. What Hell it would be to be at home alone with only books. No people – not even bores. Book-bound Hell. But poetry that plays over modern doings and the immediate, especially an urban stream of events ... ah, yes. But most important of all, a poetry that needs others to complete it, where only two-thirds of the whole, if there is a whole, is from the poet's own mind ...

She fell asleep.

10. Bi-modally Sweet Marie

More alone than free is the way with me right now. The journey did me in. They said two days; it felt like a week. None of us had food enough but we could jump out to stock up at stations where there were stalls.

Breakfast (wonderful!) in the streets today: hot sausage in a bun. Soon I will try to wash in that little sink. "Apartment for rent," it said; but it's just one room. Big, though, and with a little kitchen behind a curtain. But just a room – sorry, "chamber." The housekeeper fellow called it a chamber.

More abandoned than astounded right now. The journey, as I say, did for me. Like a fool I expected the train to bring us on to Manhattan Island. But they unloaded our flock of lost sheep in a nothing region in Jersey City called, because it had to be called something, Exchange Place. I followed the others down to the North River Ferry in the small hours of morning, looked at the black water, saw the towers of that city. Inhuman beauty. My pounding heart. It was an army massing for combat, and so too a playground for unimaginable people. As I inched down in the queue to board the ferry, it started to light up. On board the vista seemed to recede, so I closed my eyes, sensing only the varied stinks of my fellow travellers.

Then to arrive at what the ferryman called "midtown," Pier 96. No magic in these streets; like downtown Frisco, but where dark-skinned people ask you "How ya doin?" and call you "lady" as if it were an insult. The many street-poor looking like they carried rats in their pockets. Walked and walked to a shuttered Broadway: a mouse in a field of corn. I asked a policeman the way to Greenwich Village and he said, from the corner of his mouth, without looking at me, "7th Avenue then downtown trolley to Sheridan Square." Gestured eloquently with his thumb.

"The Village" is ... It was there in all its narrow red-brick streets, but I managed to get through, ha-ha. Found notice of this place in a coffee shop window. Bleecker Street "and Jones," as I'm learning to say.

Lay down to sleep. Got to know the brown-stained ceiling too well. Got up; sitting here, slowly absorbing the city, which sounds absurd till you come to have to do it. Now properly tired. It's 3.00 p.m. but let's try sleep again.

Up very early. West to the river. Blue now; sunshine outside and inside. Sleep had washed the journey away and allowed joy in. And here I am, after two helpings of scrambled eggs and toasted bread and unlimited coffee in a café on West 3rd Street, having just been to sit in Washington Square.

But the brute force of the nothing: not a single Henry James thought rose to my surface as I sat there watching birds, children, lovers, and listening to a flute player. Tomorrow the bank and write to my folks (but how?). I've spoken to next to nobody except for practical purposes, except for the fellow who lives below me. A strange bird, he. Very softly spoken. Whispery. Angelic, almost: fine blonde hair like a baby that needs a haircut; triangular face; a child's blue eyes; little rosebud mouth.

He smiled when he told me how happy he would be to help with lifting and carrying and directions and how good he was at "wielding a screwdriver." But his smile ... the smile was uncomfortable for me. Little pointed teeth like two ivory combs. No, a baby shark. Come to think of it, more like a pansy than an angel. Seemed nice enough though. Said his name was Kate. Now there's a pansy name if ever there was one.

11. Thick line between love and Kayte

Sometimes you have to throw nuance down the well. With Mister John Kayte (the downstairs dweller) you certainly do. You may wonder: Is there such a thing as evil? You may say: No, it's just having the wrong desires and a weak will. Then you hear of the acts and dispositions of Mister John Kayte. The denominator of him was a taste for himself being the cause of misery in others. His mandate was to deliver mental pain. Not exactly sadistic because he took no pleasure in it – a cold duty, rather. He had no excuses beyond the vile luck of being born John Kayte. Loving parents in Connecticut and he their hating child.

And not only could nobody be less of an angel: no one could be less of a "pansy." The possession of women was his single goal, enjoying them briefly then subjugating them, making them squirm in bespoke ways. He was an expert at finding the right kind of woman. His pretty face and fine body helped. An artists' model by profession, he exercised for hours every day before a long mirror. He sucked women in till they needed him, then he exposed them to situations that were their special nightmares, and sometimes these situations could be no more than hearing him speak ... about them. He read William James. He was a psychologist of a kind.

When he was not posing or exercising, he was cleaning and tidying his "chamber." He'd painted it light grey and white and it was as clean and unsociable as a clinic, except for the indentations in the walls, re-plastered and re-painted but leaving rough islets of disturbance. This is where he had pounded in fury (smashed chairs had been quickly replaced), bringing us to Kayte's Achilles heel ...

His aggression, as I said, was strategic, gradual, and a verbal affair; but when he was in drink, even a small amount, it was a different story. At his most dangerous then, but most vulnerable too, as there was nowhere to hide. He liked public aggression. And in it there was the beacon of his red, unembarrassable face, his biting teeth bared. He might return home from an evening of just two beers, an evening of failing to seduce a waif who looked easy meat ... then beating up his walls, going for the knockout.

As for Marie, this self-styled mental scientist had her down as "a dreamer." He could pretend to bring her dreams of integration into Village life to fruition. He almost could seem to do this (he had no friends but some contacts). He would follow her whenever he could. If she ventured out this evening he would follow to see what she liked, betting she knew nobody here. In fact, one of his skills was following people. On hearing her footsteps on the stairs, he was dressed and ready.

He saw her wander like a child in Santa's grotto. Up Bleecker to 7th, double back via 4th Street, stop in a bar there for what could be a whisky (actually a sarsaparilla), down MacDougal; then, seeing the lights of *Jimmy's* in Monetta Lane, she tentatively descends the cellar steps. He follows, but she stays for so long, gradually moving to the front row before the little stage, and he feels he knows all he needs to know (the little ninny is stage-struck for that dull circus of fiddlers and spouters!) and goes home. If they could, his walls would breathe a sigh of relief at his lemonade breath.

12. *Pencil-sharpeningly Sweet Marie*

"What do you recommend?" I'd said to the young barkeep. He sized me up. "An Alabama Home," which turned out to be port and brandy.

That was my first evening at *Jimmy's*. Knew immediately it would become the venue for my future evenings. It suits me just fine. Can't say New Yorkers are friendly folk; they talk but not neighbourly, don't give much of themselves away. The atmosphere in that cellar was my dream of Greenwich Village, but it was the acts on the little stage that kept me there. A juggler; a young fellow playing the fiddle, holding it against his chest and yodelling country songs; a wall-eyed conjurer; a schoolmaster type declaiming, no, *shouting* Longfellow and reading, no, *lecturing* James Russell Lowell. No-thank-you-very-much!

Later in the evening they all struggle. Folks can be drunk

or excited, plus more out-of-towners arrive, but earlier on less has been drunk and food has soaked up the liquor and there is space for attention, maybe, for me and my efforts. I know who runs the place. Not Jimmy but Janine. A manly wench but kindly to me. She advises me: "Watch him – don't leave your bag open." That kind of thing.

I'll ask her if I can read. No need for dollars.

I could warm them up with a little Poe, then some Emily, then, yes, my Higson's Draw poems, and then my New York poems.

All's changed utterly now with poetry since the journey. I sit down and what comes are not quite poems and they come from somewhere else in my mind. My fences have been let down and now the yard is full of strange animals.

These two efforts. What comes from this vein will seem to some, and maybe is, muddy brown water, not the sparkling Mosel of poesy. Well, these two are my muddy experiments. The first: street impressions of my first night. The second: some Pear memories.

Night Waves

I am among the many stalks in the street
seeing his or her clothes, and her hair
is ...
It's cooling enough for them but they won't
huddle or cuddle together for warmth
warmth comes from the gaskets below
in the kitchens of night.

Steam tells us to ...

If the whisky burns your throat it's time
to sweeten yourself in Alabama Home
not needing the torch of summer

in the happy caverns we suck in music
through outstretched pores.

Who would want to be stainless and brave
or flung upon dull circumstance when there are
these figures of rough usage here
animals
animals and flowers?
Their breath flatters my cheek like a ...

Behind every bar door
perched on a high stool
sex is the image rejecting
your porticos of substantial hardtack wisdom.

With grey blinking piety Mr Jones you ask
Are these "men of the night?"
Would that I could witness myself ...

How these buildings hide us
from the old winds, give us space
to work towards a definition of
the cool spirit.

Masters of contention glitter
at the corners of their own mouths
by which I mean ...?

I wander lonesome in this honeycomb
of the unknown world
threaded catacombs, illicit banquets
but it's the dried-blood hue of brick
that saves us reality
No bees for sure only the catcalls
of brilliant Indians, their "primitive"

chants and our small wishes
merge in night-waves
freshets
will bring some caramel soon?

Keeping it in the Family

It's time to draw in the cheeks
and salute the day
my thoughts so few but loud enough
to praise the dead.

I loved you so much despite ...
I loved you a little, maybe
suckled you, gave my body to you
both of you locked out of me

your wandering on Sunday with dusty guns.

You were not around long enough
to think towards what's really wrong
You? Something moved like an egg-timer
within you, your "maturer" years.

In the past, a steep time
these adobe huts, you eat your fill again
scrubland so wide and hot perhaps?
I am lost, can
you tether my heart?

Children scraped the sides of my body all day
I more than ever
behind the schoolhouse, tears
so little love you had to give.

The town streets are rutted and muddy, hard mud
the dull air, a smell of wood smoke
it's enough to make you cry out.

Such bodies pear-shaped against the window
with the kitchen dark in the early morning
perhaps a crow its wings small black cloud
then the yellow day all out of time.

The dirt track snaking up to the ridge
the warm breath failing, death near enough to touch
trying to form new words from nothing
you teeter on the threshold and you ...

brown paint in the church porch
your two white faces in
their undertaker-smiles.

Let's see now ... my penknife and pencils call. Who can that be tapping at my "chamber door"?

Well, I suppose it's a case of "poor fellow." He so much wants to make a connection – lonely, ineffectual and soft. The lisping and the failing to meet my eye ... "I thaw you in Jimmyth watching the thow, so here's thomthing that might perchanth be of inneretht." It was a hand-sized advertisement for Gerde's Folk Theatre. Not for me: playlets, political meetings, tenors and sopranos. I told him how kind he was and said, "Thanks so much, Kate."

"Oh, John, please. Nameth John K-A-Y-T-E."

He was shuffling there, tongue-tied, desperate to find the right words to keep my door open. Impertinent, though, looking over my shoulder. "Oh, I thee yor writing. Letterth home?"

I told him I was reading through my poems. I thought he would collapse with joy. "Tho yor a POET!?"

A long, long silence as he digs out words:

"She walkth in beauty like the night."

His dreadful smile. "Rather remindth me of you in your evening perambulationth." Now that gave me a chill. He could see it did. No, his hopeless blanket of "thorrys" could not warm me after that. Maybe this John is not a pansy; his eyes alighted too often on my bosom. But then he was maybe too shy to aim them higher ... I suppose.

13. Biddy Baxter Redux

If you are an outsider, better to be one in relation to a set of people you want to be within, rather than, as in Higson's Draw, outside of an alien milieu. What she was still or inevitably without was, rather, as old Biddy Baxter had described it, the louche, the bohemian, the unfamilial, improvising a rolling boil of humanity in the Village streets and taverns.

She filled her days exploring, hardly leaving the Village. There were cafés and bars set against which *Jimmy's* was a homely billet. Among the clientele of these places sat the demure Marie with her coffee and cookies and slim volume of Tennyson, too shy to pencil on her pad, unlike the others who made a show of drawing, scribbling. A far cry from Longfellow and James Russell Lowell were some of the poems she heard declaimed, usually in a room upstairs from a restaurant. The kind of poems Ned Pinker might write. But mainly there were what she called The Whitman Wanderers: hirsute, open-necked disciples of Walt declaiming the self-delighted rhetoric of prose – to the ear of Marie, at least. She could be severe. And *so young* they all were. To become *fresh* is hardly a project. Yes, the confidence deficit was still within her. She remained within a small zone of comfortable people, ventured like a tourist beyond this zone, observed it as she had observed the Grand Canyon on her honeymoon.

But what focused it all was Janine giving her a reading slot in a week's time at 6.00 p.m. "Let's see how it goes, doll. If they eat you alive, I ain't insured."

Marie was that common thing: an inhibited exhibitionist, who now made over her appearance into something in the Village way. Her hair now fell to her shoulders; she did something with darkener around her eyes that a friendly waitress had recommended; she swapped her mushroom-coloured clothes for blacks and red and whites and purples; beads, too, were added. Quality was maintained in uptown stores that intimidated her. Now that the house-sale proceeds had been wired through, she thought of buying a small apartment, but could not think beyond that to herself unanchored there, doing *what?*

In the everyday she seemed aloof to folks, not shy, not careful, but disdainful. The pellets of conversation she loosed to the server of her breakfast eggs were seen as crumbs from a high table. Danger could wash all this away.

One evening her door was not tapped but hammered. For a second she was pleased to see him and was ready to help. Then she saw the bloodshot eyes and smelt the drink. And the lisp was gone ...

    "Aren'tyagonna ask me in, muh dear?"

    "No. Go now or I'll call the housekeeper."

    "She'll *caaaalll the housekeep!!!*"

    "NO!"

    "Your funeral, sister."

When he could see she was likely to scream, he staggered back down the stairs.

Her waitress friend at *Jimmy's* explained about Kayte and told her, "Move, honey, soon as you can." She told Marie about a friend of hers who worked in a laundry on Grand Street. Kayte had cultivated this girl, up from Kansas City, then the usual happened. "At least he passed swiftly from the sweet-talking, nice-guy stage. Now you know where you are." Marie silently blessed the barkeep who'd served him his beer that night: the canary in her mine.

The next day a grovelling letter of apology was pushed under her door, plus a dreadful poem comparing her to

> *a faun in the forest who*
> *shyly out peeps.*

Then there he was, in the front row for her first reading at *Jimmy's*.

The nerves she felt before the event were not as those she faced before her class. This was an act. She hotly thought this while knowing it was false. Thinking that after just four or five syllables into her reading they would be hers, captive in silent wonder; but ... nothing. Tennyson, Emily – wallpaper to them. Then, when it was time to recite her California and New York poems, she had an idea: drop her voice ...
    "Speak up, sweetheart!"
    Well that was rude ... but positive. She did not. Indeed, grew quieter.
    "Give the gal a chance!"

Yes, something was working itself out. The unfinished utterances made them (made some of them) strain their ears for sound, or their brains for a completing sense. There were grumbling voices, of course, but they were as distant thunder in her bluebell wood. Peacefulness was being floated out. She wound up one poem early, not because she'd had enough but because she knew that the building wave of calm and friendly puzzlement would soon crash from inattention. And she flattered herself she'd set a thirst in them.

Well, it sure set a thirst in the mental scientist from the room below who, that evening, became soberly insistent, then, days later, vile enough in his drink to raise the attention of a slumbering housekeeper.

"On the house," said Janine setting an Alabama Home before her, adding "Still not sure abou'cha. Twice a week should do it, doll."

She hated terms like *modus operandi* and *modus vivendi* and all that chest-beating stuff, but she was developing a "modus" alright, and more and more of her own work found its way in, till one night she looked up and saw, two seats back from Kayte's usual perch, a corona of brown curls and Robert's subtle, slightly-smiling face beneath it.

14. Devastatingly Sweet Marie

A leap of pure joy, curdled at once by uncertainty, by the usual Robert ambivalence: how and why? How did he find me and why is he here? I rushed though two more poems, finished in a damp cloud. He stayed put; I was clearly expected to go to him. His warmth was a practised thing. We embraced, our first such. "Let's have a drink elsewhere" were his first words. Off to a bar on Grove Street that I knew would be quiet. I'd leave the questions till later. We walked through the streets in near silence, shouldering through the Friday crowds and sat in the window of the bar.

I tried the how question ..."Easy," he said. "The sheriff's office in Salinas wired the New York Port Authority. Nobody by your name had sailed for Europe. We prevailed upon the police department to go though all rooming-house arrival records for the past month between 125th Street and the bottom of the island. Picked you out in one. Went to the Bleecker Street place. Fellow in charge had no idea where you were. Then a pansy kind of creature muttered, on his way out, something about you being at *Jimmy's.* I seemed to have angered him. But then, New Yorkers aren't like us. Unmannerly."

"But why go to all the trouble?" I said. "I mean, it's truly a fine thing to see you again, Robert. I've been thinking about you. I feel we could have had a real good ... friendship, but it's like I'm being hunted down."

He looked into his drink for too long a time.

"How did you do it?" he said, clear and hard.

"Do what?"

"Kill all those people, of course."

I swallowed my whisky and asked for another. To Hell with it, I thought. Tell him the truth.

I didn't say my "advisor" was called Jocelyn, and of course I never mentioned him saying he was from the future. Did what I could to suggest I was a decent woman trapped in a poor life dropped into the maelstrom of a fairy tale. I said my visitor was a gypsy. I told him the go-figure words, being careful not to say them straight to him.

He gazed into his drink again and a slow smile grew. He looked at me ..."You look different," he said. "I like it."

At that point I knew that, sure, he was doing his duty, but that he was seeing pleasure beyond that.

"You know what?" he said. "I believe you. I mean, I believe you are telling the truth."

"It IS true!" My anger surprised me.

He was laughing, but not at me. He said, "Maybe we could prove the power of these words. Get hold of an alley cat and tell it to go figure."

"It'll need to speak English."

We chatted and drank some more. I was in a chamber between one state and another. New York does that to you. You are in a drama between two epochs of grey reality. You enjoy it as best you can, exciting, barely possible, worth it. But then a stab from him ...

"I heard about the legacy from your husband's family."

"How?"

"Higson's Draw is a village. You can't hide news."

Now I was really angry, and the whisky nurtured it. I looked outside, thinking I would cry from anger, and found myself looking into another angry face the equal of mine – Kayte's. He peered in through the window, then came in. This time he was real drunk. Swaying. He sat with us, though we didn't want him there.

"Hey, doll!" he said. "Here's a pome for yuh."

> *I see you gotta new boyfriend*
> *No I never seed him before.*
> *You sittin' pretty with him*
> *Smiling like a Jew-boy's whore*

The next thing I knew, Robert grabbed Kayte round the throat and squeezed hard. I thought he'd kill him. Only at a shout from the bar did he stop. As Kayte slumped over, I whispered to Robert to leave it to me. I had my best ever, most bad ever, most *magnificent* idea.

We waited to him to recover.

"Tell you what, John," I said to Kayte. "Why don't you get some food to ... um ... settle your stomach. I'll just round up this little bit of family business with my brother here, and then why don't you call in tonight for a nightcap of hot milk? We can" (I breathed suggestively) "finish off the evening."

He left, thinking hard, with a smile to me and a smirk to Robert.

"Now there we have our alley cat," I told Robert.

"Yup!" was his reply.

I also told him about the curtain between the main part of the "chamber" and the kitchen, where he could station himself. Nearly joked that he could nestle in the sink.

Folks laughingly say "Oh, I feel evil!" when maybe they're minded to eat the last currant bun. If I said I felt evil it was in almost that way but with more weight on the "evil." Had the Devil in me whilst still a bright-eyed avenging Angel.

We dined on fish and fried potatoes, making plans as the drink wore off. Robert told me the important thing was that we should ascend the stairs in lock-step. I should pause before Kayte's door as we went by and cough high and loud. Robert said he'd sit still upstairs, or, better still, station himself on the bed, so Kayte would not hear him. The thought excited us. We leaned across the table and kissed.

Later, with Robert squatting like an incubus on my bed, we heard an emphatic but not aggressive knock. Kayte looked confused, not as drunk as he was earlier but like somebody who has been having second thoughts and is angry you've noticed it. The original state was still alive in him.

"Some hot milk, John?"

"Snot milk I wan'... s'yew."

"Me? Goodness."

"Now you jess come here, Missy," says he, advancing.

"Go figure!"

"Go to Hell, more like! Swear you think I belo–"

He gave a crooked, smoky grin and slid down the wall to the floor. That changed to the satisfied smile as of a job well done (a fine golf putt, a *bon mot*).

I called out for Robert to help me lift him.

When Kayte saw Robert he perked up. "Shit eater!" says he. Then a shrug, a sigh, and he wanders home for his final bout of shut-eye.

After that? Well, all I can say to Robert as he snores beside me is "You never wasted time." Now it's around 6.00 a.m. and I've spent the last hour or so competing with a naked man for space in my little bed. He makes sudden movements in his sleep. He pulls himself straight, front on to me, moving upwards in the bed as if he has to give me continual evidence that he is indeed a Hebrew.

15. Sixth Avenue between 13th and 14th

They almost became a "Village couple," a walking feature, with his arm flung across her shoulders, she with her arm around his waist, the same height, the same vague smiles, often striding carelessly in the middle of the street, early snow banking in the gutters, an image of the unfettered, free-rolling life in their bulky coats and long scarves. Yes, those smiles could be a little smug (look, we've found each other, unlike you ...). But you did not have to look closely to see they were rarely in conversation. In *Polly's* restaurant they mostly sat in silence among disputatious artists and the other saucy crews.

Marie was still sparing of speech, taking her cue from others. Not true of Robert, but he seemed absorbed in his own cogitations, as if his speaking would be an impertinence, like laughing in church. There was, though, happiness. If you took a relative view, this could be said: She was much happier than before, and he was more "himself." Too bad that, out from behind the badge, this "himself" could be inert. He assimilated. He instigated little. Did he think *his* being content was enough to make her happy? Adjectives like "complacent" pile up like dirty snow.

We again have NYC as a space between two states, and they were both in it. Grey behind, grey before, but the space itself was not exactly bursting with colour. It was clear that Robert could not report back to Salinas the cause of these six deaths. He toyed with the idea of joining the Police Department in NYC, but his toying was the kind he went in for when they spoke of marriage – as if it were a third-person conjecture. He did more seriously toy with a musical career. On *Jimmy's* stage? He was "thinking of" buying a guitar. "The shops here have so many fine ones." Oh, please God, no, thought Marie. Folk music! Hyo Hooah Heya Ho, then a lyric about a wayward donkey? Please, no. She lied that playing music was not allowed in their building.

The question that returned to her, especially in the early hours when she shoved his snoring carcass against the wall and struggled for *Schlafensraum* (their shared joke – not a joke) was: Did she love him? Oh yes, she did. She desired him hotly and felt desired. And they were peaceful together. And he had an inscrutability that was kind of charismatic. "He's an enigma, but he's my enigma." And that his floating little-boy-lost look set the seal on it. But then he would irritate her in the morning with his demands from the bed for coffee, and could she fetch a newspaper; and, Oh Lord, his *singing*.

But that was not the way this morning. He was up, smartly dressed, had shined his shoes and explored what her new tooth powder could do. Oh yes, he was going to the Police Department today to "see how the land lies." She *had* thought he'd gone off the idea. He told her he'd be home for supper.

That was just fine with Marie. She relished the real freedom, as opposed to the cover-story bohemia of their wanderings. She fiddled with some poems but could not settle; decided they were better left alone, as documents, sketches of certain episodes ... but she could not convince herself of that and felt restless-bored.

After an early lunch the thought came, "I'll go shopping. When do I ever do that? I've got the money and what I really want is a warm, waisted overcoat in dark blue with a yellow or red scarf. Elegant but not *outré*."

Not so far up 6th Avenue to Macy's. As ever in these places she felt like a cowgirl attending the Duke's banquet. Admired greatly a gorgeous light-grey coat with a fine fur collar, but could not bring herself to pay the price. "Too dressy for the Village as well," she reasoned.

Then she turned to see a beautiful girl in that very same coat, twirling, delighted. Showing it off to the store attendant? Surely not. To somebody in a chair between them, occluded by the broad-in-the-beam attendant? No! It was Suzie. Suzie! Marie was not pleased so much as shocked. She'd received few replies to her letters and they'd been short and full of cold irony.

The attendant moved off to the side. Here was the person in the chair, his corona of curls. She thought she'd lip-read these words accurately (she had):

"Thank you so much, darling." They embraced.

Marie's first thought, the hard barrier against emotion:

"Yes, Robert rarely paid his way with me."

16. Relatively Sweet Marie

To a child, a jumping bean is an enigma, one that is resolved by showing her the worm inside. That much a child I felt ... and such the reflective thought I'm enjoying now, waiting for him to come home.

There were a number of cold thoughts in the emotional bulwark. Perhaps the second: How like it was the devastating-for-Hyacinth reveal scene at the end of Mr James's *The Princess Casamassima* that sparked his suicide. But this *will not spark one*: "cide" maybe, but not "sui."

And then came further bulwark thoughts: so THAT was how he'd heard of the legacy – through *her* – and THAT was how he'd learned of my address. All that nonsense about tracking me as if I were an international anarchist. His plan maybe to arrest me and return to her. What did he TELL her? The go-figuring? It all crumbled into the mote and I was not left wounded quite but with a sword in my hand and fury in my heart.

At her. Mainly her.

As for him ... well, it's what assimilating, dull men are inclined to do: grab what they can from the front row of a fruit stall while keeping their eye on the more delicious offerings at back. What loss? His sitting over a bottle of port he'd had me buy, sitting in his underwear displaying his incipient pot belly and reading the funny papers. No conversation, no interest in anything bar writing those letters to his fellow Sacramento Eagle Catcher, also known as Suzie Ancona. As for the act of … what … love? More like for him the discharging of a bodily function.

I had caught sight of myself in a shop window, striding back to the Village, leaning forward, fists clenched, and I was *cold*. I do need a warmer coat. She's warm, the bitch is warm, and PERMANENTLY cold is what she deserves to be.

Despite the cold, I had gone to sit on a bench in Washington Square. Could not stomach the "chamber" and its associations with our coming together. Cold planning, then … The go-figuring plan had woken me up, and now awake I could dispense hot justice on two deserving rear ends.

He'll come in the door – my thought ran – with unimaginative, vague inventions about events at the cop shop. I'll describe what I saw and then, in a little-girl voice, with my head down, say:

"Call me crazy, but I want to imagine Suzie now. Where is she staying? I want to go and forgive her. I wish you both well."

Once I have her address, I'll go-figure the bastard. Then wander off to Suzie with a song in my heart. I'll see her face when she opens her hotel room door … "Any wisecracks for me, Miss Ancona?"

(struck dumb)

"GO FIGURE!"

"No, not that. DON'T!" It was Jocelyn beside me on the bench. "Or rather, can't. I've taken the power away from you." He laughed: "Not much of a Sweet Marie now, are you? But still – sweeter than most. Relatively Sweet Marie. Flesh is weak, after all."

I'd been habituated to surprises by now and could feel

my anger being spent on him.

"But why give me the power of death? I didn't want my son to die. I only wanted to tongue-tie them, give them a taste of what it's like, not finish them off!"

He turned away and spoke quietly, in profile: "It was a malfunctioning of our system. I should have told you to tell them: 'It is what it is.' Sorry about that."

"SORRY!"

"Ah, but we've made a few much-needed improvements to our system. I have words for Robert tailor-made for him. Leave Suzie be; the new Robert will be torture enough to her. I promise, these words won't kill him. They are: 'It's all gone pear-shaped.'

"When Robert speaks in earnest, or with even the slightest passion, the words that issue from his mouth – phrases, clauses, sentences – will be very different from the words he meant to form from his thoughts, and they won't be weighted words but light words, from the future, often more British than American – centrifugal words."

"*Scentifugal?* What the Hell are you talking about!"

"Relax, Marie. Breathe deeply. Go home to your poetry. It's really who you are – oh, damn, there's another future-cliché we like to weaponise (sorry, I mean another future word just popped out)."

I can't say I was warming to Jocelyn, and that was not the point of him. He was an efficient (mainly) executive, humane in a weird way, but bloodless. I told him I had found myself that morning, and not for the first time, losing faith in my writing, even finding it ridiculous. Now his familiar half-smile was gone.

"Don't lose faith in it. You are of the future. Actually, so too is Robert, 'but not in a good way' (another of our future clichés). Your poems? Yes, they tend to cluster around a prose idea that can be simple, even banal, but they have intimations, fruitful ones maybe, for other, better writers. Yes, you are a minor talent only. Sorry! But you point the way, the way that can lead to solipsistic blather but also to something wonderful. You are doing the right kind of thing, albeit not quite well enough, if that does not sound too much like your beloved Henry James."

He looked straight at me for the first time ever. His grey eyes showed some warmth at last. I liked him then a lot and watched him walk away along 4th Street.

17. You what!

Robert entered the "chamber" somewhat after suppertime, initially with a hunted demeanour, immediately switching to a toothy grin and a "Hi, honey. Good to see you!"

"Who else were you expecting?"

"Ha-Ha," and on he forged.

"Successful day?"

There followed an excruciating account ... how intrigued by him they were, especially old er Joe er Smith, the Station Sergeant; but they were not sure they had any vacancies at the moment.

"And that took *all day?*"

"Um ..."

"And anyway, why on Earth would they give a job to a lawman who'd absconded when sent to track down a possible murderess?"

"Well, you see ..."

"Never mind. I guess it's all above my head."

"Sure. And how was your day, sweetness?"

"It's all gone pear-shaped."

"Huh?"

"Never mind. Let's go eat."

They ate at the place of their first ecstatic night; ordered the same thing as then.

Now her assay …

"Let me be straight with you, Robert. How did you really find my address? What you told me has not the tiniest ring of truth. Spit it out, man."

He meant angrily to say: "You don't understand anything about police work. You're an ignoramus, doll." Actually he said:

"Now here's a funny thing: My wife, I say, my wife, is so ugly I'd rather take her with me than kiss her goodbye."

His anger turns to horror, as if he's watching these words march out of him. He splutters, a look of terrible panic is on him, so much so she feels some pity (but not much).

"And another thing, Robert. No doubt I'll be paying for this meal as usual. Are you saving up? Maybe for a winter coat?"

He meant to say: "How dare you. You're rolling in money." He actually said:

> *"My specs are splashed with lobster*
> *My lobster's splashed with snot*
> *No woman makes my knob stir*
> *A bloody cold I've got."*

"Sorry, I can't see the relevance, Robert. Can you repeat, please? This is not lobster but haddock"

"I said," he said:

> *"I'm Chippy Minton and this is*
> *my son Nibbs."*

"Let's eat up and go home, honey. You're over-tired after your long day."

He managed a few disconsolate words now and then before they reached the "chamber."

She sat him down, saying ... "Alright, I know you have betrayed me. I saw you with Suzie buying the coat this afternoon. You are beneath me. Beneath most people, in fact. Now get your things and scram!"

He meant to reply: "Glad to, you little nobody. She's a goddess compared to you," but actually said:

> *"Now the next number is called*
> *'Looking through the knot-hole in granny's*
> *wooden leg.'"*

"Sorry, Robert, that's too complicated for me. Can you repeat, please."

> *"Half man, half biscuit."*

"Still not with you, darling ..."
"I SAID:

> *Spare ass Annie. Spare Ass Annie."*

Then he tried to say "What have you done to me, you evil goddamned witch?" But said instead:

> *"Oh foolish heart, silly thing, silly thing*
> *You hear any old tune and you sing."*

"Just trying to make you out, darling ..."
"I SAID:

Love again. Wanking at ten past three."

She'd already packed his bags, which she threw at him. "Now your key!" He passed it over in silence and she held the door open for him.

Leaving, he tried to say: "You won't survive in the Village without me. You're a lost little school-marm." But actually said:

"*Haven't you been to a Harvester before?*"

"What?"
  "I SAID:

The Siamese twins are coming to town."

She waited by the open door and heard him bump into old Mrs Stein from the room below.
  "Everything alright, Robert?" she said.

"*Don't forget the fruit gums, mum,*"

was his reply.

When he reached Suzie in Gramercy Park, he meant to say: "That bitch, Sewell. I'll swing for her!" In fact, he said:

"*I've just been down the Rue de la Paix
looking for rude day lah postcards.*"

"What the hell are you talking about, you fool."
  "I simply said:

*Ladies and gentlemen. It's all about to happen.
Let's hear it for the fantastic Rolling Stones.*"

Suzie was a determined women, wanted to stay in NYC and needed a man in her life, so she trained him only to speak when he was detached from the content. It worked, sort of. People attached the word "cool" to Robert. He had to be cool; if not, the gibberish fountain spouted. He was marked out by it and it seeded a long-lasting fashion; no fun for him, though.

Suzie helped him write folk songs from his strange discourses. He strummed along to them in bars but it never really took off. Unlike Suzie, who did take off, with a younger, less "complicated" fellow.

Marie? She felt the pull of Columbia, having come to dislike the Village. Founded a poetry magazine called *The Pear* that nurtured the talents that nurtured the talents that eventually would impress the world. She died in the Spanish Flu pandemic of 1918, much loved, and not just for being a "minor" miracle.

Souvenir from a Dream

For Betty Smith

You were living five lives in one
Taking everyone's coat,
Why can't you show them
What you've got in your cloak?
Cold hand on my shoulder,
A star begins to beam,
That's when you show me
Your souvenir from a dream.

Tom Verlaine

Day 1. 60% cocoa solids

Here goes nothing ...

As you probably know, there's this little sister of Alexa called Anissa, and when you say "Anissa, record!" she records. She'd better be recording now, as seeing a red light or any visible signs of activity is beyond me – as you know or will come to know. Mugs away, then. Here come my sentences.

The researcher girls said they wanted me to talk about the so-called *phenomenology* of going blind while also pressing on with the *everyday narrative* as it develops ... or not. I'll find the second one easier to manage, and there will be more of it. I won't, though, find this process easy because it's just not my kind of thing. I'm too young for it. Too fuzzy-edged and messy. In too much rude health and too full of unpredictable competences. Yes, and too full of bullshit as well.

In fact, given the tendency just revealed, I'll try for a tone that is stark and Beckettian, at least when it comes to phe-nomenalising. I'll shoot for restraint, constraint, sans taint of self-pity; and of course I'll keep failing.

I won't fail as a Beckett stoic, I'll fail as somebody dis-tracted, who cannot take this stuff seriously.

I'll fail, too, because what some call my "gibbering" will keep breaking out from time to time. I natter and digress. I give asides that become headline stories for next-to-no rea-son.

I also have spasms of chair-kicking-over negativity and, I admit, self-pity.

Phenomenology, then. I've been thinking about this, and it turns out there are pluses as well as minuses here. But in pass-ing I'll let you into a secret: it's a blinking dratted nuisance hav-ing no visual input. Blindness isn't all it's cracked up to be. Vision has my vote every day of the week. *Look,* what do you think the "phen-om-en-ol-ogy" of being blind is? (in loud mock cockney) "*It's faaaahrrkin' 'orrible*" is what it is!

This is my way of coming out as somebody who dislikes the invasion of psychology "research" into private life and dislikes words like phenomenology tripping off the tongues of teenage researchers.

There!

And so I sound like a crazy old man in a waiting room. Back into his box he goes.

Now, I'll surprise you by saying that I'm being serious about the pluses. Sorry, folks, let's regroup. Blindness almost lib-erates you from what I'll call "the prison of the solo perspec-tive." An illustration ... One morning, shortly before the much-debated medical incident, I was wringing out my flannel in the washbasin as I prepared my face for shaving. It was like watching a film, a dose of grim bathroom-sink realism. I was a camera alighting on a blue flannel mangled in the hands of a man in early middle age in a basin that sorely needed cleaning. But what lay beyond? For God's sake, widen the lens! Pan! Tilt! Shoot from a drone! And of course there is no escape from the solo perspective. No Cubism on offer. The visual comes, given the eyes stationed in our heads, with an ego-tag, and at that moment I longed to escape it.

Why? It's lonely. It's lonely because it rubs your nose in solitude – our being condemned to unique experience.

People who report back from good acid trips talk about becoming one with universal consciousness. They report its blissfulness. Actually, I don't think that's balls. This feeling didn't linger beyond my finishing my muesli, but it remained as a residue. Only an idiot would say blindness is "tantamount to slipping the ego chains." (laughter) Perhaps you see what I'm trying to get at.

And yes-yes-yes, there is an auditory-spatial perspectivism too; but it's a relatively feeble thing, isn't it?

This has a knock-on effect, on music. Unless it was an exciting rock or a jazz solo that pinned me to my chair, I was quite separate from the music I listened to. Classical music, in particular, was always *over there*. I liked it well enough – especially French stuff, Ravel, Debussy, Poulenc – but it was an art object in a vitrine as my mind wandered round the perimeter of the room. Now, though, I am WITHIN the music. It's a breathed-in element. So there you have it.

As for the negatives. What a joy it was in the early days to crash around the flat like a trapped fly in a bottle in piss-wet jeans. What a joy in the feeling of absolute impotent dependency while sitting in a "easy" chair with smashed crockery at your feet. But let's talk about *order*. That sounds abstract but it's not remotely. When you have a visual field, when you – I have heard philosophers use this phrase – *enjoy* visual phenomenology, it's easy to choose to experience things in your own order – look at a face, then a window, then the scuffed toecap of one of your shoes.

There are imposed orders, too (the waitress approaches *before* she gives you the bill), but you can have your own order and you can reverse it at will.

What larks!

Of course, the blind can touch things in any order and reverse that if they so wish, but you've got to know where the things are, about which you are frequently *in the dark*. Anyway, touch … not much of a sense, is it! Unless it's flesh we're talking about. The sound world – need I even say this? – is a world of imposed orders, refractory and irreversible … one word after another, the car-door slam, the driving off.

Enough! Oh please, enough.

Phenomenology is shrinking in the rear-view mirror as we race towards facts and contingency and the blessed stream of behaviour and identity.

My name is Alvar Pullen. Alvar? I think my parents were fans of the newsreader Alvar Lidell and his mellifluous mahogany tones that reassured the listener, just as my sharp, cantering chatter grates on them; boo-hoo. It's my only first name so there's no escape. Alvar Pullen. Alvar Pullen. Alvar Pullen. You can imagine it as a Polish dish of meat and mash livened by a sauce of yogurt flavoured with mustard and dill.

More? I live in a basement flat and have a girlfriend called Priscilla who still comes to see me, her heels clattering down the iron steps to my cave. Not much in it for her, but she comes anyway. I also have a brother, Seb, and a sister, Amanda, both a bit older than me.

At one time my family occupied the entire house. Which is in Barnes, by the way. Then it all went wrong. Our dad was some kind of moneyman in the city, then mum died in an accident, an accident that precipitated the birth of me. Shortly after this, pappy just upped and buggered off, leaving money in trust for us three. Not enough money, because not enough reality in his so-called investments. A Dickensian misery of a paternal aunt brought us up, Blanche.

As it turns out, Seb has just been to see me. Unlike Priscilla, you can never hear him coming, this soft-shoed entrepreneur. He is also softly spoken so I have trouble locating him after he's finally made it into the flat. Luckily, Magda, my carer, was here to let him in. He's so grand now, he rarely opens doors for himself. He asked me how I'm doing, after which I have learned to reply "Fine. How are you, Seb?" And then he's off. The poor lamb is suffering under a less-than-ecstatic review of his latest book. There can be no blemish on his perceived excellence, of course.

Look, I think I'd better tell you about Seb. It's well away from the how-is-it-with-you? mandate, but here goes. The trajectories of he and his sister, who are both authors of a kind, describe a diagonal cross – a saltire cross, the law of supply and demand cross, the pirate crossbones cross. Hey! How's my *stark*ing? Not so great, is it? He started low and rose high, and vice versa for her.

He was about two when I appeared and not long after I reached that age I could see what he was like: moony, inert, desperately dependent and marbled with aggression. Consequently he found it very hard to make friends, and consequently every area of his life suffered. As he grew into adolescence, he tried various personas to hide behind or raise himself on, but the only one that worked was "the intellectual." This is surprisingly easy to pull off, because you don't need to be particularly intelligent as long as you steer clear of the technical and keep your utterances wordy and niche. He managed to get a place on a university course. This lasted just a year, a year of social isolation and academic struggle, then he gave it up and came back to the house. We had enough dough for him to live – if you can call it living – rent free. More like suffocating on the island of Radio 4. All his trust money went to pay for therapies. Not the Freud-style ones; those he couldn't stretch to.

He tried all the others, though. Spent his days filling his days with them. All the mainstream players were accounted for: Cognitive Behavioural Therapy (CBT) and Mindful-ness-Based Therapy, while Self-Compassion Therapy acted as a gateway drug to Existential Therapy and towards a nest of "eclectics" who let him do all the talking while they played games on their phones. It was mainly online. It made him worse, and the day-long drudge exhausted him ... until there came an epiphany in the form of a puff of wind.

Mindfulness, as followed from book and CD, had always been a mainstay (like trying to fill up on that foam Michelin-starred restaurants go in for), and one Friday morning there he was, shoeless, on a rug before his CD player, following the instructions for "mindfulness of action." Left hand on hip, right hand outstretched; and as his body curved gently rightwards and downwards, he heard, on the recording, "and if you like – if it's what you feel you want right now – you might pay attention to the way your eyes *drink in* the colour field through which your hand passes."

At this point there came from him a loud, almost vocal, high-pitched and interrogative fart. He collapsed in ecstatic laugh-ter, and while falling to the floor his eyes "drank in" his CBT booklet, open at the page for The Five Areas Model. He kept repeating "drink in" and "the Five Areas Model," sounding (he imagined) like an hysterically corpsing actress. He could only squeak, and through the wall the neighbours must have thought he was having energetic sex. If you have ever corpsed in rehearsal, as I have – actually, I was holding a woman's hat as a prop, coming on as George Deever in *All My Sons* on the line "There's blood in his eye ..." – you will know that it's not a matter of *everything* being suddenly funny, as it is for a stoner. There are instead unplumbable depths of glorious craziness in a phrase or a sight. But it was not *quite* like that for Seb, because from these twin sources radiated the thought that mental therapy as a serious adult procedure is a thing to be laughed off, a sign that the world's silliness goes all the way down. All forthcoming examinations cancelled due to our suddenly seeing the funny side. This was the first time the poor guy had ever felt joy.

He changed utterly. He got himself a job serving at the local deli. He made friends and got a steady girlfriend. You could hang out with him. He was not like somebody on happy pills, he was like a cool, funny *stranger*. Cool, yes ... but cool and calculating. It was around deli-time that he met Ted Bilco, a PhD in social psychology and – I love this word and have been dying to use it – a *scion* of a big family of West London restaurateurs. Bilco had the needed spark, I'll give the arse that. He got his dad to rent Seb and some easily-recruited therapists an office in Brentford. Easily done, because London was full of semi-trained practitioners who couldn't keep a straight face. So this was the famous Therapy of the Laughing Buddha, or TLB.

Now the beauty of it is that I don't need to tell you about TLB. The world knows. And everybody, apart from a few children, calls it the For Fuck's Sake Therapy or Fuck 'Em All Therapy or Enough of this Bollocks Therapy. In the early days, sessions used to kick off with a big glass of Amontillado or a joint or a bar of Waitrose Orange and Almond 60% cocoa solids chocolate. (laughter) Shaun Ryder needed the money so they got him to record his version of the *Mindfulness* CD, with ad lib swearing. That together with the Amontillado: pure magic! As for the thing itself, it contained a hard kernel of truth and it worked, bearing in mind that the exact opposite kernel is also true and that all therapies work at the beginning, placebo-style. But it's still going strong, isn't it? My God, he's making money from the books, the courses, the personal appearances and endorsements. And the miracle of it is that he's retained his naiveté and softness. Seb is still as soft as you-know-what but not – absolutely not! – a *soft touch*.

So, were I to say something to him in answer to his usual, "Is there anything we can do for you, Al?" it would be:

"Yes, there is. Please could you pay for me to spend time in a good hotel with a professional carer rather than poor put-upon Magda while my flat is being made fully blind-friendly at your expense? Oh, and can the carer be fit as well as super-competent. I know I'm blind but, well … use your imagination."

To which he'd reply: "Now that's a really *creative* suggestion, Al. I'll put it to the board. You know my hands are tied."

Anissa! Stop recording!

Day 2. Come on like a dream

Hello! And on the bombshell that's looming, I begin. In fact, I DO enjoy a visual phenomenology – oh yes! – one that is rich and standard issue. I do so because I dream. I dream of having a normal, independent life in which I am my real and prior self. So there you have it, researcher girls – didn't the Beach Boys write a song about you, by the way? – not only can I serve up the purest phenomenology of sense data without objects but also a *narrative* phenomenology – the perfect intersect of your twin desiderata. My God, I sound like one of Iris Murdoch's unreliable narrators. But I *am* reliable. Seriously. Just not to myself.

That said, I cannot "enjoy" dreaming, as if I were on a kind of night-release from my prison, because I don't know I'm asleep. So there can be no fairground wu-hooo or yee-ha! And, more darkly, I awake to the same black dawn, always early, and always with a longer wait each morning for Magda to get me going, despite the fact that she's completely punctual.

You asked for it, girls: a tsunami of boredom from this dedicated dream-teller. That's what I aim to do. Oh, and one further thing: the dreams are totally different now. Most dreams most of the time are divorced from reality, whereas mine are awash with the everyday.

Just to give you a taste of my dreaming *before* the debated medical event ... I was riding upstairs on the bus towards Kingston. Lovely mid-summer day. I was relishing the way the sun was turning gold the topmost tree branches in this suburban Eden. We had just passed the Tiffin School, when who should come and sit beside me but Matt Hancock.

Without a pause, he related to me a sequence of pathetically minor successes, all of which were Hancock-centred.

I looked into his eyes as I heard the wheedling corporate phrases skitter from his lips, and steadily began to weep.

In the dream I felt that my life had been a failure, leading up to this moment.

Hancock smiled a smile at my tears.

Well, none of that nonsense happens now, thank goodness. While at the same time, it must be said, I never have anatomically impossible sex with Angelina Jolie.

Last night's dream, then, was an exemplar of the tyranny of the solo perspective mentioned yesterday. Or am I just recalling it that way? It was a pleasant dream of a stroll down to *The Bull's Head* to hear Art Themen play. Me, Priscilla, my sister Amanda, and her current guy, Mike Kahn. Pleasant but for Kahn. He personifies the loop that the poor girl is perennially stuck in – I nearly said "the vomit to which she is chained." What I mean is that the men she chooses are always more fans than lovers.

This was blindingly true in the days of her great success. But now they are fans *of what she used to be.* And because she used to be a successful and ubiquitous poet, they are all poets, though always now of the manqué persuasion.

At least the success-era ones were good-looking and personable ... but *Kahn,* he's a nasty loser-runt. Look, I think I'll break off now and tell you about Amanda. It will emerge how this sibling, like the other one, has a calculating side to her.

We have always got on well, Amanda and I, so it made me sad when she went up to York to do a course on sociology or something. She did little work and associated mainly with a literary crowd, started to write poetry and publish it in student mags, then later in national outlets like *Poetry London.*

This amazed me, as she'd never before shown the slightest interest in poetry, or even in literature, sticking to films and social-theory tomes. But she joined *The Poetry Society* and became the leading light of the local branch of Stanza – a subgroup of some kind. She published more and more and actually managed to bring a book out with Cape.

Now, call me irresponsible, but this surely wasn't just down to her writing (which, by the way, I never read, not liking modern poetry). You see, Amanda – or rather "Mandy," her poesy name – is a looker. She's an attractive long blonde, like a cool drink. (No-no, be still my churning mind and block these images of her walking by the river with the dark, hairy runt, Kahn.) And she comes on like a dream (as in the song), having an intimacy of voice, patent niceness and patience, which indeed she has for real. And all that was helped on by her collection having a *theme* – the theme of the wounded woman. A *sexy*, wounded woman. Roll up, roll up! The nature of the wound was obscure and yet, apparently, universal.

She was featured in *The Guardian,* striking a pose before Barnes Bridge. The book sold. More, not too many, followed, as did presenting stints on Radios 3 and 4. As each of her books had a theme – feminist, socialist, concrete (as concrete as the routines of a bricklayer, say) – each theme was an entre to a radio gig ... "And now poet Mandy Pullen reflects on Emily ... um ..." (Her name escapes me for the moment; that suffragette who jumped in front of the King's horse.)

Then all changed with her collection called *A Bobbin a Pedal*, inspired, so she said, by the racing cyclist Beryl Burton. With the critics she could do no wrong, and early reviews had ranged from the admiring to the ecstatic. And this despite the fact that the Beryl story had already been well mined in Maxine Peake's truly excellent play that Pris and I saw the year before. Now that was more up my alley!

She did not, however, impress John Carey, who did more than fail to admire. He commissioned a review of the book by a young novelist and ex-poet who shared his scepticism. It was the centrepiece of the Arts Section, full page, entitled "I'm Mandy. Buy Me." The name of the novelist – Bethany Fear – gave the lie to her calm, sunny, unhurried – like laying tiles – style and more-in-sorrow-than-is-good-for-you tone. In content it was a rapier to the heart.

She began by describing the state of modern poetry in terms of the stark choice facing one who fancies trying to excrete some pomes. Do you join the unintelligibles, who range from the high priesthood of Late Modernism to the anything-goes hopefuls of loose experimentalism? The drawback with them is that their stuff is unreadable and so they only write for and are only read by one another and academics. Or do you roll up your sleeves – the "you" is likely to be a female – and join the writers of overwrought, ever-open, confrontational, confessional *prose* with short lines to make it pass as poetry, and with a few rhymes here and there to the same purpose? The name of the game here is *energy*. However, unlike the punk rock on which it's loosely modelled, the result is boring. Sure, it makes sense, but nobody cares much about the sense. Same drawback as before: nobody likes it. Not really.

Or do you do what Mandy Pullen does – write stuff that absolutely looks and sounds like poetry while presenting the reader with little jumpable hurdles to interpretation? You give them the flowers of poesy plus the satisfaction of being able to pluck them to their heart's content. The punter can safely give books of them to one who may become – to whom they want to become – a loved one. Giving poembooks betokens sensitivity, you see.

The formula here has two main elements. First, pile on imagery, all dressed up in metaphors and similes that look bold but are actually sloppy and approximate, while having the safety net of them seeming "surreal" if they badly misfire. These must be like codes with built-in crackability. Ms Fear gave some devastating examples here. Second, you really must end with an epiphany of some kind, an epiphany with echoing and phony resonance. It's as if somebody offers you an ice-cube or a cheese grater and says, "So what about THAT, then!" – somebody who has worked hard to earn credentials as being on a higher art-intellect plane than you. The huge advantage of this stuff is that it sells. The drawback is that this kind of poetry can only be written in what she called "a counterfeit spirit." Many of the unintells and the prose-shouters are sincere. But writing as Mandy does "mandates a cold strategy," so there!

The piece was done with a novelist's skill and it was unignorable. It had the *ring* of truth. Of course, it was also highly debatable, simplistic, and very, very cruel; and for this reason it was weatherable. Mandy did not try to weather it. Later, she was approached by the *Guardian,* to be interviewed for a feature on victims of stinging reviews ... *No Turn Unstoned* ... the title of one of my favourite books, edited by dear Di Rigg. She was asked, "Do you think there was anything in what Beth Fear wrote?" The reporter claimed that a "downcast Mandy mumbled this: 'There was a lot in it. Has to be faced.'"

This did for her.

Her never writing another poem after reading the review did for her just as thoroughly.

Look, I was so proud of her giving this response. Never loved her more. So proud. (he breaks off) To tell the truth, and to completely contradict what I said before, I don't think she is remotely "calculating." At least she wasn't at the time of writing the poems. It was, I'm sure, only on reflection that she could see the calculating source. Or did she just hate how her kind of poetry so blatantly *affords* the charge of calculation? My sister is no counterfeit.

As to why her boyfriends continue to be poets after this ... no idea. Maybe to remind her how fine it is not to be one any more. Yes, Kahn. The dream! At the end of the first set, Kahn gave us his critique: Themen's playing was "derivative," "over-complicated," "with low energy in the ballads." Adding, snarkily, "a cushy way to earn a living, though." I told him Themen was retired from a lifetime of working as an orthopaedic surgeon, then bustled off to the bar. Pris followed. We'd recently seen a movie in which this line is said by a redneck matron: "Ah think Hitler was right about you people!" She repeated it in her best deep-South and through laughter said, "Why don't we say this to him in unison?" "It will wash over him," I said.

Then guess what? Next day there was a knock on the flat door – I mean for real, not dreaming. Magda was not here. I shouted to ask who it was. "Mike!" "Mike who?" I knew, of course. "Mike Kahn ... Man's chap." (He calls her fucking "Man"; I mean, really ...) But I let him in anyway. He at once (no How-are-you? or anything) said, "I've written you a poem. Do you mind if I read it?" "Delighted!" I'm much nicer in real life.

Anissa! Stop!

Day 3. Justin's flighty wife

Hello and yes, you could say I've been playing fast and loose. Saying something on my tin and then pouring the golden varnish down the bog. Didn't I say at the beginning that I'd aim for the stark and the Beckettlike? Stoicism was mentioned too, I believe. OK, I did add a little camp ho-ho to the effect that I was bound to fail a bit here and there; but I said it like a bad father who says, "I've been a good dad, I mean within the limits of my character." No, of course it's not like that at all. Let's calm down, shall we? I should have told Anissa to switch it on only when I was ready. (long pause) Right, then here we go again ...

The fact is, there could have been something like stark dignity, even a bit of philosophic clarity-truffling, if I'd stayed away from the dreams and stuck with this film noir directed by a teenage nihilist that is my sorry life. You vowed to leave me free of feedback for the duration, so thank you ... so you're partly to blame, I suppose. That said, let's scrabble up some continuity with Day 1 and what I was saying about blindness imposing orders of sound unlike the chosen orders you get with the scanning of a visual array. Now just imagine THAT as an introduction to a *Blue Peter* story. It gets worse; I wake with a thirst for a chosen order of experience. A tactile one could almost be in sight if I ever really got to know my newly invisible flat and if Magda never moved things about. Instead, I talk to myself. I sing to myself. "How cow brown now" is an atom of freedom and an Alvar contribution. Magda sometimes hears me, so I've got to keep it pretty corporate within her hours. In fact, it's like training yourself to be an introvert – which, let me stress, I am NOT. Never had one of those "inner voices" folks talk about. I want real-world dialogue, not sodding inner dialogue. Yes, and dreams give me that; so here we go, back to the dreams. I'm like somebody giving in to the need to scratch an itch, choosing the orgasmic pleasure of it, the islet of relief, while knowing the itch will multiply times five thereafter. What, pray, is the "itch"? How's my simile-ing? The itch – playing with a straight bat here – is the torment of desire to tear the black veil away and ENJOY the world as it is, in silent radiant colour. Sense data of touch and sound? *Do me a fayvah*! (broad Cockney, in case you weren't sure)

Dear listener, you will have detected by now that I'm on edge. Very. And the *reesin as fur woi* (West Country) is last night's dream. I cannot not tell you about it. You'll see that it smashes my hopeful generalisation about my dreams post-the-debated-medical-incident being realistic. This was not remotely realistic and it left me a bitter souvenir to carry into the waking day.

In the dream I had gone to *The Bunch of Grapes,* on the corner of our street, for lunch – not a routine thing. Was sit-

ting at a table by the window, tucking into my pint and looking forward to my curry and chips, when I saw at the bar a
familiar – what Auntie Blanche used to refer to as a "funny-
osity." Recognised him immediately as one of the renters
from the house.

(I should explain, by the way, that the business of rent-
collection, maintenance, and all the rest of it, is taken care
of by an agency. I'm totally hands-off. This leaves the family
with a pathetic secretion of money, a squirt of income. I do,
though, make it my business to know who lives upstairs and
in which apartments.)

This particular "osity" lived in the cheapest studio, the
smaller of two tucked under the roof. He was tall and lithe
and old, an American who dressed like a Southern grandee,
with bootlace tie and cream suit. Imagine a long-haired
Francis Crick cosplaying as Colonel Sanders and speaking
like an academic. He rode a bike but mostly wheeled it while
wearing a crash helmet, telling all who would listen that he
was "on heavy-duty blood-thinners" and so was "virtually a
haemophiliac." He had that embarrassing kind of charisma,
the kind that obliges people to say "He's a bit of a character." When they really mean, "He's a bit of a bore."

Shit! (thinks our hero) He waved to me and wandered – like
a big-fight promoter wanders – over. "Hi there!" he
drawled. "I hear my fellow 'inmates' call you Justin, but I
know you as Alvar Pullen. Can I get you another pint? You
may know me as Clint Duveen, but my name is actually
Frank Pullen. I'm your dad, in fact. Bitter, was it?"

Let me break off to explain the "Justin" business. As you
may also know (that phrase again), I'm a thespian, and not
a particularly successful one, a foot soldier among the character actors of London. I specialise in waspish but easily
undermined authority figures with islets of funny or dan-

gerous incompetence. I'm a "Justin" because I had a long stint in *Eastenders* playing a dentist of that name who had moved onto the square with his flighty wife and who was making a total arse of renovating his house. I'll add that I never wanted to be an actor – it was a philosopher's life for me – but I'm a show-off who's easily addicted to the camaraderie of the troupe and not clever enough to be a philosopher. As for the implications of this thespian-fact for the business of my blindness? Hey, folks! If there can be colour-blind and sex-blind and age-blind casting, then why the hell not blind-blind? How about *Hamlet* or *The Homecoming* with an all-blind cast? Actors looking past each other, falling off the stage. Check it out. I am not available for voice-overs!

Oh, forgive me please for being so human. Press on; must press on. So I asked this creature, more irritated than shocked by what he'd said, why I should believe him? He told me my mother's name (Jonquil) as well as giving a rough account of why I'd never met him. My gob was smacked to the core. After this, he dug into his grubby big cream pocket and produced his "proposed lunchtime reading," which was Amanda's novel entitled *Expectant Rain,* that she'd written a long time after her poetry career had topped itself.

Once again I must pause to expand on something. Amanda had been secretive about writing this book and had struggled hard and long to publish it. Her name still had *some* cachet, so the publishers made it look as much like poetry as possible, with tiny print to slim it down, a wispy abstract on the front cover, reviews of her poetry on the back, and the strap-puff "Mandy Pullen breaks her long silence." The style was maximum prose. A police constable could have bashed it out on an old Imperial typewriter on a sturdy iron desk.

Almost no figures of speech. Almost no modifiers. I suppose it had the starkness I had begun by aiming for. It certainly had none of the Beckettian humour I was after – but then, who else can do that? (I did once play Estragon, by the way. One critic said my performance lacked nuance.)

You felt Mandy's book was *supposed* to be compelling, like those people who dress all in black. No, I don't mean nuns. (laughter) In fact, to the family, it *was* compelling; at least the first half was, being clearly reportage rather than invention. Good readers could probably tell this from the writing alone: a lack of hesitancy and craft, like a breathless confession.

It told the story of a warring couple living in a large riverside house in South-West London along with two children, the narrator (Jill) and her little brother (a happy brat). The mother was beautiful and vague; the father mostly absent, but when present still absent or noisily dissatisfied. The pivot blade on which everything turned happened one May morning, when Jill is busy marshalling her dolls in the hallway and her parents are descending the grand staircase (now an uncarpeted, uncleanable track), mother before father. Mother is heavily pregnant and they are having one of their usual shouting matches, today's with special venom. Jill looks up to see her father push her mother down the stairs. She lands heavily at the bottom. The fall itself is undescribed. She lies screaming as a red stain blossoms below the waist of her maternity smock. Dad steps calmly over the body, not pausing to comfort Jill, calls an ambulance and then his broker. Mother dies giving birth to, well, to yours truly, I suppose. After this, father absconds; the little brother hides from the world within himself; the martinet "Auntie Betty," the father's sister, moves in to rule the house; and the new baby develops into a bumptious me-first merchant who knows which buttons to push. The remainder of the book is forced and lifeless.

Basically, Jill quits her university course, lives on the streets, and eventually wins through to some transcendent whatsit at the glorious bottom of the heap. Shining through the careful resolution by the Thames mud is the light of implacable hatred.

"Enjoying it?" I said. This caused his rather smarmy smile quickly to fade.

"Not a light read," was all he said.

Then I asked him why he was here.

"Sacramento is no place for an Englishman. Never has been a home. I'd had enough. Just wanted to come home and see my kids and explain the lot, while there's still time."

His drawl was absent now and his tone sharp:

"Can you fix up a meeting with all of us? You, me, Amanda and Sebastian. I know they live in London."

My dream-self is not my usual self. I behaved like an official – a border policeman, say – but a kindly example of one. I said Amanda could well be a hard nut to crack but that I'd arrange a meeting with Seb at my flat.

"Seb ..." He tried the feel of it in his mouth.

Then my curry and chips arrived. No pint was forthcoming from him. Something about him told me he had to be careful with his money.

Anissa! Stop!

Day 4. His grubby socks

I did a single-hander once, a weird mixture of *Krapp's Last Tape* and one of the later interviews of Keith Richards. "Overpowered," said one reviewer of my performance. "Some desperate shouting in the dark," said another. You get halfway through the performance and it's like swimming a river, in that excellent cliché. You must *sustain* at all costs but you panic, being the farthest you'll ever be from dry land.

Well, that's roughly how I feel now. I feel that things could fall flat at any moment. I could, of course, pump them up with more straight-dream narrative; but that's not me *brief*, innit? And yes, you will have spotted that unlike your common-or-garden dream stuff, each night's dream is continuous with the others, like in a soap. Or is it that I impose – more imposing, vicar? – continuity in recalling them. Who knows?

The dreamwork, as he who Auntie Blanche used to refer to as "Floyd" called it, beckons sirenlike. But I must tell you – the show must go on, apparently – more about my waking life.

As I said at the outset, Priscilla still comes to see me. Surely that's not news? We've been together for 15 years, and if *she* had gone blind I would be round there every single day, helping her to choose dresses and tights – Jesus, that sounds *creepy*. She too is an actor, a little younger than me and certainly a looker. Didn't I call Amanda a looker too? Oh dear. She is certainly a *speaker*, too, a fine speaker of gratefully-received pronunciation, so fine perhaps that there's little room for the imperfect nuances of an actual individual. I can't help saying her speech is "actressy"; though, thank God, she doesn't look it ... by which I mean she lacks the actress mask-smile. At this point I hear the more medically-inclined listeners straining to wonder, "How is their *vie de couple*, their ... um ... bedtime habits?" None of your bloody business!

No, we never married, and for a variety of reasons. Perhaps I should have married her – in the words of Larkin's jolly poem, "to stop her from getting away" – because, as it turns out, I want her "here all day." If only she could fill Magda's role. No! For her to have to lend a hand *to all I need doing?* No! No-no-no. It's wonderful having her here, in fact. It's the only real continuity with my sighted life. It feels like we love each other, too. That thought had never forced itself on me before. Not 100% wonderful, though. I don't know whether it's part of the actress persona or part of the actress soul, but she has a hard core of upbeat in her, and this despite the fact that she's not a particularly happy person ... *persona*, then? She over-enthuses, over-detects the bright side; half-filled glasses are always on the verge of spilling over. Plus she's a jolly-hockey-sticks force of can-do.

"Why not do some voice-over work?" (Recall: this is already a sour joke.) "Your voice has deepened since it ... um ... happened."

Like telling a lifer it would be good if he could spend an hour a week in a MacDonald's queue. And how would I know the text? Learn braille? Memorise it from audio? I'd rather sip tea to Radio 4 Extra. She stays four nights a week; I'll tell you that.

Thus far, I've never dreamt of Priscilla. I want so much to look into her eyes, but no dream has ever given me the chance. Instead, it's dream tunnel-vision on my siblings and this Colonel Sanders in a cycle helmet. A frustrating element is that in the dreams Seb is – how shall I put this? – out of focus, like Woody Allen in that film of his. His invisible self is more real when he comes down the steps to soft-soap me in the darkness.

So ... as people never stop saying ... the dream meeting between Frank and Seb did take place, took place, in my flat. A firm knock on the door and there was a burnished young woman, all smiles and tits. Seb's PA, of course.

"Hello there! I have Sebastian here for you. Just to check you're in and everything's cool ... Ciao!"

My guess is that she didn't want him to have a wasted journey all the way down the steps to my basement. *No, can't 'ave thaaat.* (West Country, for what it's worth)

Then, eventually, Seb appeared. Funny how he's taken to wearing too big and emphatic scarves, like shawls, in the way literary types do as if to say, "Look, I'm not just a lap-top-jockey, I'm an artist." Though, come to think of it, Tim Spall does too.

We chatted as if we were waiting for the dentist. When Frank arrived, a little late, he was all confident comfort and warmth. No emotion, just bonhomie laced with little under-glances of humility.

Instantly, he congratulated Seb on his brilliant career, then I missed a few exchanges while making tea. He had clearly decided to prevent Seb from saying much in the face of his onslaught of curated memories.

He produced some ancient "snaps" taken on a beach near Folkestone. "What a little handful you were, right from the start. In this one you'd gobbled down your ice and then fisted Amanda's into the pebbles. That's why you're laughing your head off and she's scowling."

I was so surprised at Seb; surprised by his passivity, by his generic remarks and weak jokes. He was actually *deferring* to this clownish man. Yes, Frank's possible dadness made no real impression on me, me being, of course, my dream-self; I'm not so cool in reality. (laughter) I did, though, watch it unfold with near disgust: the corny display and the deflating audience. Until I couldn't help but say ...

"That's all very well, Frank, but can you tell us why *exactly* you pissed off to America after mum died?"

All he had to say for himself was that he couldn't really "step up to the 'exactly'" and to ask that this be left for "further discussion and elaboration when all four of us are assembled."

I said that was a politician's answer and insisted that we wanted something explicit.

"I'll tell you now, it was nothing to do with the family."

"But it *affected* the family – all of us."

"What I meant is that I had to get away due to events outside the family."

"*Events*, dear boy?" (I couldn't resist)

"I'd done things outside the family, the consequences of which had to be faced or ... in my case ... escaped."

"And now you sound like a *drowning* politician."

"Listen, friend–"

"Do *not* call me friend!"

At this point Seb stepped in, and when I say "stepped in" I mean stepped in with a professional swagger and a smile. Here he was in his therapy zone. Here was his true genius. The very thing he claimed to find hilariously empty was what he practised. The word "Orwellian" springs to mind here.

"It's a fine irony" (beatific smirk) "that putative father and putative son are bickering on the brink of some perhaps beautiful realignment.

Realignment!

"Why don't you relax into these thoughts: A, that we are who we say we are; B, that the past is past; C, that higher humans have huge reservoirs of forgiveness."

Between us we took the wind out of Frank's sails, and Seb alone gave us the full glare of his competence.

He said he would ring Amanda, and then the cheeky toerag said that as I seemed to be "err ... *resting,*" perhaps I might have time to nip over to Mortlake to talk her round to a meeting.

"*Yass'm, boss!*" I said. At which Colonel Frank pretended to laugh his grubby socks off.

You'll have noticed that in dreams we're usually spared the boredom of transitions. Dreams are episodic, and scenes change with the frequency of that Spike Milligan sketch, "A play for actors with small bladders." Not in the dreams I dream, they don't. I dreamt the whole walk from here to Mortlake, felt nostalgia for the hoppy aromas en route, found myself wondering how the tooth of the old brewery would finally be pulled.

But I'm an editor now, so – to work.

Amanda's house was finally reached. Although there's nothing actually *wrong* with the place, since moving in she's done nothing to it but clean it obsessively. One imagines her taking an old toothbrush to awkward corners and skirtings. But the kitchen is 1970s; much of the furniture is what was left behind by the previous owners; the paint is nicotine-stained (a sparkling, varnishy brown). She did, though, buy an elegant drinks cabinet from a junk shop, and all her domestic energies seem to go into keeping it well-stocked. There are – amazingly – no books to be seen on the premises because, she says, she doesn't happen to have a bookcase. *Happen to have?* – as though all bookcase owners become so by sheer good luck and nothing but.

Where the dream-Seb is slightly out of focus, the dream-Amanda is maximum crystal presence. By the by, I love the little book on presence by that acting coach whose name escapes me. She sees a production in which the only actor with presence happens to be a dog. I know *just* what she means. Oh, I'll solve the mystery for you researcher girls: Amanda lacks self-consciousness (doglike), whereas Seb is awash with the stuff.

Anyway, it was early evening and an already opened bottle of Shiraz sat between two balloon glasses. The three sat on a veneer of *Pledge* beneath which was a real veneer cracking quietly away. It felt somehow too good to be true.

Imagine if it had tipped into a nightmare at that point ... I might turn to my right and see Kahn on a beanbag holding out a glass and wearing a T-shirt emblazoned with the slogan "It's wine o'clock."

I can add that she's finished with him. The last straw was when he introduced her to somebody as "the Forward Prize shortlisted poet ..."

And talking of reality, now it bit. A dream reality this time for sure; but it was *my* reality. God, I hate this way of talking. "I'll tell you *my* truth ..." Pass the sick-bag, Alice.

This is what bit:

"Al," Amanda said, "I am not – repeat, *not* – meeting that fucker! It's perfectly possible that he is our father. What I'd do is tell the police about him if I thought they'd give a toss. Look, I've spent nearly all my life putting him into a manageable compartment in my mind, and I don't want the fact of him coming and shitting all over the little life I'm now managing to make."

"You know he's read your novel."

"Yeah, and he's brazen enough to go ahead with this anyway."

"Go ahead with what?"

"Getting his hands on Seb's money, of course. You know what Seb's like; he's a marshmallow at heart. Maybe the bastard doesn't know that's what Seb is, but he's betting on it."

"But Seb's tight-fisted, too."

"And will he be with his *long-lost pappy*? Look, this has nothing to do with my not wanting to meet him. I tell you: it happened *exactly* as I said in the book. I saw him kill mummy! I was seven, not a baby. I saw him push her down the stairs with all his might."

"So TELL him this! Make him suffer! Threaten him with the police! *Confront him!* I don't like the guy, father or no father, and would love to see him being given some ... *feedback* from you."

She drank deeply and we talked in a lower key. Then, in the end, she agreed to meet him at Seb's, to do pretty much as I'd suggested. I should say that this forceful weapon of argument I describe myself as being is, as ever, the dream-me. Deferring is my reality mode.

After this I woke up sweating. Funny how the sounds of morning inspire blind visions of morning light at the edges of my curtains. Is this a case of synaesthesia, researcher gals? Invisible light to go with your blind-sight? I've heard of blind-sight but don't know what it is ... story of my life.

Anissa, enough! Stop recording!

Day 5. Becoming responsible

I could force myself to squeeze out some phenomenological reflections on the blind life but, sorry ladies, no can do. My way of getting through this is to turn my mind from absence and incompetence and towards some other, brighter stuff. It's like my brother's take on therapy: the goal of therapy is to encourage the client to ignore the bad stuff that's he's cuddling up to and laugh and say "So fucking what! – does it matter in the wide blue yonder of life?" If you want to know about blind phenomenology, just use your imagination.

And so, in the interests of ignoring the centre, here are some reflections that I'll steer towards an account of last night's eventful dream. Some years ago I was in a production of *Playboy*. It wasn't a success, mainly because the director seemed to think that his beloved *pace* would come from rapid articulation alone, while allowing many of the cast time for a cigarette break between cues. So we gabbled, ran around like blue-arsed flies, and our Irish accents were poor; and most critics slaughtered us. Well ... at the sad after-show party, as the set was being struck and the corks pulled, I made a little speech in which – thanks to a scholar friend of Pris' – I was able to recite a six-line poem by Yeats called "On those that hated *Playboy of the Western World.*" I can recall it perfectly, so here goes something ...

> *Once, when midnight smote the air,*
> *Eunuchs ran through Hell and met*
> *On every crowded street to stare*
> *Upon great Juan riding by:*
> *Even like these to rail and sweat*
> *Staring upon his sinewy thigh.*

Of course, we were hardly expressing Don Juan, but it's fair to say that these pen-pushing naysayers were eunuchs, not doers. It lifted us all, my little speech, and here I am again "shouting in the dark." Which is all, as ever, by the way.

The point is that the collection in which this perfect little thing appeared was called *Responsibilities* (1914) and the first of two dedicatory quotations on the cover page was this ...

> *In dreams begins responsibility.* (*Old Play*)

But which old play? I'd love to be in it. Of course, most people know this sentence (with "responsibilities" plural) from the title of a short story by Delmore Schwartz, teacher of Lou Reed. It's a pretty unexceptional story. Could be mistaken for an episode of *The Twilight Zone.* (laughter) Also, the "responsibilities" of his story has or have no resonance beyond the little fancy he'd dreamt up.

But the dream I had last night, with its revelations and tears and humiliations and hot heat, was surely my responsibility. Who else's could it be? It came from my mind's downtime with its waste matter and desires. Why did I dream it up? It contained no truths from the world. The news from voices that comes down my iron steps doesn't contain these items. No grubby Franks to speak of. No Amandan intransigence. Pris and various friends come down into the dark; my near and far family come and pretend to do their duty. Not a word of it from them. So it's my responsibility, while not being something for which I can *take* responsibility, in the sense of doing something about it. The dream impinged on me. It did so in the way that the monster wave in Victoria at the end of *Point Break impinged* on Patrick Swayze. I wish to be, and am, more suited to being wan pale Keanu Reeves watching from the shore. But – to keep on pushing this envelope till it falls into the wood burner – imagine the wave coming to shore and treating Keanu like flotsam. Enough already! Time to relate the dream. I could not, did not "compose myself for slumber" last night. I told Magda to leave the remaining little puddle of Scotch within reach and let sleep creep up. No Priscilla last night. That might have helped.

There was Frank, wobbling across Kew Bridge. In the dream I'd decided to bike it over to Seb's, who lives in West Chiswick, and as there was a bridge closure to the east I'd gone west to Kew. Frank had had the same idea. He was actually *riding* his bike, just about, wearing a new helmet, one of those that look like WW2 German infantrywear. That and his Colonel Sanders outfit gave him the appearance of a very, very incompetent German spy on a mission in Deep

South USA. I rode behind him for a bit, watching the shards of fear shoot off from his body. Eventually he stopped and decided, as had I, to cross the road and go down to the riverside, east of the bridge, and make his way from there.

"Hi, Frank!" I called from behind, expecting him to be ruffled; but he was dead-eyed. It was a hell of a job helping him get his big old bike down the steps to the riverside; and when it was done we rode together at walking pace for a while, and then walked at crawling pace.

I tried some general remarks as an alternative to silence, but he had clearly decided to engage reminiscence mode (to beef up the case for being who he said he was?) ... tales of carousing with Uncle Harry in *The Steam Packet*, which we were struggling past; and so on. His voice quavered, and the American accent – was it ever genuine? – was fading.

Eventually we stood before Seb's splendid grade II residence (one of his two London ones) and all he could say was "My-oh-my-oh-my" over and over again.

Amanda was already there. She barely looked up when we arrived and it was clear that no form of polite greeting was on the cards.

"Well, I guess we all know who we are," breezed Seb.

"I know who I am," was Frank's sad attempt at lightening the atmosphere.

There followed awkward, irrelevant chit-chat, during which Amanda continued to watch Frank unblinkingly. Then, once the drinks had been served and half-consumed, she spoke.

"OK," she said calmly, "I think you are in fact our dad. You look like the man I remember and move like him, despite being a physical wreck. From photos, too, I can tell you're him."

"Thank you," said Frank. *Thank* you?

"So, tomorrow I'm going to phone the police, in fact I'll go to see them and tell them I was witness to a murder in the 1980s."

This energised Frank. "And you think the Met in the hopeless state it's in would do anything, Amanda? I really–"

Which energised and enraged her.

"Shut up, you seedy, murderous *creep!* Look at you. You shuffle in here stinking. You want to heave your stinking self onto out lives. Why are you here? To grab a bit of Seb's money is why. He might buy you a one-bedroom flat around here, give you a little allowance, and then he might publicise it to throw a spotlight on his wonderfully generous but interestingly *wounded* side ..." She clearly had much more to say but wanted to see the impact of these words.

"If I can just tell you what I came here to say. What I crossed the Atlantic to say."

"'Crossed the Atlantic.' Give me a break."

"Please, let Frank speak." (Seb)

And he did ...

"The context is this: Alvar is not my son. I told Blanche to register that name if the baby was a boy, that's all. I know this because Jonquil and I had not had physical relations for about 18 months prior to the birth. Do you remember that we had separate bedrooms, Amanda? Maybe Sebastian remembers too. I knew who the father was, a guy by the name of Chris Miles, whom I'd known since Oxford. He became a sort of friend of the family as he lived nearby; certainly a *very* good friend to your mother. He was a penniless sponger but handsome and a brilliant raconteur, funny in a Peter Cookish kind of way. It was goddamned obvious what was going on between them."

"I fail to see what this has got to do with–"

"If you will just LISTEN!"

His anger was stronger than Amanda's, so, reluctantly, she listened. Probably she also remembered Miles.

"In the end, Jonquil confessed, saying she wanted a divorce so she could marry Miles. I refused. I knew that at all costs I had to keep the family together. It was my LIFE! I mean, even if the baby wasn't mine I had to keep the family together. I won't say a word against your mother, but she could be hard. She would not and could not allow herself to be thwarted! She told me that if she didn't get her divorce, she would tell the City's Office of Financial Regulations (or whatever it was called then) what I'd been up to for the past couple of years. I admit, misdirecting government loans and asset-hiding was illegal, but it made me a cool million. (All legal now, by the way; but in those days it carried a maximum 30-year jail term.) I kept on refusing, and bugger me, she did what she said she'd do. The sword was hanging over me.

"Well this was the set-up on that day … We were coming down the stairs. I didn't notice you at the bottom, Amanda; not at first. She had just spat out, "Well, none of us will be visiting you in prison." I then said something pretty nasty back at her, at which she wheeled round to strike me with the back of her left hand. This was a speciality of hers, as her engagement ring was guaranteed to draw blood. That happened often. Remember when I used to say I'd been scratched by the cat, kids? I caught her wrist to protect myself, she struggled to free her hand, lost her balance and fell."

"Not as I remember it."

"Why do you put such trust in your memory, Amanda? Memories are not like little videos you carry round and consult." Frank seemed sure of himself now; younger, more vigorous.

There was then what seemed like a very long silence. Seb was moved, that was obvious. Even Amanda showed signs of melting. Then I saw – OK, dream-saw, but saw just the same – something I hope I'll never dream-see again. Frank imploded, uttering the following in almost a single outburst of air: "I remember your dolls, Maggie May and Belle, waiting for your pretend friends Micky and Hannah to come to tea, a cup cake ready to be divided, four little paper plates ... Oh, my Lord ..." Tears sprang from him pathetically. He fell to his knees before Amanda, clung to her and sobbed his heart out.

At what seemed like the right moment, we helped him up and sat him back in his chair like a Guy Fawkes. Seb gave him a big brandy. He stared out into space for a while, breathing hard, eventually telling us, all trace of Americana now gone, that he had been faced with a terrible choice: "the kids" would have either a jailbird dad or a vanished one, and the latter option was "better for all concerned." Funny kind of better, I thought. But then, who can blame him for wanting to avoid prison.

What am I doing here? I reflect on this as if it's real. I suppose it is real, but real like a radio play. (Peter Tinniswood's products are alive and real to me these days.) He then actually said that he could trust his sister Blanche to do a good job. Now that really *was* funny.

We got him back here. Seb conjured up a driver and a huge people carrier, which took us and the bikes, exactly as would have happened for real.

During Frank's Guy Fawkes phase, Amanda sat beside, him holding his hand. And she was the first one to call him "dad." She even helped him up to his eyrie. What to make of her, eh? What to make, rather, of what my dream-mind makes of her? What to make of it all? I'm solidly rooted in this John Lewis easy chair while talking to you lot; solidly at home, as wooden and safe as the chair. But I'm Keanu driftwood too after last night's dream ... Ah, but the upside: who would want grubby Frank – I sound like Trump – as a father, even in within the hidden wellsprings of my dreaming? And yes, I've always been a huge Peter Cook fan. My wit and satirical heft has to come from *somewhere*. It's OK, girls, I'm joking.

Anissa! Please stop recording!

Day 6. Five lives in one flat or mind

Now the parallel between me and Sammy Davis Jr is far from obvious, but I'll do my best to explain it. We both have or had a surface competence and swagger that we cover or covered by a smokescreen. Of course, Sammy had his portfolio of brilliances – the fastest draw in the West End and all the rest – but gluing it together was a desperation. When I was an actor I could be excellent, sometimes supremely right for a part, memorable even; but there was always, always the desperation. This was why I could never be what Orson Welles calls a *King Actor*. Sammy was a smoker, whereas I don't indulge. But I surround my accounts of myself with wreaths of smoke; and you surely know what I mean by that.

In the 1960s Sammy did a season in the West End, at The Palladium. He was, of course, good; but there was a falling short, a routineness, a lack of occasion. He smoked incessantly, *desperately*, on stage. And, stupidly, he would sing out plumes of smoke into the spotlight. The heading of one broadsheet review was "When the smoking had to stop." Well, you didn't need to read the review to realise its tenor. Now is the time for me to stop smoking. I'm stubbing my fag out right now.

Here is the dream narrative for last night. I won't bother with the three previous nights, which were routine stuff: an audition, the unbearable unfamiliar lightness of the three sibs, plus old Frank's obvious happiness. Yes, he'd bought himself a smart linen suit and proper shoes to replace the cowboy ones, and a nice white shirt or two. The thoughts of dream-Alvar during these nights were pretty much the thoughts of me now. But I've already metaphored them, and that will just have to do. I was essentially an observer anyway, watching the metamorphosis of Amanda.

Was she happy now? Happy, yes, in her self-appointed mission to float something good away from the wreckage. She didn't seem to have much to do directly with Frank, but she did – all done by phone and texting – persuade Seb and me to hold a party for all of us in "the house" – meaning, of course, my flat. To do what? And why? I forget quite what she said, something about taking the bad taste away. And although she'd never use the expression "find closure," that's what she meant.

Seb provided top-class savouries and a chocolate fondue and champagne. Amanda came round with scented candles and multi-coloured throws to go over my dull grey sofas. She said, "We should bring our partners too."

"But Kahn is no more, surely."

"Ah, but there's a new guy, Piers." (oh no)

"What about Seb?"

"I think he's between supermodels right now."

"Well, be sure to bring Pris."

"OK."

So ... to last night's dream. On the phone, Pris – the dream-Pris – said yes, she'd love to come and that she'd come early to help me get the place readier. She didn't sound very chipper, and on arriving was far from it. Amanda had just texted to say she was going up to the attic to fetch Frank.

"Alvar, we've got to talk now, before they get here," said Pris. "No, I don't want a drink."

Weirdly, she lifted Amanda's colourful throw to make a point of sitting on the grey upholstery. Symbol of something, or what?

"I haven't said anything before now because I didn't want to upset you. The time never seemed right. And what with the Frank business, and your dad being not him but Chris Miles, and with everything being up in the air, and now, on top of all that, with this God-knows-why party, I thought a better time is unlikely to come, so it had better be aired and resolved, and quickly."

"Please don't be so breathless, darling. You've got something to say. Why don't you say it. Just say it."

"It's about you, at night. Your dreams. At first I thought you had another woman, one or more. Cries of 'Magda!' and 'Anissa!' But then you were barking at her, demanding help for instance with your socks or finding the sugar; so I thought no, not that. And you wake up every two hours or so sweating like a pig, terrified, saying things like 'There's a light. A light! I can see, *of course* I can.'

"Sometimes you get up, turn on all the lights and stand in a rapture before things like that photo of you in *Cabaret*, full of joy, saying things like 'I can see perfectly. It's rubbish this blind bollocks.' You tell me not to let you go back to sleep, saying 'I'm not going back to blindness. I'm too young for it. Too fuzzy-edged and messy, in too much rude health, and too full of unpredictable competences.'" (yes, folks, that may ring a bell) "Or 'I'm not blind! Keep me awake, Pris!'

"Then, in the morning, you've forgotten all about it, saying you slept like a log. Every night this happens. Every night I'm here, and the nights you stay at mine, too. I can't go on like this, Al. It's torture for me. I hate to see you like this. I want to share a bed with you; but even if we just did it then slept in our own beds there's the next day's hangover from the night. You are so serious and heavy, and a kind of free-floating spite seems just around the corner ..."

She went on like this, listing all the evidence, thoroughly exhausting her case for my dreaming every night that I was blind. "You have a separate life as a blind man," she said, as if accusing me of keeping a secret mistress. She was drained. I was frozen in fear and disbelief. We looked at each other till she said that actually she would have a drink. We both did, and had barely clinked glasses when I shouted, "Oh, hell!" It looked like some kids had *again* pushed the blue recycling bin, full to the brim, down my metal stairs. That was the first image that sprang to mind, followed in a trice by the true one: Frank crashing down my steps in his new blue linen suit – propelled with major force!

What surprised me was how unsurprised I felt. I ran out-side, and, before looking down at Frank, I looked up the steps to see who I knew I'd see – Amanda, speaking through that satisfied half-smile of hers. "Let's just say he was in a bit of a rush and tripped, whoops-a-daisy!"

And there was Frank, just moving, groaning slightly, maybe knowing that a massive brain bleed would be just one of his "challenges." A steady stream of blood was trick-ling from one ear.

"Why?" I asked Amanda. "Why did you do it?"

"I know what I know," she said. "Hadn't you better phone an ambulance. He's blocking the entrance." After which, she beetled in and busied herself with the chocolate fondue, ignoring Priscilla who was white and silent with shock.

I went in to cuddle Pris. She clung to me hard as I dialled 999. Seb's arrival was *de trop*. He seemed to feel *de trop* as he frantically phoned all the private medics he could find in his book, because the ambulance people had said "up to an hour," which of course meant *more* than an hour.

Amanda piped up again: "Don't bother with the private bods, they'll only take him to the West Mid. Won't get priority over the NHS ... Oh, and look: it's starting to rain. That'll cool him down."

Was she suppressing laughter? Certainly she spoke through mouthfuls of chocolate, which could hardly imply seriousness.

Well, I know what I DON'T know. The one big thing. Was dream-Priscilla right, or is this real – the blind-me talking to you? I WANT her to be right. Are you mad? I want the real in which I can look into her eyes. This black-real is shit ... which is my phen-om-en-ol-ogy in a nutshell. But it feels real. Which isn't enough, of course. Dreams do feel real at the time, don't they bloody just! Have you noticed, by the way, that speaking is the one thing we need consciousness to do? The rest can be done without it. At a pinch. I'm speaking-real and chock-full of consciousness. And what if it's all an illusion, huh?

Yes, yes, even those of you researcher girls who've never had a philosophical thought in your life will know of Descartes and his *cogito ergo sum*. I'm pretty sure too you all noted down my confession that I was not clever enough to be a philosopher; but I was *on the way to* philosophy, so I know what I know here. Descartes grounded all human knowledge in the fact of being conscious – the single certainty. Well, girls, *fuck that certainty and fuck that foundation* is my prize-winning essay précised. "All I want is the truth, just gimme some truth," sang John Lennon. Descartes never answered his own worry: *What if the contents of my consciousness were put there by an evil demon?* – a kind of Noel Edmonds or Jeremy Clarkson. Sorry, I must stop "smoking." The reason Descartes could not answer it is because there is no answer.

My invisible hands on the invisible chair arms. My sensing, because of the way it's tight at certain points, my shirt has been done up incorrectly, one buttonhole up from the correct one. My wondering about whether I would be able to find a croissant or bit of cheese in the kitchen. My wanting to pee and wondering whether my aim would be true – true *enough*. It SMACKS of the real because the greater the constraint the greater the reality, perhaps. Recall me on "refractoriness" on day 1, said the bore. In dreams we fly and ... recall me on Angelina Jolie on day 1, or was it 2? But the gaudy wonder, the flesh-tones and coloured weather of these so-called dreams! I just don't know.

But I do know that there's – how to put it? – a paradox or a structural flaw or self-negation here. What about the thousands of words I've spoken? (At least ten thousand, I'd say. Actors are geniuses at word counting.) If Priscilla is right – oh, please be right, girl of my dreams – the text they leave is your souvenir from a dream.

Also available from grand**IOTA**

Brian Marley: APROPOS JIMMY INKLING
978-1-874400-73-8 318pp
Ken Edwards: WILD METRICS
978-1-874400-74-5 244pp
Fanny Howe: BRONTE WILDE
978-1-874400-75-2 158pp
Ken Edwards: THE GREY AREA
978-1-874400-76-9 328pp
Alan Singer: PLAY, A NOVEL
978-1-874400-77-6 268pp
Brian Marley: THE SHENANIGANS
978-1-874400-78-3 220pp
Barbara Guest: SEEKING AIR
978-1-874400-79-0 218pp
Toby Olson: JOURNEYS ON A DIME
978-1-874400-80-6 300pp
Philip Terry: BONE
978-1-874400-81-3 150pp
James Russell: GREATER LONDON: A NOVEL
978-1-874400-82-2 276pp
Askold Melnyczuk: THE MAN WHO WOULD NOT BOW
978-1-874400-83-7 196pp
Andrew Key: ROSS HALL
978-1-874400-84-4 190pp
Edmond Caldwell: HUMAN WISHES/ENEMY COMBATANT
978-1-874400-85-1 298pp
Ken Edwards: SECRET ORBIT
978-1-874400-86-8 254pp
Giles Goodland: OF DISCOURSE
978-1-874400-87-5 302pp
Rosa Woolf Ainley: THE ALPHABET TAX
978-1-874400-88-2 182pp
John Olson: YOU KNOW THERE'S SOMETHING
978-1-874400-89-9 192pp

Production of this book has been made possible with the help of the following individuals and organisations who subscribed in advance:

Rosa Ainley

Christopher Beckett

Paul Bream

Andrew Brewerton

Ian Brinton

Jasper Brinton

Peter Brown

Allen Fisher

Giles Goodland

Penelope Grossi

Randolph Healy

Lindsay Hill

Kristoffer Jacobson

Sharon Kivland

Don Lawson

Heller Levinson

Richard Makin

Michael Mann

Shelby Matthews

Peter Middleton

Paul Nightingale

Sean Pemberton

Lou Rowan

Alan Singer

Carol Watts

www.grandiota.co.uk

Milton Keynes UK
Ingram Content Group UK Ltd.
UKHW042038031123
431812UK00004B/149